Veil of Synnor

Scott Thompson

This is a work of fiction. Names, characters, places and incidents are either the product of the author's imagination or are used fictitiously. Any resemblance to actual persons, living or dead, business establishments, events or locales is entirely coincidental.

Text copyright © 2023 Scott Thompson

All rights reserved. This book or parts thereof must not be reproduced in any form by any means – electronic, mechanical, photocopying, recording or otherwise – without prior written permission of the publisher.

To everyone who ever wondered how hard it could be.

Ask no questions, and you'll be told no lies.

Charles Dickens

I

The Crowd Favourite

As he stared down the firing range, Acalan drew in a breath. The tension would have shaken an inexperienced performer, but the seasoned bowman stood unfazed. His narrow perspective in the darkened corridor ended with a small canvas target. The stretched fabric was illuminated by torchlight, making it a simple focal point for him and his spectators above. Countless eyes watched in anticipation as he stood resolute and lifted his bow. With absolute focus on the task at hand, he drew back the string and released his first arrow. The venue fell silent. Only those seated at the distant end of the venue could pick out the sound of the arrow sinking into its mark. Acalan smirked with self-satisfaction and acknowledged the familiar roar of the crowd. Another perfect shot.

Without hesitation, he selected a second arrow from his quiver and fired. The air vibrated as the spectators reacted to the arrow sinking into the target, but Acalan remained still, his gaze fixated on the two arrows that he had embedded in the canvas. They seemed to overlap one another, with no measurable gap separating them. Acalan entered a comfortable state of flow as he prepared his final shot. The sound of the crowd faded. Maintaining his composed demeanour, Acalan released the final arrow. There was an audible click as the projectile pushed aside the two that were already in place, finding enough space to sink down between them. The stands erupted with cheers as the spectators recognised the placement of his shots. Acalan swung his bow onto his back and nodded to the crowd, who showered him with praise. He could never tire of the euphoria that accompanied this moment, even after many years of participating in the trials.

Then, the black curtain beside Acalan fell, revealing an identical corridor containing another bowman. This parallel range was indistinguishable from Acalan's, with one exception: its occupant was much less comfortable with the setting. Acalan's heart sank when he recognised the shaky individual opposite him. Myrin Maiseros was a lumber merchant from the city's Grand Market. Acalan had never had a bad experience purchasing materials from him or his daughter. They had always been pleasant to him, which was why he chose to trade with Myrin even though his prices weren't the best on the market. Acalan attempted to suppress this thought as he took in the scene before him. It was immediately clear that his opponent saw this task with different eyes. Where Acalan had nocked each arrow precisely, Myrin shook with his bow and struggled to line up his first shot.

Acalan was experiencing a paradoxical emotion that he had only felt a few times in his life.

Recognising Myrin forced him to tolerate an uncomfortable feeling of guilt-ridden relief. After all, by necessity, he would always hope to win a trial, and knowing Myrin was not an archer allowed Acalan to have a rough idea of his own odds. Nevertheless, he couldn't enjoy the moment as he was greatly aware of his conscience.

Meanwhile, having finally drawn his bow, Myrin shrunk into place but did not yet dare release. The crowd fell silent for a second time. While Myrin looked ahead, Acalan spotted the glistening of a tear as it escaped down his face.

Myrin's first arrow left the bowstring and flew down the corridor. At this moment, it became clear to all who watched that there would be no upset on this day – Synnor's finest archer would be victorious again.

Though unable to witness the wider context, Myrin knew that he had sealed his fate with his first shot. Although he had managed to sink his arrow into the third of his target's five rings, he knew it was not enough. The crowd also seemed to recognise the significance of the moment and watched with bated breath.

Myrin's vision was now almost completely blurred by tears, yet he persevered. It seemed that he was unable to maintain focus when he released his second shot, missing the mark. Maddened and desperate, he tore his final arrow from its flimsy quiver and launched his final shot. The arrow soared clear of the mark.

Myrin's unremarkable attempts reflected that he had gained nothing from his training week, a detail not lost on the spectators who had watched as the two shots missed the target completely. Myrin dropped his bow in disbelief.

The enchanted curtain around Myrin's corridor fell to reveal to him what all others there could already see. His view expanded to include Acalan's target, decorated with three perfectly grouped arrows. Acalan looked across at his defeated opponent, unsure which reaction he would see on this occasion. Some of his adversaries over the years had shown dignity in defeat, but some could not. Acalan shuddered upon unintentionally making eye contact with Myrin; it would be easier if he didn't have to watch. This fragment of time was shattered by an explosion of sound from the crowd above. Outmatched and defeated, Myrin fell to his knees and then, to the floor. Acalan avoided looking any longer and turned towards the crowd, whose applause intensified as they were acknowledged by their champion.

Two guards stepped onto the open stage and began to approach Myrin. Hearing a disturbance, Acalan turned towards his opponent once more, but Myrin was not the source of the commotion. Instead, it seemed to originate in the stands. Acalan's heart sank once more; he recognised her too. The youthful profile of this girl exactly matched the one from behind Myrin's market stall. Acalan had never surpassed small talk with Myrin's ambitious daughter Amara. On several occasions, he had found her buried in a different book. She was always friendly to him once he was able to get her attention, but it was always clear that she was doing work that was not her own. Looking at her here, it was clear that the humble budget of a Synnor trader's lifestyle had limitations. While those around her wore fine robes, her plain clothes took no note of the occasion. In his memory, her hair was always straight and tidy, but parting the crowd headfirst had ruffled it. Hysterical, she had managed to barge through to the railing that separated the spectators from the trial.

'You must stop! He is an honest man; he has broken no law!' she pleaded with the guards, but they continued.

'These trials are not in the name of the Titans, you can't take him!' she cried.

Then, despite some members of the audience attempting to dissuade her, she vaulted over the sturdy wooden barrier and tumbled down into the rough sand pit at the edge of the arena.

Amara clambered to her feet and sprinted towards the stage. Although Acalan had seen this happen once before, it was too late to avert his gaze. Her wailing was brief as a hail of arrows showered down upon her. A murmur of disbelief from the spectators lent no sympathy to the scenario. Amara's corpse lay still, a lifeless doll studded with pins. Myrin only managed to muster a breathless yelp before the guards were on him.

Whether unwilling or unable to stand, Myrin's

feeble protest was for naught as the guards overpowered him. They peeled him from the splendid metallic floor and dragged him backwards by his arms across the stage.

On the far end of the stage, opposite the two sets of targets, a final curtain dropped. Acalan's perspective now included a marble stairway. The guards began to climb these stairs, dragging a limp Myrin, who appeared to have succumbed to despair.

No further intervention could be dreamt of, Acalan thought. He wasn't convinced that Myrin had anyone else, and even if he did, what could they do? Although they had fallen on deaf ears, Amara's last pleas were genuine; her father had committed no crime. Myrin had led an honest life and acted within the law throughout. Yet, these details were irrelevant, and no mercy was given as they approached the top of the stairway.

Desperate to catch his breath, the trader displayed no combat experience when they threw him to the floor. He hit the upper stage face first, and the crowd's chanting intensified without sympathy. Acalan was expressionless as he watched the scene before him unfold. He faded into obscurity, standing in the background of Myrin's ordeal. The crowd jeered as Myrin crawled across the stage. Though all eyes were on the main event, anyone taking a glance at Acalan would notice his discomfort. While the audience encouraged and supported the guards, Acalan stood in solemn silence. As far as he was concerned, the trials were a cruel but necessary evil.

Even though it troubled him at times, this was how it must be. This sacrifice, and the innumerable ones that came before it, were there to maintain the favour of the Titans.

'One must suffer for the greater good,' he reminded himself.

Still, something was different when he recognised the person suffering. As he looked around the venue, he tolerated the weight of morality and remained motionless. His lifetime contained countless victories in the trials, so he knew that there was no alternative. Losing would have placed him in the gut-wrenching scene he was witnessing. It didn't usually affect him, but this time, he didn't see a nameless loser: Acalan saw Myrin, a person. Only now did he question if the blood was on his hands.

Myrin raised his head and looked towards the crowd. His attempt at a brave face was marred by his tear-streaked cheeks and eyelashes heavy with barely contained droplets.

Myrin suppressed his self-pity as he lifted his head towards the audience. He had never even lifted a bow until the week prior, yet this was his defining moment. Everything he had ever done had led to one bow and three arrows. Every decision he had ever made and each crossroad at which he had struggled meant nothing now. Both competitors would have had hopes, dreams and talents. Unfortunately for Myrin, though, whatever his talents might have been, they were of no use here.

Acalan watched as the guards grasped Myrin's arms and lifted him, forcing him upright. From this stance, Myrin had an unfortunately close view of the marble table that was the apex of the upper stage. The surface extended upwards from the platform, adorned with intricate designs of the Elemental Titans. From where Myrin lay, he would have only been able to see the Fire Titan, Igneous. This depiction portrayed a male figure who controlled a flame in his cupped, outstretched hands. If Myrin was paying attention, he would have also seen the Earth Titan, Terros. His was a quieter depiction. The man portrayed was of a smaller build, and he was sitting cross-legged, meditating in a rocky garden. On the opposite side of the surface, the crowd was able to see representations of the Water Titan, Aquiris, and the Air Titan, Cyclos.

These four murals each bled their respective elemental colour up towards the carved surface of the table. The design of the carving differed from that of the murals; a lone humanoid figure was depicted without much grandeur. Though outlined in gold, little was remarkable about the man. The figure stood in plain clothes, without any of the armour or adornments the Elemental Titans featured. He stood with a simple bow drawn towards the sky. The vibrant colours of each Elemental Titan surged from their respective murals and centred on his bow; each Titan was lending a hand to the archer for his shot.

The fine craftsmanship of the table was lost on Myrin when the guards shoved him onto it. They pressed him down onto the surface, facing upwards and into the skylight. Myrin's ineffective struggling only added further unpleasantness to the situation. Each guard had a firm grip on an arm, locking his torso in place. His legs kicked uselessly against his oppressors, only expending any remaining energy. The crowd's chanting ceased, and unintelligible muttering rose up once again. Approaching from the edges of the arena, a mysterious group began to assemble at the stairway. A spectrum of four cloaked individuals, each draped in a rich elemental colour, illuminated the steps. They advanced as one, taking each step in perfect harmony.

Leading the cloaked individuals was Queen Alanis Virrel, flanked by two more guards. Her ruby-red hair cascaded over her shoulders, its loud style tamed only by the fine circlet that embellished her temples. Extravagant robes trailed on the floor behind her and over the steps while she moved. The vacant black of her mantle was devoid of any pattern, contrasted only by the exquisite gold finishing that decorated its edges. All eyes were on Virrel as she moved with certainty in each step. A great deal of orderliness remained clear throughout the procession's entire movement. The people roared for their queen.

'People of Synnor, I thank you again for gathering here in honour of your Titans,' her commanding voice boomed around the venue. 'I am delighted to announce that our next offering has been selected. Under the guidance outlined in the Titanic scriptures, the defeated combatant will now pass into the afterlife. It is only there that they can deliver our message to the Elemental Titans.'

She paused for a moment before solemnly intoning, 'We live in worship of Eden Synn. We owe our existence to Synn, and we continue to prosper under his watchful eye. Praise Eden.'

'Praise Eden,' the crowd repeated.

'As is our duty, we have gathered the Titanic representatives to bless this sacrifice,' she continued, causing the four hooded figures to approach their respective side of the table. 'I would now like to request that the champion of the day performs the rite of the Prime Mover.'

The crowd's attention shifted to Acalan, who had not moved from his spot since the trial began. He jumped upon noticing the figure standing beside him before hastily attempting to conceal his surprise from those watching. As always, he was unable to see the face hidden beneath the hood. Arms extended towards him, offering up an extra arrow with open palms.

This was the victor's arrow, only ever accessible for this purpose. Although it was elegantly decorated on its fletching, what always stood out to Acalan was the smell it emitted. The scent was akin to the blaze of a campfire but with an acrid kick. It was a synthetic odour that was non-existent outside of this arena, but it always awoke a sense of nationalism in him. Where before there had been guilt and anxiety, now, he felt omnipotence. To

Acalan, it was as if he had become Eden Synn, the Prime Mover himself. He placed the arrow against the drawstring of his bow, shuddering under the full tension as he drew it. Acalan couldn't be sure if the crowd had indeed fallen silent or if it was his ego taking over. Either way, he didn't hear a sound when he released the arrow skywards.

The crowd erupted into celebration as his shot left the arena and hurtled into the sky. Several seconds passed before the magical bolt exploded outwards. Four vivid elemental colours filled the heavens as far as the eye could see. This effect darkened the arena as the sunlight failed to break through the visual effects of the ritual.

Virrel's voice cut through the celebrations to command attention. 'Now that your champion has performed his duty, we can begin.'

Following this, each of the Titanic representatives placed a hand on Myrin and clutched him tightly. Ignoring his pleas stone-facedly, they fixated upon the queen. She stepped towards them without urgency in her gait, produced a small dagger in its scabbard from her robes and unsheathed it. After placing the scabbard on the table, she examined the dagger for a moment before thrusting it into the sky.

'Praise Eden!' she cried without reservation. Her free hand shot up to grasp the hilt of the blade, and she turned it to face downwards between her palms.

'Deliver our message,' she whispered to Myrin with a smirk before thrusting downwards.

Myrin's screams as his life was snuffed out were inaudible over the chanting of the crowd, but this made it easier for Acalan. Though he could not see everything from where he stood, Acalan watched in horror as the limbs he could see thrashed and spasmed. Myrin's arms and legs flailed about desperately, grabbing at the air in a hopeless attempt to cling to the world.

'One must suffer for the greater good', Acalan reminded himself once more.

II

Ghosts in the Grand Market

Acalan awoke as the sunlight crept through tears in the aged curtains. The bleak brownish hue filled the room with the sort of pseudo-daylight that would be expected when the drapes fail to keep the world out. He noticed fine dust particles illuminated by the main light beam shining through. This provided a spotlight on his prized longbow, displayed in a case mounted on the wall. The door to the case was ajar by about an inch, providing the perfect angle for the light to refract. A comforting spectrum of light shone over the bow, a beacon signalling that it was time for Acalan to make a move. Instead, he rolled around in protest before pulling the sheets back over his head.

Although it was warm under the sheets, Acalan could not get comfortable. His mouth had dried out, still tasting of the cheap wine from the previous evening. He recalled the friendship he had discovered in the scuffed bottle that lay on its side in the corner of the room. A slow but steady drip flowed over its lip into a reservoir that had formed overnight. Watching the droplets ripple through the pool only intensified his thirst, forcing him to sit upright. The movement caused him to feel the full severity of a well-earned hangover in the back of his head. His new glass friend had betrayed him.

Acalan looked at the modest table that sat below the ornate display case. Relief flooded him as his eyes alighted on the gift that he had left himself: a simple glass jug of water that he had been diligent enough to grace the desk with before retreating to bed. Acalan hauled himself across the room and swiped at it. In doing so, he caused yesterday's arrows to roll off the table and click across the floor. Despite this, his full attention remained on gulping down the contents of the jug. In his haste, the water sloshed down his front, and he jumped at the sudden cold, only switching to choking on the water once the alternative was to drown on land.

After draining the jug –with more precise sips this time – he placed the empty vessel back onto the table and turned to retrieve his arrows. He had no trouble with the first and second arrows, which had only rolled a few feet away from where he was standing. The issue was the third arrow, which had rolled under the bed and into the darkness. Retrieving this further irritated his fragile condition.

Acalan found himself sprawled on the floor, stretching out beneath the bed to grab the arrow and managing to coerce it back with his fingertips. After gathering all three arrows, he hauled himself back to his feet. As he stood, he felt his stomach cramping as it struggled to process the water it had just received. His nostrils flared as he resisted the urge to cough and splutter, instead clearing his throat cautiously.

When he stepped towards the display case, his frame blocked the prism of light that had refracted into the air. He opened the door fully and slid the arrows onto a set of hooks below the bow. Satisfied, he clicked the door shut, locking it at the side with its polished golden latch.

Acalan's persistent headache was then worsened by the thumping he now heard on his front door. He considered the possibility that the Synnor Royal Orchestra's percussion ensemble was on his doorstep.

'They must be here to perform a rousing composition to help celebrate my latest victory', he thought.

'Wait! I'm coming,' was his intended response to the visitor, but his throat could only manage hushed, raspy grunts. The thumping on the door continued as Acalan crashed around the kitchen in search of a key. Although yesterday's Acalan had gifted him water, the same man had also been generous enough to leave him a battlefield in the kitchen. The casualties were the filthy pots and plates that littered the surfaces around him. The cracked windows above his simple washing area lit the disaster that he was scanning.

The sound of a keen visitor intensified, and with it, the associated pain in Acalan's skull. At this point, he reached a lapse in patience. It was only when he swept the pots and dishes off the countertop that he found what he was looking for, as the tinkle of the key against the floor cut through the crashing of metal and the smashing of ceramics. When silence descended once more, the throbbing in his head subsided, returning to a dull pain.

The key stood out against the grimy tile floor with a glare, picked out by the natural light where Acalan had failed to see it.

In the aftermath of his outburst, Acalan took care not to cut his bare feet as he made his way across the minefield that was the kitchen floor. Once he had seized the key, he turned towards the door, and as he did, locked eyes with his visitor, who had made their way around to the kitchen window.

Iverissa's unmistakable white hair hovered on the other side of the glass. A subtle piece of silver-tinted hair was combed into an arc around her face. Natural leaf green surrounded her pupils, which fixated on Acalan and the disarray in his kitchen. Pushing her large round glasses up the bridge of her nose, she raised her eyebrows at him. He froze on the spot as if she might not have seen him standing right there in the middle of it all. Embarrassment set in when he pictured the scene from outside. In response to Iverissa's questioning gaze, Acalan held up the brass key that he had retrieved. A muffled laugh could be heard through the pane.

Acalan inserted the key into the lock and waited for the click of the tired mechanism before turning it home. As he unlocked the door, it swung open inwards, and Iverissa swept him aside upon entering.

'I was worried about you! That's not okay, Ack,' she scolded.

He tried to interrupt her, but his exasperated friend spoke over him.

'I thought you were freaking out again, and it looks like I was right,' she went on.

Acalan waited for an opportunity to respond. He hadn't had this sort of lecture in a while, but he knew that he deserved it.

'I didn't realise it was going to be him,' he finally said, attempting to justify his disappearance.

This failed to satisfy Iverissa, who grasped his shoulders and shook him. An earthquake crashed through the hangover party that was being held in his skull.

'Who?! Myrin?!' she demanded. 'Use his name, Ack. You knew him. It's worse if you don't.'

'I know,' Acalan conceded. 'It's just th–'

'It's harder when you know them?' Iverissa prompted. 'I know. We had this conversation the last time, and the time before that.'

Acalan acknowledged Iverissa's frustration; she understood him best. Although his parents had been proud to see him do well when they were still around, they were just that: proud. Iverissa was the friend who was always supporting him, though differently from the crowd. Behind her oversized glasses, there was something about the way she looked at him that was unlike any other. Her gaze was clear of the naïve admiration that most people looked upon him with since she had no interest in his talent with a bow. She knew he was more than that and recognised his thoughts and feelings – legitimised them.

'I couldn't find you afterwards,' she continued.

'Wait,' he interrupted, 'you went?'

'Well, you aren't the only one who reads the boards, Ack,' she reminded him. 'I saw it was you and Myrin, so I thought I should be there in case it was too much.'

'Don't,' Acalan warned. 'I don't want to talk about it. I'm fine.' Noticing her eyes widen at his words, he corrected his tone. 'It was an easy trial, and I am in the best form of my life.'

Iverissa raised her eyebrows at this last remark; Acalan's current form was that of a hungover tavern bum. This unconvinced look from his friend niggled at him as the silence stretched between them. Iverissa then broke it with a sigh as she began to gather up shattered crockery from Acalan's kitchen floor.

'I'm glad you're okay,' she said in a concerned tone.

Time passed as the two worked their way through cleaning up the mess. Iverissa placed the broken pieces of dishware into a small brown sack, which she placed beside the washing area before sitting next to Acalan as he wiped the floor down with a wet rag.

'I haven't eaten yet,' she announced. 'Breakfast then shopping?'

'Shopping?' Acalan squinted back at her, unsure what she meant.

'You need new dishes, Ack,' she elaborated, causing him to nod.

She was right; not a single plate had survived his rampage.

'Good.' Iverissa sprung to her feet. 'Breakfast will help.'

***

The pair burst out the front door about an hour later. An excitable Iverissa led the way for a recovering Acalan. Although he was still suffering from the same dull headache he had awoken with, breakfast had indeed helped. The significant difference was that he no longer feared a sudden onset of vomiting. Although they were heading out with new plates in mind, Iverissa had also insisted that fresh air would solve the headache. As he followed her onto the cobbled city streets, it dawned on him that he had slept the morning away. The bustling streets indicated that he had slept well towards noon. The blinding sun approaching its zenith in the sky confirmed this. With this in mind, Acalan wondered how he could still be feeling so rough.

Soon, they approached a small gap in the masonry of the wall. A black metal hatch was riveted into the old wooden fixture that connected Acalan's house to its neighbour. The sack of broken crockery clattered when Iverissa grabbed it from him. As she lifted the hatch, the full stench of this week's waste assailed Acalan's nostrils. He clutched at his chest and turned as the fear of vomiting returned once more. One of the things that set Synnor apart from other cities was its unique waste disposal system. This involved a dedicated sewer-style network of tunnels deep below the city streets. Each week, the city would perform a divine ritual to the Water Titan, Aquiris, who would clear the sewage with a single elemental blast. Acalan choked against a clenched fist as he barely managed to hold down his breakfast.

Always here at the wrong time, he thought, since the smell was almost always unbearable when he came. Had they come later, the ritual might have already taken all the waste out of the city and into the ocean, breaking it down in the process. Iverissa used her entire frame to fling the bag into the chute before she noticed him retching.

'People of Synnor, witness your champion, Acalan Izel!' she teased, giggling as he bent by her side.

Acalan shook his head in his hands as part of a failed attempt to conceal his grin. Having disposed of the plates, they began to make their way towards the Grand Market. The streets became busier as they descended through the districts together. Although Iverissa was shorter than the crowd that surrounded her, she continued to lead the way with her elbows. Following closely behind, Acalan kept his head down, and together, they shuffled their way through the dim alleyways. The road ahead widened, and soon, they joined the main promenade. They paused at its edge for a moment, as they often did, and took in the dazzling view of the Synnor-Jasebelle Sea. What was stunning was that the city of Synnor was built at the top of a cliff, with the promenade suspended far above sea level. The pair leaned against the railing, silenced by the breathtaking horizon.

'Do you think it's true?' Iverissa speculated, breaking the silence. 'That Eden Synn had an eye so keen he could see the Jasebelle shores from here?'

'I believe,' Acalan stated, unwilling to have another argument about what Iverissa may or may not have been reading.

Working full-time in the city library made Iverissa one of the select few in Synnor with elevated literary access. She was able to access all recorded lore and research within the city walls, much of which was deemed too dangerous for the general public. Although she had access to sort and file these books, nobody was permitted to read them, not even her. It had been almost a year since Acalan had stumbled across an agnostic scripture in her home. They hadn't spoken for months after he had immediately destroyed it in the fireplace. Acalan had decided that on this occasion, ignorance was bliss.

'Standing here makes me wonder what's out there,' Iverissa said, further worrying her friend.

'There's nothing out there, Iverissa,' Acalan said emphatically.

He was just like the rest of Synnor's population: neither permitted nor interested in venturing out in the knowledge that the Titans watched over Synnor but not Jasebelle. This was all thanks to the Prime Mover, Eden Synn, ancestor of the sitting monarch of Synnor, Queen Alanis Virrel. Following the great famine in Jasebelle, only those who followed Synn across the water and did so in belief of the Titans survived. These brave followers were the first founders of Synnor. They would have watched Eden Synn win the first-ever trial and make the first-ever sacrifice.

As Acalan squinted, trying to pick out the distant shore, he couldn't imagine how it would look after all this time. The unblessed soil would reap no crops, and even if it did, the spiteful elements of the Titans would kill them off. This was what the trials were all about: an offering from Synnor to the Titans. One that facilitated centuries of safety and prosperity. If anyone could even survive the barren wasteland over there, they would do so alone.

'Some days, I feel like I need to go out there,' Iverissa confessed. 'I feel trapped as if the walls are closing in.'

Although misinformed, Iverissa's sense of entrapment was understandable. After all, the lanes surrounding her home in the Lower District were narrow and claustrophobic. Acalan stayed in the Upper District, the only point in the city high enough to be surrounded by land. This would have been unsettling to him had the towering wall around it not comforted him. This was what separated Synnor's blessed people from the dangerous wasteland outside.

'Hmm.' Acalan did not indulge her and instead turned towards the gate of the Grand Market. He stepped through the colossal concrete gateway, trailed by the ever-curious Iverissa. The looming gateway widened into an oval court surrounded by inward facing buildings. The structures darkened the marketplace since limited light could get in from above. The light at street level came from iron lampposts dotted between thousands of stalls. Acalan flicked up his hood and pulled a thin cloth section of his robes across his face as they entered.

'Well, alright then, Mr Celebrity,' Iverissa joked, before shoving her way back to the front.

She took point as the pair tried to navigate the hectic market layout. Acalan followed behind but noticed that they passed the same merchant twice. Despite Iverissa's superior knowledge, she was struggling to find the stall she sought.

'Are we lost?' Acalan asked, acknowledging their

third pass around the same stall.

'I swear this guy has moved; he was right here,' she insisted, allowing Acalan a glimpse of her frustration. 'A man was trying to sell me soup bowls!' Iverissa gestured towards a jeweller's stall manned by an older gentleman whose eyes were vacantly half asleep from the lack of interest in his stall. Acalan's makeshift mask obscured his smile when he recognised the opportunity.

'Good mo– afternoon, sir!' he said as he approached the merchant. 'I see you have an outstanding selection of jewels on offer today!'

The older gentleman sprang out of his stool and lunged at the pair. This caused Acalan to jump backwards instinctively before trying to play it off. The pace of the merchant's movement completely outmatched the physical body that they were looking at. This was before he launched into what may well have been his first sales pitch of the day.

'You're quite right, sir! We have the finest jewels in Synnor right in front of you!' He gesticulated enthusiastically. 'You won't find a stone cleaner or a gem more polished anywhere in the city, and that's my guarantee to you!' The merchant leaned on a short staff and looked around Acalan to shoot a glare at a competing stall across the way.

Acalan was amused by the similarity of these two stalls and their apparent rivalry. From where he was standing, their wares seemed identical.

'Y'know, Iverissa, I was starting to suspect that

the market would let us down today. I'm so pleased that you have brought us to meet...'

'Daylor Daerie at your service, sir!' the merchant responded.

'Daylor,' Acalan repeated, completing his sentence. 'Would you be able to help us find some nice new plates for my kitchen?' he inquired. 'My friend here insists that there was a merchant here days ago selling the best ceramics in the city.'

Iverissa couldn't help but grin as he teased her. He was acting like himself for the first time today.

'Plates?' Daylor responded, puzzled and disheartened. 'No sir, only jewels.' His shoulders sank.

'And I wouldn't expect to find plates near here?' Acalan pressed, making his point to Iverissa without an ounce of subtlety.

'No sir, for your homewares and the like, you would need to be on the east side of the marketplace. You are on the wrong end,' the merchant replied. Oblivious to his role in the joke, Daylor remained keen to help.

'What a terrible misunderstanding, Mr Daerie,' Iverissa cut in, defeated. 'We must be on our way.'

'Indeed,' Acalan agreed. 'But first, we must choose one of Synnor's finest gems to adorn my friend's neck?' Acalan's enjoyment wasn't over yet.

'Yes sir!' Daylor seized the opportunity.

'Couldn't agree more,' he added.

Iverissa flashed Acalan a playful scowl when Daylor turned to swipe up one of the largest gems on his table. Acalan's amusement remained obscured by the cloth that still covered his cheeky grin.

Daylor's first suggestion was a garish ruby attached to a weak and dainty gold chain. When she finally got a word in, she insisted that something more modest would be suitable.

'You're not funny,' Iverissa scolded Acalan as they left the stall. A beautiful emerald stone decorated her neck, suspended by a glistening finely crafted silver chain.

'You like it, no?' he responded, still smirking under his cloth mask at his ability to find ways to tease her. She sighed; he was right.

As they manoeuvred their way back through the market, Acalan caught a glimpse of a detail that he had missed before. Iverissa only noticed it after he froze on the spot and stared at the empty display table. It seemed invisible to everyone around it, and yet, it had captured Acalan's full attention. There was something poignant about the table, and little set it apart from others around it. Its design was identical to many of those close by. Its defining feature was a partially torn fabric tarp draped over it. Acalan couldn't determine if it was a gesture of respect or an act of ignorance.

The hole in the fabric showed that the table

underneath had been picked clean. Acalan hoped this was at least the result of family or friends. Sadly, though, he suspected that an opportunist passer-by was a likelier culprit. The stall sat frozen in time as the world dashed around it.

'They aren't even looking,' said a bewildered Acalan. 'Nobody notices.'

Bodies continued to pass the ghost stall without giving it so much as a glance. Only one day had passed, yet the space had faded into the background completely.

'It's not right, they should still be there,' Iverissa added, palming an elbow as her physical stance closed in on itself.

Acalan felt discomfort as he stared at the consequences of his actions. He knew the sequence of events objectively: Myrin was gone, as was Amara. This wasn't what stymied him. Somehow, he couldn't process it. He was looking at an anomaly in reality; it was like the timeline didn't fit right. It was as if there was a mistake somewhere, and the ripples had led to this.

Deep in thought, he pictured Myrin and Amara there today as usual. A range of veneers completely covered the stall in an array of coloured columns.

'I've been waiting all morning for you to roll out of your bed!' Amara scolded Myrin. 'I have places to be, Father!'

Although her shouting was causing a scene, the

public continued to pass, unable to hear what Acalan could. Myrin's stained clothes and scruffy hair suggested that he had indeed come straight from his bed. He swayed in front of his daughter before leaning against the table. Amara stood with her arms crossed while he shrugged through a half-hearted apology. She rolled her eyes and stormed out of the picture, vanishing once again from existence.

What Acalan could see wasn't perfect, but to him, the scene felt right. He couldn't grasp how to unpack this vulnerability as he considered powers greater than himself. A faint breeze shuffled the cloth tarp that lay there now. Reality manifested once again as Myrin and his wares faded away. Something was wrong; he could sense it.

'He's delivering our message to the Titans now; this is how it has to be,' Acalan said, vocalising none of the thoughts that raced through his head. They would only encourage Iverissa, and that was the last thing she needed. He turned his back on the scene and began to move towards the east side of the market.

III

Selection Carefully Made

Acalan stared into the bleak soup he had prepared himself in the morning. Turning his spoon created ripples through the uninspired colour but did little to motivate him for the day ahead. He leaned in closer to the bowl and squinted, having noticed an imperfection in the ceramic. He slammed his spoon onto the table in frustration; there was a small chip in one of his new bowls. It had only been a few weeks since he had replaced the set. His purpose on earth might be to rid it of the ceramic scourge of handcrafted dishware, he thought. His attention then shifted to the citation that sat next to his bowl.

The official seal of the City of Synnor glared at him as the brilliant red foil caught the light that shone through his window. The detail was lost on him as he popped it open absentmindedly.

For the immediate attention of Acalan Izel,

It is with deep regret that the city council writes to inform you that you have been selected to represent your people in the traditional Synorri archery competition. Your determined opponent is:

Cornaith Heiberos

You are reminded of your duty to represent the people of your city if you are defeated. This entails passage into the afterlife, where you must deliver the Synnori message of worship to the Divine Titans.

If you have any queries, we urge you to reach out to your city council representative during your preparation week. If for any reason you believe that you qualify for an exemption, you must discuss this with your representative as a matter of urgency. You are also reminded to check the council boards for the full trial details.

We wish you the best of luck in your preparation.

Synnor City Council

Since he had read the boilerplate text of countless identical letters before, Acalan skimmed through the letter. His eyes were fixated on the name of his competitor. His main source of relief was his confidence that he had no idea who Cornaith was. Any amount of real danger was trivial since he didn't fear the selection process. He believed that he could win against any opponent, and he hadn't been challenged in many years. With this in mind, he swept the letter aside. He lifted the bowl to slurp the remaining soup, taking extra care not to cut his lips on the chipped section.

After placing the empty dish back onto the table, he moved through to his bedroom to collect his bow. The cabinet was spotless, which struck him as odd. A fine layer of dust would usually form between his selections, but they had become more frequent lately. He was aware of the trend of the top performing archers in the city seeing more frequent selection. It was a nice thought, but he didn't flatter himself with it for too long. Regardless, he couldn't change his selection since he was still many years away from exemption.

He clicked the latch loose, allowing the cabinet door to swing open before lifting the unblemished bow from its hooks. When he examined the tension of the bowstring, he was relieved that his bow seemed ready for another performance. He had been putting off this work, so he was pleased it was not yet required. After placing his bow on the desk, he then proceeded to inspect the heads of his three arrows. He realised that just like his bowl, the top of one of his arrows was chipped on one of its three corners. Unsure how he had failed to notice this, he suspected that the missing fragment was on the floor.

Instead of searching for it, he retreated into his kitchen cupboard and slammed the door shut behind him. Any visitor might expect to find this insignificant room littered with mops and cleaning supplies. Instead, they would discover Acalan's workshop. Acalan took a moment to light the half-used candle that sat on a ledge above his head, and the flame lit up the small space. He lowered himself onto the tiny stool and got right to work.

The walls surrounded him with countless compact storage drawers, each with a purpose of its own. While pressing his wrists into the practical crafting bench, he used his thumb to guide a small craft knife underneath the arrowhead. Taking great care, he pushed the blade away from himself like his father had taught him. As a result, he managed to remove the tip from the arrow and toss it into a small metallic junk bin.

Acalan smiled to himself as he slid out a deep drawer from behind him. This compartment was filled with a few dozen flawless replacement tips. The arrowheads sat in perfect rows like chocolates in a box. Selecting one, he attached it to the headless arrow shaft. Since he always crafted his own gear, he would never consider using the flimsy equipment provided by the city. Getting up, he blew out the candle and swung the door shut behind him. His solution was better.

***

A week later, Acalan was once again standing in the dark corridor, looking down the range at two arrows embedded in a bull's eye. This was when he pulled the final arrow from his quiver. He paused before placing it against the drawstring, realising that the final shot was going to be with his mended arrow. With this at the front of his mind, he took a moment to inspect the arrowhead. When he applied a minimal amount of pressure to the tip, he was pleased to find that it stayed in place. Then, he noticed a tacky substance on his fingertips. A small amount of glue had run out of the arrowhead and onto the shaft. He cursed this realisation as it had come far too late. After drawing the bowstring, he did his best to compensate for the leaked substance before launching the arrow down the range. His heart sank as he realised that the arrow was fishtailing: the balance was all wrong. Only when the arrow landed askew in the outermost ring of five in the bull's eye did it dawn on Acalan that he might have put himself in danger.

For the first time since he had emerged in the arena that day, he acknowledged the thousands of eyes burning down upon him, particularly the eyes of his opponent, who had already taken his shots. Acalan directed his attention towards the crowd for some indication of the result. The stunned silence at his awkward shot revealed nothing. In his arrogance, he hadn't listened to the crowd's reaction to his opponent's shots. It hadn't seemed relevant until then. For the first time in many years, Acalan felt mortal. The wait for the curtain to drop felt unbearably long. Soon enough, it did, and his perspective expanded.

Acalan's stony mask slipped for a split second, allowing the crowd a glimpse of his unnerved scan for arrows. Panicked, he looked straight through his opponent and towards their target. A crushing sensation developed in his chest when he couldn't locate the arrows. It took several seconds before he realised that no arrows were on the canvas of the target. Only then did he look for Cornaith.

Acalan saw that the guards were already escorting his opponent up the stairs. He had been oblivious to the shift in the room's attention: it was no longer upon him. This realisation allowed him to regain his composure. Queen Virrel and the Titanic representatives moved into the scene, and a flawless victor's arrow was thrust in his direction once more.

***

Sometime after the celebrations concluded, spectators were still exiting. The crowd flowed towards the square and dispersed outwards into the surrounding streets of the Upper District. Acalan sat atop the peaceful hill looking into the crest of the arena. The alcoves of the arena's concrete pillars were darkened at this late hour of the day. The commotion of the day had mostly subsided, and from this spot, only the chirping of birds in the nearby shrubbery could be heard. Acalan finished explaining the experience to Iverissa, who hung onto every word. She was sitting in stunned silence, having been unaware of the danger her friend had been in.

'It turned out fine, but for a moment, I thought it was my turn to go up.' Acalan paused, catching a lump in his throat.

'You're an idiot for risking that, Ack!' Iverissa broke her silence. 'You could've bought another arrow; your obsession nearly killed you.'

'I'm not obsessed,' he protested.

'You've used those arrows for how long?' she

asked rhetorically. 'You sit in a cupboard for hours on end mending them.'

'What if luck exists?' Acalan responded. 'There isn't a way for me to test that. If I go out there and I'm wrong, I don't get a second chance.'

'I know you're scared, Ack; I would be too,' she admitted, startled by his vulnerability.

'I know you would, we all are.' He was glassy-eyed, each breath less disciplined than the last.

'Somebody has to lose. If it's not them, then it's you,' she reminded him. 'I need you to be more careful,' she said gently, backing off as she recognised that he was struggling with the emotions of the day. She attempted to reassure him. 'It's okay to be scared, Acalan.'

That was the thing, he thought, the moment when he would see the fear in their eyes. He needed to know what scared them in their last moment. The council? The Titans? He latched onto a deep breath but did not speak. Was it him that they feared? A droplet escaped his eye, but he swiped it away with a keen hand before Iverissa could notice. He wasn't willing to cry in front of her. He rocked back onto the grass and stared into the sky, seeking an answer from the Titans above. No divine response was obvious among the blurry white specks scattered across the clear dark sky. Then, two green spheres were above him as Iverissa leaned over him from above.

'You don't control the selection, Acalan,' she said,

appealing to his sense of logic.

When he sat upright, movement at a temporary wooden section of the outer arena caught his attention. The wood on the external façade was out of place in the grand stone structure. Acalan watched as a small group of construction workers resumed restoration work on the arena's damaged section, a result of the continued unrest in the city. It seemed that this was worsening as of late, although he couldn't understand why. The Synnor council and monarchy provided stability and security. These disorganised riots seemed only to destabilise the city and spread fear.

'Would working this late make you eligible for exemption?' Iverissa joked, noting the shift of Acalan's attention towards the construction occurring below.

The unrest greatly increased the demand for qualified builders and engineers. This led to a temporary exemption clause in the selection process. It involved working unpredictable hours, but for many, it was worthwhile. Some people would do almost anything for that exemption.

'To think that you get yours for free,' he remarked, acknowledging her attempt to restart the conversation.

'I'm essential in that library!' she protested, to his amusement. Only then recognising his cynicism, she shifted her tone to imitate him. 'I'm a valued council associate,' she joked, but technically, it was true.

Her intelligence was essential to the administration process of managing restricted literature. Only Iverissa and her colleagues had such access, which made them essential to the council. The sensitive nature of her occupation made her difficult to replace, thus exempting her from the trials.

'You're brilliant. Just don't be too brilliant,' Acalan concluded as he stood up and began to make his way down the grassy hill.

'You're heading home already? We barely got here!' she called out, causing him to stop after only a few paces.

At some point over the years, it had become a tradition. They would sit together at this vantage point after his trials. Usually, though, they would stay much later into the evening.

'Well, I need another drink...,' he explained, 'but not alone. I was hoping you'd join me this time.'

After the unforeseen intensity of the day, the invitation needed no justification.

IV

An Error in Judgement

As he was stepping out of bed, Acalan didn't bother to plan the day ahead. Thanks to his recently stitched curtains, the absence of daylight brought him great satisfaction. It was only when he flicked the curtains open and they slid without resistance along the railing that the early morning light surged in.

He sighed when he looked towards the ornate display case affixed to the wall and saw it awash with the light of day. It was in perfect condition except for a thin layer of dust along the top. Boredom had pushed him to replace the drawstring of his bow several times, yet it had done nothing but sit in the box. The arrows, in particular, were in pristine condition. Following his scare, he had retreated into his workshop to refurbish each arrow.

As he stared through the glass, he felt a conflicting mixture of relief and disdain. On one hand, it was a blessing to escape selection for so long. He had grown concerned by his repeated selection, and this break made it look like a coincidence. Yet on the other hand, it was boring loafing around while his identity sat in its box, waiting for another call to the crowd. Shadows enveloped the landing as he wandered across it. The spiritless plaster of his walls did not inspire for his day ahead.

He had just delivered a bow that had taken several weeks to finish and was between contracts. He had no dependents, and odd jobs for bow repair and customisation provided him with more than enough income to sustain himself. There was plenty of business thanks to his reputation in the arena. Although he had just been paid, he considered searching for a contract to fill the day. Just then, he saw a small red circle fall to the foot of his door, interrupting his thoughts. The council's red wax seal caught Acalan's attention as it screamed at him from its envelope. Acalan smirked; at least his arrows were ready.

He swiped up the envelope from the grubby doormat and flipped it over. As anticipated, his name was written in a substance unlike any traditional ink, as if etched by enchantment. This matched all the citations that had come before it, confirming his suspicion.

As he stepped into his kitchen, he flung the envelope towards the table. It twirled with grace through the air, its equilibrium maintained by the wax seal, and landed neatly on his dining table. Disinterested, he grabbed the used tankard that was waiting beside his sink and filled it with water. The misty drizzle outside distracted him, and the tap water overflowed, cascading over his fingers as he looked out into the bare morning streets.

Delighted that he now had plans for the day, he turned back to the table and took a seat. He tore open the envelope and extracted the single folded sheet enclosed within. Flicking it open, he skimmed the typical format of the citation. It was only when he processed the relevant line of the citation that Acalan froze. For perhaps the first time in his life, he gave the council his full attention.

Acalan knocked aside his steel tankard as he brought his hands to his face, stunned by the words before his eyes. It slid along the table, stopping only to add a crack to the chipped bowl. Upon impact, the water in the tankard sloshed up and outwards in an arc. Acalan was oblivious to this, remaining fixated on the name of his next opponent. The splash of water smudged the boilerplate text but did not blur the magically imprinted name.

Your determined opponent is:

Iverissa Zyrel

This wasn't possible, he thought; she was exempt. Acalan stumbled to his feet and folded the letter with the utmost care before placing it in the front of his robes. Disconnected from what he had read, he stepped backwards towards the door. After a few slow steps, he reached behind him for the door handle. He clicked the lock and removed the key before opening the door and letting the world in. The morning drizzle sprayed his face coldly, but he did not react.

Must've been a mistake, he thought as he locked the door, a clerical error. He turned towards the street. It can be overridden, he assured himself.

Acalan stepped onto the cobblestone street to find it free of foot traffic. The only movement was that of the rainwater flowing down the stone gutter at the roadside. It seemed to drain at a steady pace, which Acalan matched. Getting to Iverissa's house was a short journey as the crow flies, but for a person walking, it was a bit more complicated. They were much further apart by foot since he had to descend through the districts. This wasn't a problem, though. Acalan visited Iverissa all the time, so he knew the quickest route.

Acalan continued to follow the rainwater as he turned onto a steep downhill alley. He was just starting to process what was happening, and his thoughts began to spiral. He had never heard of a selection error, so he didn't know how this one would be handled. He quickened his strides to keep up with the flowing rain, which was then setting a brisk pace downwards. The wind was blowing a chilly mist up the alley and into his face. He could see the giant stone tower of the Lower District's Titanic church, its tip peeking into the end of the tight lane that he was then running down. A legal challenge to the council would be completely unprecedented. Acalan didn't know what he would do. He didn't even know what he could do.

As he reached the end of the alley, the buildings that flanked him also came to an end. He stopped on the spot as his perspective widened to include the Lower District. The tiny buildings conformed to a strict structure. As the majority were council-funded buildings, they had identical dimensions. Each dwelling had a window and a door, but not much else. Despite their incredible blandness, a complex web of tight lanes linked them. Morning light from above crept over the district, bleeding through the narrow alleys. The rain grew heavier, lashing down over the rooftops.

Acalan gazed out from his current position, taking in the obstacles that lay between him and the city's edge. Situated on a cliffside, Synnor's construction catered to a vertically oriented society. The desolate wasteland at the peak of the cliff enforced this unique architectural approach. Countless steel bridges and stairways connected the districts together. Standing on one of these bridges, he observed the scattered cottages of the Lower District. The only exception to the low-lying landscape was the prominent church tower; it was as if the Titans were speaking directly to him. He prayed that this was them attempting to reassure him, but maybe they were taunting him. He shuddered, pushed the thought aside, and directed his gaze downwards, towards Iverissa's little cottage in the west.

The gutter system alongside him culminated at the city's edge. The resulting flood burst over the edge and ran down the rock wall between the districts. The purpose of the rusty gate he stood at might have been to restrict public use of the aged metal staircase. Yet, without a lock, it was open to anyone brave enough to risk using it. He shuffled in a clumsy rush down the spiral, taking extra care not to slip on the soaked grid under his feet. It was easy as long as he didn't look down.

When he stepped onto the cobbles of the Lower District, he lunged into the rain, and it lashed back in his face. He was losing a race with his mind as it sped through all possible future outcomes. By the time he approached Iverissa's home, his robes clung to him like a second skin.

Upon arriving at her door, he sought limited shelter under the overhanging stone archway. It was time for Synnor's royal orchestra to perform another composition; he hammered his fists into the door. The sound of fearful slams reverberated, eventually slowing into thuds of despair. The woodwind ensemble then continued the movement with a chilling breeze that pushed him inwards.

'Iverissa!' he choked out, clawing at the door. 'Let me in!' His voice didn't carry as he gasped for air, having lost control of his breathing on the rapid, albeit short, descent.

After receiving no response, he braved the full force of the weather once again and made his way to look into her window. Only then could he see that she was sprawled across the dimly lit carpet. He was only able to recognise her dainty figure by its contrast against the aged leather of the armchair that she was propped up against. She looked disturbingly vacant, with her eyes hidden behind her unmanaged lily-white hair. Her tear-soaked jawline peeked out, exposing part of the face that was cowering behind her unruly locks. While one hand clenched her glasses, the other clutched her corresponding citation. Acalan's racing mind ground to a halt. This was real.

Iverissa swiped her hair behind an ear, revealing the bottomless green of her right eye. Her pupil was swimming in dread as the pair locked eyes through the window. Nothing could be heard through the pane. The rain continued tapping on the glass on Acalan's behalf.

'Let me in,' he mouthed, shivering against the pane.

Letting her glasses roll onto the floor, Iverissa raised a hand to wave him in. Surprised to find the door sealed shut only by the latching mechanism, Acalan let himself in and approached her, but she remained on the floor. The tip-tapping of the raindrops outside diminished and came to a sudden halt as the door clicked shut. A sniffle marked the end of the Orchestra's performance.

'It's a mistake. We can appeal it,' Acalan thought aloud.

'No,' she answered, revealing both eyes as she shook her head.

She avoided Acalan's eyes, keeping her own fixated on the envelope that lay on the carpet, its red seal barely clinging to the ripped paper.

'I know it's unprecedented, but we have time to explain. It's going to be okay.' He tried to calm his friend but noticed that her eyes still wandered across the carpet as if seeking sanctuary from the conversation.

'Look at me, Iverissa. They got it wrong. You're exempt.'

'I'm not!' she snapped. A fresh tear escaped her eye when she made eye contact with him for the first time. 'I've been selected to represent my people,' she said, feigning honour with an ironic shrug.

'I don't understand,' Acalan said, bewildered.

Iverissa was gifted; it was her unique intellect that had kept her exempt from the trials throughout her life. He had always thought it was fortunate since her genius would have done nothing for her in that arena. Since she had always been safe from the invisible hand of selection, Acalan could never have anticipated this.

'I was about to tell you,' she whispered. Her false smile was incongruent with the shimmer of the tear that dripped from her jaw.

'I need you to tell me now,' Acalan responded, tolerating the unexpected, albeit minor, sense of betrayal.

Somehow, he felt responsible. He thought he knew everything about Iverissa and had assumed she was safe. If nothing else was clear to him, he knew he had been wrong about that.

'I'm not exempt,' she explained. 'Not anymore.'

'The library?' he interrupted.

'I'm not welcome there anymore. Although I don't suppose that matters now,' she continued. 'I was learning about the Jasebelle people and–'

'Iverissa, what have you done?' he interrupted again, and then, it aligned in his mind.

For one endless heartbeat, Acalan had absolute clarity. The disappointment he felt screamed outwards and inwards simultaneously. She did not respond, instead remaining silent like a child who had been caught breaking the rules.

'Why?' he pleaded for an explanation, unable to tolerate her silence.

'I needed to know. This place is a prison.' Iverissa looked to Acalan for encouragement but found his head cradled in his hands.

She should have known better, he thought. Yet, this could have been avoided had he been brave enough to confront her sooner. It was too late.

'You don't know that!' he argued, his face re-emerging from the confines of his hands. 'We're safe here.'

'Are we?' she challenged him, matching his argumentative tone. 'You can fool the crowd when you go out there and hope you're not next...,' she went on, equipped with all the details of his experiences. '...but I don't believe you.'

Acalan stopped speaking, allowing the tension to subside before joining her on the floor. The warning signs began to sink in. When they had stood on the promenade and looked out towards Jasebelle, she had stated it explicitly. He could only see this for what it was in hindsight: she had cried out for help, but he hadn't wanted to recognise the ugly path she was taking.

'I've been doubting it all for about a year now,' she confessed in the face of silent judgement. 'We're told that it's dangerous out there, but we aren't allowed to know why.'

'Does it matter?' he muttered dejectedly, before falling silent once more.

He remained speechless while she explained to him that she had been going to work and investigating for herself. Her research consisted of whatever books fell into her hands when a good opportunity arose. Generally, this meant her sneaking a book out of the building amongst her paperwork. After speedreading it at home, she would return it the following day to avoid its absence being detected. Restricted or not, she had been absorbing as much knowledge as she could.

'I felt invincible, people weren't even looking at me.' Her words were proud, but her defeated tone indicated fresh humility. 'Even if they did, I was sure they'd have given me the benefit of the doubt,' she added with a shrug.

'They didn't though, did they?' Acalan asked,

failing to resist the urge to cut in.

'Nobody even asked,' she argued, before returning to her explanation. 'It was just small talk while we locked up for the night, but I panicked.'

'Who knows?' Acalan cut in once more.

'Just Talmu,' she said quickly. 'Everyone else had left.'

'...and what do you mean by panicked?' He pressed for more, without concern for sensitivity.

'I was rushing, a trailing bag strap looped around my ankle and I didn't feel it,' she admitted, lifting her robe to reveal a trivial graze on her leg. 'Everything scattered across the floor,' she continued, and he listened intently. 'He was quick to help me gather my things because he's a gentleman, but when he saw it, he didn't hand it back.'

'Then what?' Acalan demanded once again.

'He seemed very surprised at first. He told me to leave and never come back,' she answered, causing Acalan's tense core to relax against the armchair; he had anticipated far worse. 'I guess he wanted to give me a second chance,' she surmised.

'Why didn't you tell me?' Acalan shuffled towards her as he spoke.

'I've been hiding here for the last few days, trying to figure out what to do.' She looked down at the citation she held. 'I suppose I don't even need to do that now.'

Acalan fell silent and evaluated the situation. It was difficult for him to appreciate the compassion Talmu had shown to Iverissa by looking the other way. Losing a trial was not the only reason a person might be delivered into the afterlife to face the Titans. Had Talmu informed the guards, Acalan was sure that she would have been immediately detained and executed. With the trial in mind, his attention fixated on the envelope in her hand. It occurred to him that any selection had two sides, and he had never seen this side before. This wasn't a game for most people; he knew that she wasn't prepared for it, and she didn't have enough time to learn.

The continued tapping of the rain on the windows cast his mind back through the scenarios he had considered on his descent. It was an uncomfortable realisation to him that none of them were this dire. Under normal circumstances, he would be preparing his bow, blissfully oblivious to the impact on his opponent. Given this unimaginable scenario, he evaluated his priorities, then he pulled her close. Her face retreated into his shoulder, where she could bury her anguish.

'It's okay, we can figure this out.' A white lie. 'We're in this together,' he added. Technically, that much was true.

V

Fight or Flight

As she stared down the firing range, Iverissa drew a breath. It was silent, a pleasant reading environment if not for the task at hand. Daylight from above lit her targets down the imaginary corridor. In theory, this was a simple focus point for her and her spectator. Only one set of eyes watched in anticipation as she lifted the flawless sylvan bow. Her open stance was amateurish, and she shook under the tension of the bowstring until she released her first arrow. The training ground by Acalan's house was hardly comparable to the arena, but he had replicated the distance and the target.

Acalan observed the arrow as it flew, and his shoulders dropped when he heard the arrow clicking along the stone. He grimaced as he imagined silence from the crowd who would soon be watching. Though Iverissa had managed to get the arrow onto the improvised canvas target a few times, Acalan remained concerned. His analysis of her performance noted inconsistency in her style as well as her results. A hit seemed to him the result of luck much more than skill. It further unnerved him that the target wasn't even placed at tournament range. With only a week to train, there wasn't enough time to bring her up to scratch.

It wasn't long before Iverissa was selecting and firing another arrow. She cursed as she watched the shot miss. Ripping a final arrow from her makeshift quiver, she struggled to nock it. Predictably, she then sent it flying past the target to join the rest. Acalan remained silent as this last arrow disappeared from view. The thudding of the bow hitting the ground might have been satisfying had he not put so much effort into making it.

'I can't do it,' Iverissa stated irritably, making no attempt to contain her exasperation. For her, it had been hours of ineffective practice. 'This is a waste of time.'

Acalan had never used a preparation week like this before. Usually, he would do minor repairs or simple practice drills; this was the first time he had ever feared the deadline. Acalan recognised that an hourglass had always been there once selection for the trials had been made, but he had never watched the sand deplete. This was the first time that he experienced the anxiety of feeling his time draining away. Every moment that passed was one closer to competing against Iverissa.

None of this was in his best interests, but he had decided he wouldn't be able to live with himself otherwise. Since there was absolutely no hope of an exemption ruling for Iverissa, he had decided that morality could only be found in fairness. With this in mind, he had decided to help Iverissa with her preparation ahead of their trial, but a fair competition was seeming increasingly unlikely.

Following the revelations at her house, Acalan had peeled her off the floor, insisting that they at least use the time that they had. That afternoon had involved a trip to the Grand Market for materials for him to hastily craft her bow. It was almost as good as new since it had just collected its first scuffs from the stone at its feet.

Ignoring Iverissa's frustration, Acalan walked up the range. He approached the target and made a minor adjustment to the position of the fabric. Doing so allowed it to sit flush on its cheap wooden frame. Then, he stepped around to collect the arrows that Iverissa had launched. While doing so, he realised that she was right: this wasn't working. He clutched the retrieved arrows as he walked back. When he tried to hand them to her, she refused.

'It's over, Ack,' she insisted.

'Well…,' he attempted a response with his arm still outstretched.

'I want to spend a night together,' she stated.

'We're together now,' he said, misreading her tone.

She scoffed as she kicked at the ground, spraying muck over the bow at her feet.

'Just us,' she clarified. 'No shooting.'

Acalan looked her in the eyes and watched as

they explored their surroundings.

'They will take one of us, that much is certain. It doesn't control the time we have left unless we let it.'

Acalan was starting to understand. They hadn't separated since they had received the news. Yet, this was under the constant awareness that judgement was looming. Their citations had shackled them together with an imminent deadline. Hopeless as it might have seemed, it wasn't upon them yet. If they chose to spend all of the remaining time training together, it wouldn't really be their choice.

The idea of losing her didn't feel very liberating either. Iverissa had made reasonable progress with her new bow, but it would never be enough to compete with him. Even if she was able to hit a couple of decent shots on the day, he would still outmatch her. Her eyes latched onto his, eager to hear a response to her suggestion. Winning against Iverissa would be easy, he thought, but it was also impossible.

'What do you want to do?' he conceded, much to her relief. One of them would be facing the Titans soon enough, but not yet.

Iverissa sprang onto Acalan and pulled him into a tight hug.

'I want to go back to before all of this mattered,' she said wistfully. 'Do you remember when we were kids?' she began to expand. 'We used to walk the promenade after school, too young to worry about any of this.'

Acalan cast his mind back. He reflected on his innocence at the time, on how little he had seen. She pressed her head into his chest as she spoke. Acalan stepped back to look at her face and saw that same innocence in her. She had never done this, but he had competed more times than he could count. Perhaps it was his turn to lose.

'I'm going to let you win,' he confessed.

Iverissa's figure was modest, she stood well over a foot shorter than Acalan. She had been a full-time librarian, and she was built like one. It must have been the shock that amplified the impact when her hand slapped across his face. His eyes watered slightly. It wasn't the response that he had expected.

'No.' She rarely spoke this concisely. Doing so reinforced the response that her hand had made clear.

He searched through the sting on his cheek for words to rescue the moment but found none.

'You're not hearing me,' she said. 'Just let me forget about it.'

'I'm sorry,' Acalan backtracked, unsure what else to say.

'Don't make it weird,' she brushed off the awkwardness, allowing him to detect acceptance from her. Not acceptance of his apology, but acceptance that the trial would come regardless.

'Meet me down at the promenade,' she went on, seemingly at peace that it would likely become her responsibility to deliver the message to the Titans.

He focused on her instructions when it became clear to him that there was no honour in conceding. The only honourable thing he could do was allow her to enjoy the precious time they had left.

***

Only an hour had passed since they stood together beside his house. Acalan was walking towards the east end of the promenade, where he expected to meet Iverissa again. She had advised ho, to go inside and get changed before meeting her there.

'Clean up well. Make an occasion of it,' she had said.

Her words echoed in his head as he turned into a lane that would end at the edge of the city. He was completely out of place wearing a black two-piece suit and walking through the back alleys of Synnor's Lower District. He wasn't used to such attire since his basic clothes fit into two categories: function or comfort. His suit jacket provided neither, but he wanted to impress, and this was the best he could do.

His field of view broadened as he left the tight confines of the city streets. The ocean came into view as he walked out onto the main esplanade. The setting sun that peeked over the horizon filled the sky with warm orange hues. Gothic iron fencing running along the front of the promenade accented this backdrop. Ahead was a gap in the fence where one part was missing. Although not by design, the space was a viewpoint at the cliff's edge from which to stare off into the distance.

Acalan's eyes fixated on the focal point of the scene: a lone figure who stood looking out to sea. She was wearing a teal dress that clung to her figure at the waist before flaring out. The hemline, like a painter's brushstroke, dared to flirt with the boundaries of convention. The heels on her feet lent her several inches of height that she usually lacked. Her white hair was arranged elegantly on the top of her head, exposing her shoulders. The only disruption to her sophisticated aesthetic was a bulging leather satchel slung across her shoulder, hanging at the small of her back.

Acalan approached the fence, taking care of the steep drop at the edge, and stood beside her.

Sensing his presence, she turned. He could then see a glimmer between the cross-front style of her dress as her emerald necklace gleamed in the setting sun's rays. The silver chain that supported the stone was pristine, hanging loosely around her thin neck. Iverissa smirked at him, her eyelids fluttering, not showing any signs of fear. All he could see was the curiosity he had always known her for, wrapped in a bundle of nostalgia. Even though her silhouette was unfamiliar, he couldn't help but smile back. She exuded elegance as she stepped back from the cliff's edge and walked along the front of the promenade, her gait unhindered by the heels that clung to her feet.

Neither was thinking of the future as they walked together through the past. A sacrifice was still due, but it was as if the hourglass had been turned on its side, and the sand had ceased to flow. The moment stretched as they laughed together. Problems and insecurities from their youth seemed so insignificant. Even their recent worries seemed much smaller. Their outfits earned them confused looks from passersby, but neither Acalan nor Iverissa noticed. The world moved on around them, and they were refusing to participate.

The duo slowed as they approached the giant stone gateway that led into the Grand Market. This also served as a sign that they were halfway along the promenade. Multi-storey towers flanked the gate through which Synnori nightlife would soon pass. Acalan gestured towards a small café with quaint tables surrounding its entrance. In response, Iverissa's white teeth revealed themselves in a half-smile.

'Very classy, but I had another idea,' she said as she flicked open her leather satchel and produced a small corked bottle of wine. Acalan withheld his laughter but did not speak. Instead, he looked downwards and released an exhale through his nostrils. She coerced him back towards the fencing and they stood at the edge of the world while she thumbed the bottle's cork free. Then, without much care, she flung the cork over the cliff's edge. It plunged towards the water below. Turning to Acalan with a shrug, Iverissa took a swig from the bottle. It was undeniable that gulping from the bottle detracted from her elegance, but this didn't matter to him. When she extended it towards him, he swiped it and took an equally classless swig.

'I was going to ask if you would escape with me,' she stated abruptly, causing Acalan to choke on the wine.

He lowered the bottle and looked towards her with his eyebrows raised.

'Doesn't matter now, though,' she added, maintaining his attention.

For the first time, intrigue entered his mind, replacing apprehension.

'What do you mean?' he asked, finally humouring her after all this time.

'I wanted to see what was out there. That's why this all happened,' she explained, opening up. 'I was going to make a plan, but I couldn't even do that.'

'What did you find?' he asked, resisting the urge to lecture her any further.

'Nothing worthwhile.' She avoided the question, but this only intrigued him further.

'I won't tell anyone,' he teased, mindful that they were long past the point of such concerns.

'Well, it's either up or down.' She forced a

defeated exhale through her lips.

'Down is probably off the table, right?' He squinted over the edge and down to the distant waves.

'Very perceptive!' she congratulated him sarcastically. 'If Eden Synn had any chance of seeing the Jasebelle shores from here, then it must be close. Still, it would take at least ten hours to swim…' she paused a moment, '…but perhaps much longer with shattered ankles.'

'Fine.' Acalan took the hint. 'Why not up?'

'Turns out there's a good reason nothing out there has ever gotten in,' she answered, turning to lean backwards onto the fencing. 'The walls at the peak of the Upper District don't really have weaknesses.'

'The settlers would have had nothing when they got here.' Acalan tested her. 'Surely, they made a mistake somewhere, and you found it?

'Sure,' she responded immediately, 'but we've had a lot of time to improve it since then.'

'Oh, right,' Acalan mumbled, having missed something so obvious to her.

'Equal distances of stone above and below ground,' she continued, oblivious to his embarrassment. 'Several feet thick…'

'I get it,' Acalan interrupted before taking another gulp. As the wine flowed down his throat, he considered the irony that he would jump at the chance to get out of Synnor. Only then did it seem to be a matter of perspective.

Iverissa placed her hand on the back of his shoulder, finally noticing his frustration. She didn't speak, instead allowing him to process it all. Eventually, he passed the bottle back to her and stared down at the waves below. With the recent awareness of his mortality, he entertained some irrational thoughts – what if he were to jump? He could have done it there and then. Stepping off would be an instant escape, there would be no dilemma then.

As he mulled over this option, he turned to face the gate of the Grand Market. Leaning on the fence and looking into the marketplace, he remembered the desperate actions of Amara, the trader's daughter. Her death had achieved nothing since her father had still been taken. After all, somebody had to deliver the message to the Titans. He wondered if anyone else would even remember her final moments; they stood for nothing more than to remind Acalan to be rational. Still, he continued to dwell. He looked at Iverissa and relived the sting of her slap across his cheek. He couldn't leave her behind.

Acalan lifted the bottle to his lips, but only drops met them.

'Now what?' he asked, seeking impossible guidance.

Her expression tightened.

'Can we stay a little longer?' she answered with another question.

'Good idea,' he encouraged. 'I'll be right back,' he added, and then meandered away with the empty bottle.

Iverissa supervised from a distance as he stepped towards one of the city's refuse chutes by the gate of the Grand Market. He only realised that he was tipsy when he peered into the tunnel and his balance faltered. He watched the bottle disappear, listening for the satisfying sound of shattering glass, but there was no delight to be found in the silence that followed. Disappointed with this, he stood upright and scratched his head. Even a splash would have justified sticking his head in there. Although the world around him was spinning a little, for a moment, everything stood still. He had an idea.

VI

Heist in the Upper District

Acalan rushed back over to Iverissa. 'How's your swimming?'

She jumped, and her hand darted onto her chest. 'Don't push me over, Ack,' she joked, attempting to divert attention from her embarrassment. 'You promised a fair contest!' she added.

Acalan's eyes widened in puzzlement. He was still awaiting a response to his question. Though she didn't answer, her face went blank, and she tilted her head slightly.

'I don't understand.' She conceded to break the silence.

'It's a long swim, but it would be possible?' he queried.

'Well, sure, but that doesn't matter; the fall would shatter every bone in your body.' She leaned over the railing while she tried to explain.

'I get that part.' He disregarded her explanation and continued to vocalise his thought. 'Are you sure it's possible?' he emphasised.

'If Jasebelle is where the story says, then yes – it's possible, but only just.' She squinted at him. 'What's your point?'

'I know what we can do,' he stated, causing her to lean forward, intent on unpacking whatever theory he had. 'I'll explain on the way.' He pushed off of the railing and sprang into a brisk walk.

Acalan's shoulders tensed as a chill crawled up his back. The ghosts of the emptying Grand Market were a tailwind, helping him to lead the way at a healthy pace. Iverissa was trailing behind him as they passed through the lit market. Instead of slowing for her, he continued to dart through the fabric-covered stalls. They were passing through after the bustle of shoppers had dispersed but before the drunken foot traffic arrived. Trading had ceased and the merchants who remained were attending to their stocks.

'There should have been a noise,' Acalan rambled as he darted onwards. 'It was the silence that gave it away.' His rushed speech matched the urgency of his steps.

'Slow down, Ack!' Iverissa tried to get his attention, but he continued forwards. 'What should have made a noise?'

'The bottle.' Still, he did not turn. 'It should have smashed.'

'The bottle?' she asked, trying to catch up with him.

'Why didn't it smash in the chute?' He froze on the spot and spun round.

Iverissa's momentum carried her into him, but he caught her by her arms and avoided a collision.

Her frame locked up as she drew back in shock but relaxed once more as she mulled it over.

'Water?' She stabbed in the dark.

'That's what I thought!' His tone encouraged her. 'I'd hear a splash though, right?'

'It disappeared?' she guessed.

'If I can't hear it, then…' Acalan paused for the penny drop.

Iverissa's eyes widened, and her jaw dropped. and then she closed her eyes as she shook her head.

'It goes the whole way down,' she said quietly, completing his sentence.

'Maybe.' He leaned in close, keeping his voice down despite no bystanders being around to overhear him. 'I have no idea.'

He had always just thrown bags into the hatch. The disposal system existed only to unburden him of his refuse; he had never considered where it went.

'Then we need to find out,' she said, with no trace of emotion.

'If we can get down there, then we won't need to take part in the trial,' he proposed. 'We can run.'

Having ascended partway through the districts, the pair continued crossing the city. Acalan focused on moving forwards, but Iverissa's eyes were scanning the area. She couldn't help but notice the metal hatches littered around the city. They were tiny cogs in a vast machine, each providing a miniscule amount of functionality. Such a simple detail of their city usually blended into obscurity, but not that night.

Absent-minded folk pulling carts were the only foot traffic as they re-joined the main road. The late hour of the day was clear on each apathetic face that passed. The final deliveries to the warehouses around them were moments from being complete.

'We don't have much time,' Acalan shouted back over his shoulder when they dipped through the industrial back streets of the city. The intimidating spiral stairway back up to the Upper District remained a test of Acalan's resolve. It had only been a week since he had descended with his citation against his chest. Last time, he had been running towards Iverissa, but this time, they were together.

'What's the worst that can happen?' he thought, continuing to rush forwards, using the railings at his side to pull himself upwards. One of the corroded steps could crumble and send them plummeting to their deaths at any moment, but one of them was already doomed. Only getting out of the city in time would save them both.

'I need to make a quick stop,' he insisted as he sprang from the top step of the staircase and back onto the cobbled street. The street widened as they progressed, and the claustrophobia of the Lower District lifted in this more affluent area.

'Give me two minutes.' Acalan burst through the door of his house, causing it to slam against the wall, and vanished inside. He ran through to his bedroom and pounced on the glass cabinet, swinging its door open. Just as he lifted his bow, the door of the case slammed against the wall and smashed, scattering shards of glass across the floor at his feet. He stepped backwards momentarily to avoid the sharp debris, then swiped the arrows from their hooks.

'Everything okay in there?' Iverissa asked cautiously upon seeing him emerge from the house with his bow and quiver slung over his shoulder.

'Absolutely fine.' He breezed past her, leaving the door ajar.

'I guess you don't need to lock it.' Her tone dripped with sarcasm, but she spoke only to herself as he continued up the street.

They then turned onto a vast, albeit empty, cobbled plaza. The end of the square was dedicated to the towering library hall, its façade adorned with golden arches exhibiting Titanic lore and symbolism. Four of the arches sat above the giant public entrance, each framing a stained-glass depiction of an Elemental Titan.

A larger arch topped the formation sitting a floor above the main rooms. It had a matching space that would fit another window, but brick sealed it away. Acalan stared at the painted mural. It seemed to him that it was only there to accommodate what was otherwise a confusing design. Somehow, it failed to deliver on the expectations set by the glass displays on the floor below.

The mural portrayed a group of hooded people in dull clothes, crowding around a woman at the foot of the city's palace. Four elemental rays shone upon the figure of the woman, who stood looking towards the sky. To Acalan, this vibrant depiction of Queen Virrel was much less compelling than the artful glass displays beneath.

'Why have you brought us here?' Iverissa asked, looking at her former workplace across the square.

Acalan looked at her and away from the giant wooden doors that sealed the public entrance.

'I'm guessing that books about the sewers aren't even restricted.' He exhaled a partial laugh through his nostrils. 'I want to find out how deep it goes.'

'I fail to see the point in that, Ack,' she snapped.

Her tone caused him to realise that this was the last place she wanted to be. Still, that fact made it no less necessary.

'Well, they probably need to be maintained.' Acalan unveiled his plan. 'There must be a way for us to get down there.'

If they cut a significant chunk of the fall away, then Iverissa's math for jumping had significantly more wiggle room.

'If we can get in there and follow it down, then jumping might be an option.'

Iverissa's brows furrowed for a moment as she processed his words before her jaw fell. He was finally making sense. Acalan smiled; he had noticed something she had missed.

'So, how do we get in here?' He pushed her for details.

'That shouldn't be a problem,' she replied without hesitating, taking the lead as they approached the building. 'They'll have closed at least an hour ago.'

Now, it was Acalan who trailed behind as she dodged the main entrance and slinked around the building. 'I need you to understand, Ack, that we're crossing a line here. If we do this, you are throwing everything away. If we get caught…'

'You said they can take one of us, and that much is certain. Well, I'm saying no.' Acalan dismissed the topic, unwilling to discuss the risks the pair were about to take. Awareness of the danger only made him more certain he was right. He was about to defy the gods, and he was going to win; the council would be seeking its sacrifice elsewhere.

The entrance that Iverissa selected was almost obscured from view by its simplicity. Acalan didn't even notice it at first, as it blended into the brickwork around it. They descended a cracked stone step to the doorway, and Acalan ducked, minding his head on the lintel.

As Iverissa pulled down on the door's basic steel handle, they heard the dull sound of the mechanism resisting. She continued tugging at it, but there was no further sound from the door, and the handle remained still despite her efforts.

'Okay, I'll kick it in,' Acalan announced. This wasn't supposed to be the hard part, so panic was already creeping in.

'No, Ack. Stop.' She shushed him as she looked back into the main plaza, ensuring that their ongoing crime had gathered no bystanders. 'It's fine, it just does this,' she assured him.

In one swift movement, she flicked the handle upwards then pulled it down again with a satisfying click, and the door swung open. Now, the heist had begun.

The pair entered a darkened room. Acalan froze, unsure of his next step. Though Iverissa was invisible to him, she moved instinctively towards a simple hand lantern. When she lit it, Acalan could then see that they were standing in a small room that preceded a short corridor. Confidently, Iverissa led him through the short passage, which was lined with steel locker doors. Some of the doors were ajar, so he could see that many contained paperwork and personal effects, but only one of them caught his attention.

It stood out because it was open and empty, yet it was located almost along the middle of the corridor.

Surely, any unused lockers would be at the start or the end, he thought.

'Yeah, that one was mine,' Iverissa said, noticing his puzzlement. 'I cleared it out, so don't bother checking for money,' she joked, seemingly unfazed by her surroundings.

Acalan didn't respond as she walked on, instead considering what the coins could even do outside of Synnor. Pondering this detail brought on the realisation of how little he knew. An ounce of curiosity replaced his fear as Iverissa's silhouette led the way.

This must be just a taste of what she felt like, he thought. For the first time, he empathised with her desire to learn, if only a little.

They continued ahead, and the lantern's flickering flame soon cast its light outwards into the main library hall. With its shelves tightly stacked, it was like a warehouse of knowledge waiting to be absorbed. It was clear from the orderliness of the rows of books that a strict organisation system was in place. Acalan squinted at the signs carved into the wooden fixtures, struggling to make them out. This prompted the realisation that the strength of his light source was diminishing: Iverissa hadn't stopped.

Picking up his pace as quietly as possible in his formal shoes, Acalan rushed to catch up to Iverissa. He found her already engrossed in a manual she had lifted onto one of the communal tables in the centre of the room. She stood over the pages, flicking through them rapidly before stopping with an index finger on the page.

'Maintenance!' she announced, oblivious to Acalan's nod of agreement.

He felt it was appropriate at this moment to stand aside; Iverissa was doing what she did best, but his confusion was sudden when he heard her whimper. He couldn't see the page; the lantern's glow was obscured as she bent over the table.

'What's wrong?' he asked, fearing the worst.

She turned back to him, the light reflecting in her glassy eyes. His anxiety did not lift until she spoke.

'I think it's possible.' Her bottom lip quivered, although a smile pushed through.

Acalan swivelled the book around, desperate for confirmation. After a moment of processing, he pulled her into a firm hug. When he stepped back, Iverissa's partially lit expression of hope was as warm as the tiny flame that illuminated it.

Suddenly, the hall was plunged into darkness as the lantern's wick expired. The silence in the library was broken only by a gasp from Iverissa, who pulled him close once more.

VII

Run

They stood in the darkened hall, with only the dim light of the plaza creeping in through the windows. Although the shadows concealed her, Acalan sensed a shift in Iverissa's demeanour. She appeared alarmed as she looked past him and around. He felt his arms growing sore before realising that her grip on his arms had tightened considerably.

As his eyes adjusted to the darkness, the hall's organisation lost all meaning. He squinted at his companion while he awaited further instruction. A distant click interrupted the moment and echoed around the room. Both their heads swivelled around, scanning the shadows urgently, but they could see nothing. No further sound followed, so they remained frozen in the middle of the hall.

Iverissa swiped the manual from the table's surface and stuffed it into her satchel. Acalan readied his bow before leading them back towards the lockers. As they shuffled up the corridor, Acalan began to accept the continued silence. They were being paranoid, he decided. Since Iverissa had walked this corridor countless times, she was the perfect guide for the unseeing archer. It was only when they approached the exit that another sound caused them to freeze in their tracks. The crack of a striking match sounded mere inches in front of Iverissa's face.

A modest flame burst into existence, held by a lone male figure, illuminating widened brown eyes. The man was an obstacle to their freedom, yet he carried no weapons. The patterns on the sleeves of his robe were familiar to Acalan; they were similar to those on Iverissa's old uniform. The difference was an extra level of embellishment and the man's aura of superiority. Iverissa had managed to surprise her former superior one last time.

Acalan readied his bow and trained an arrow on Talmu, who did not react, but instead stood bewildered. The three stood in silence as the flame crept along the matchstick. Talmu's eyes scanned the flickering shadows for options before letting out a sigh.

'Why would you come back?' he asked in an exasperated tone, searching for an explanation. He coaxed the flame from the half-burnt match into a lantern above, illuminating the scene.

'My bag, I left it in my locker,' she lied. 'I thought it would be awkward to see everyone again.'

Her head sank down and away from the lamp, casting a mask of darkness over her face in an attempt to obscure her deception.

'Your locker was empty, Miss Zyrel,' Talmu corrected her abruptly. 'Do you think your actions and subsequent departure have gone unnoticed?' he pressed her.

'I'm sorry! Is that what you want?' she lashed out in response, but her desperate tone only earned her a further sigh from Talmu.

When Acalan evaluated Talmu, he feared he recognised a man reaching his limit of helpfulness.

Iverissa's words hung in the air, and the seconds seemed to stretch endlessly. The flickering lantern light burned down on the pair like a spotlight, exposing them as the convicts they were becoming. Yet the more Talmu evaluated the scene in front of him, the less they behaved like criminals. They continued to stand there and wait. There was no arrow in his chest, and they did not vanish into the night.

Acalan remained on standby; his inaction was action. Their vulnerability became increasingly undeniable with every second that passed. Only when Talmu appraised his former colleague once more did he notice the bulging satchel over her shoulder.

'What have you taken this time?' He addressed Iverissa as if she were a common thief. 'Whatever it is, you can't escape selection.'

His words cut into her with the truth they seemed to reveal. Talmu tilted his head to the side knowingly.

'So, you heard about my selection?' She changed the topic. 'Well, you're wrong. We're leaving Synnor,' she stated. 'All we ever did here was conform; we always stayed where we were told, looked where we were permitted. From now on, I'll decide what the truth is.' Her tone was uncharacteristically serious.

Acalan had never seen her speak to anyone like this, let alone a superior.

'Nobody can dictate that to us now. Not you, not Virrel or the Titans, nobody.'

Talmu took a step back towards the door as Iverissa concluded her point, and Acalan tightened his grip on his bow.

'We aren't going to be here to tell anyone,' she pleaded. 'Turn a blind eye? Once more?'

'If anyone finds out I have done this…,' he conceded, dropping his head in acceptance.

Acalan released a breath, his grip on his bow slackening.

'Okay.' Talmu placed his hand on Iverissa's shoulder before allowing friendliness back into his tone. 'Nobody knows how dangerous this is, so I can't warn you of anything within my understanding,' he said, addressing the both of them and giving approval to the best of his ability.

'Why didn't you try to talk me out of it?' Iverissa asked.

'You think you're the only one who wants to know what's out there?' he responded rhetorically with a chuckle. 'To leave these walls, you must do so knowing that you are no longer welcome within them.'

'We know.' Iverissa smiled at Acalan, who noted the similarity between Talmu and his apprentice.

'I hope that you find your way,' Talmu stated profoundly, without any signs of reservation. 'I will leave first. Wait five minutes and then go.'

The bliss of ignorance shocked Acalan. Once again, inaction was a course of action. Iverissa had confessed that they were going out there, yet Talmu seemed happier not knowing the specifics. He seemed so wise, yet he had opted to overlook rather than learn, and this unsettled Acalan.

Talmu turned towards a coat hook that held a single noble overcoat. He slung it over his shoulders with a shrug. Acalan cursed internally at the timing of the whole situation; a coat was to blame for their discovery. They would have avoided the encounter completely had they been a few minutes faster.

'Thank you.' Iverissa's statement of gratitude interrupted Acalan's thought.

It occurred to Acalan what this might have meant for her. She had needed somebody to confirm that she wasn't the problem, and it was saddening that it hadn't been him. Her curiosity had been validated.

'Good luck.' The door slammed shut.

Acalan looked over Iverissa and towards the door. It was outlined by the light that crept through the edges of its frame. As the seconds began to pass, he reflected on his decision, considering the person that he was, and its impact on who he was trying to become. With the tension ramped up, he had chosen to place his trust in Talmu instead of an arrow; that had to mean something. There was, of course, every possibility that this was a mistake. A cluster of council guards could bash the door down in the coming seconds. They would rush in, and this would all have been for nothing. He simply had to wait to find out if trust was the right choice, but patience did not come naturally to him.

Only around thirty seconds had passed since the door had shut behind Talmu. Without a word to Iverissa, Acalan stepped forward. Iverissa pulled on his arm, clearly alarmed by this, but he shrugged her off since he needed to peek out into the street.

The door handle didn't budge when he tugged at it, and he reached an alarming conclusion; *they were locked in.*

'Ack!' Iverissa clung to him, but he didn't stop. He ripped at the door handle with all his might, causing it to swing open forcefully. The crashing sound broke out into the darkness and reverberated through the streets. They lay sprawled across the cold floor of the librarian's quarters. A draft blew in at floor level and crept right up through Acalan's clothes. Although he shivered, he dared not move. Both Acalan and Iverissa lay motionless on the floor in a desperate bid to be ignored. Acalan finally found patience, fearing guards who would place shackles on his wrists and lock their futures away.

A moment passed. Then two. Then three. Slowly, a sigh of relief escaped his tensed lungs. If the Titans were acting here, it seemed to be in their favour. The noise had resounded in the Upper District's main plaza, but apathetic silence met it. Acalan was unwilling to test this luck any further. He sprang to his feet and presented a hand to Iverissa, who was still struggling to regain her composure. She tutted at him as she found her feet and clutched him with a sense of acceptance. Iverissa did not find a moment to scold him before he whisked her through the open doorway and out into the night air.

VIII

The Blind Leading the Blind

The cast iron door merged completely with its surroundings. Its inoffensive gunmetal grey blended with the bleak stone wall it stood in. Rivets surrounded the frame, creating a gateway for its users. Having hurried back to the Lower District, they had selected this door as their entrance into the sewer network.

Acalan walked on the tips of his toes, avoiding puddles of mysterious industrial waste. His awkward dance around the pools went unseen in this dingy, deserted back alley. The stony façade ahead of them stretched up to the Upper District, and factories flanked them on either side. The only sound came from dripping gutters running overhead.

Acalan was not prone to claustrophobia, so the narrow space didn't bother him. What did make it particularly unpleasant was the stench that permeated the space. The oily residue from above ran into the cobblestones at his feet and filled the cracks between them, resulting in the distinct scent of death. He looked towards Iverissa and saw her with one sleeve pressed into her face to cover her nose and mouth. The fabric only left her face for one moment when she yanked on his arm to hurry him towards the door.

Corrosion had eaten away the keyhole of the rusty padlock. Acalan tugged at it, hoping that the aged metal would give, but the bar held tight. He was reluctant to take another breath of the toxic air but did so before bracing his foot against the door as he pulled harder.

The only give under this force was from the door itself as it relented under his improved leverage, offering a crack but no more. Acalan's fingers burned as he clung onto the padlock and pulled until the sting forced him to loosen his grip. As the tension throughout his body relaxed, he drew in his first uninhibited breath. He realised his mistake immediately as the offensive air flooded his lungs, causing him to choke and splutter.

Acalan then frustratedly flung his entire mass against the door, resulting in no more than a slight inwards dent. This only exasperated him further, and he stepped back, defeated. All he had to show for his efforts was a cut in the skin at the crease of his index finger.

By the time he composed himself, Iverissa had already taken his place and begun to inspect the lock with her free hand. The other continued to press a sleeve over her nose and mouth. She stared into the mechanism for several moments, looking at the hole that might have once accepted a matching key.

A clang sounded when she released the padlock, and it swung back against the metal door. Her hand shot into her satchel, and her eyes rolled upwards in concentration while she rummaged.

Acalan watched the crease in her brow deepen as she searched, eventually producing a flat silver clasp. The small rectangular piece of metal was roughly the size of a small coin. It had a little hinged prong that she flicked upwards and gripped in her fingers. She inserted it into the keyhole, and with some convincing, it clunked into place snugly. After taking a deep breath through her sleeve, she used both hands to twist her makeshift key. Acalan watched her struggle against the rusted mechanism before tutting and changing her approach.

Her hand returned to her satchel once again and scrabbled around for a while. This time, she pulled out some paper. Acalan squinted to identify it. She was holding a corner of the front cover of the stolen instruction manual, which she had ripped off.

'We won't be able to return it like that!' he joked. Even in their current circumstances, he knew she'd be a little uncomfortable with damaging it.

Despite the sleeve obscuring her face, her eyes had no issue with casting him an unimpressed look. Unfazed by his comment, she attempted to fold the paper with one hand before giving up and using both. She grinned with contentment at her little origami cone.

Squatting down, she lowered the cup into the oily pool that filled the space of a missing cobble. This solution was then poured into the lock with caution, to keep it off of her hands. Then, she twisted the makeshift key once more.

Acalan couldn't contain his smile as he watched her turn the device and receive a welcoming click. Iverissa unhooked the open padlock with her thumb and forefinger then threw it aside. The door's latch flicked open without resistance, and Iverissa swung the door outwards. Together, they rushed into the darkness and pulled the door shut behind them. All light remained outside as it slammed home, plunging them into complete darkness.

Acalan found the darkness calming, as it meant they were alone. He stood and listened for any disturbances, but the only sound he picked up on was the frantic rummaging by his side. The next sound was the scratchy crack of a match being lit. A tiny flame burst into life, dancing at the end of the short matchstick. Iverissa gripped it tightly between her thumb and forefinger and held it out at arm's length.

This moment of illumination allowed them to see the damp old office they stood in. A basic wooden desk covered in splinters defied the space by sticking out from a jagged, rocky wall at an angle. To the left of it, a cave-like tunnel led off into nothingness. Acalan and Iverissa separated as they explored the space.

'What was that key?' he quizzed Iverissa, still blindsided by her quick thinking.

'It's like you said. You can't return books if you damage the pages!' she joked, revealing the broken piece. It seemed like she wasn't too attached to the metal bookmarking device.

'Clever,' Acalan complimented her tonelessly, not making eye contact as a sheet of aged paper preoccupied him. Affixed to the inside of the door, it listed the surnames of engineers as well as 'Hours Logged'. What he found curious, though, was that each engineer also noted a 'Reason for Visit'. There was a myriad of entries scrawled onto it, such as 'Pipe #XXXX', followed by a basic description, such as 'blockage'.

'I thought they worked around the clock in here?' Acalan pointed this out to Iverissa. It struck him as bizarre since he knew a constant team was in place to keep things moving in the complex system.

'Ah!' Iverissa yelped as the match she held burned her fingertips and fell to the floor, plunging the pair back into inky blackness.

'I only had one left,' she said.

Acalan noted the desperation in her tone, more than a little darkness should incite. He knew that something was bothering her, but they were in this stressful situation together, so he elected not to make any comments.

It took several minutes for Acalan's eyes to adjust to what was near complete darkness. During this time, he could barely make out her silhouette as she felt around the area for a light source. Unfortunately, all she seemed able to find were more old files and papers. Her hands pushed these bundles out of their places and searched further around the room, but she found nothing. Acalan became increasingly aware of her discomfort as he felt sheets of paper brushing against his legs before falling around his feet.

'This is fine,' he said, attempting to reassure her. 'We planned for this,' he added. This was true. Based on the map they had read, they only had to walk in a straight line before reaching an escape platform. This platform would then have a corresponding stairway down.

'I'm scared, Ack.'

Iverissa's vulnerability remained unseen, but he could hear it in her voice. There was nothing to be afraid of, though, nobody was there. The plan was going perfectly, but he resisted the urge to say so.

Walking up the tunnel was simple for Acalan since he knew to walk straight ahead; it was only the hand grasping his shoulder that held his attention. They had agreed he would be their leader through the darkness while she held onto him from behind. He felt along the cold walls that surrounded them; this was the blind leading the blind, in the purest sense.

As they made their way through the void, Acalan and Iverissa were completely isolated. The city and its people were behind them, as was their responsibility in the Arena. They took every step as it came. Each one was a leap of faith towards the escape they had planned, as the path ahead was only visible in their minds. Acalan realised that there was no crowd anymore. From this point onwards, he had one ally in the world, and her fingernails were digging into his shoulder. It hurt, yet once again, he elected not to comment.

Even though their pace was slow, there was no way for Acalan to anticipate the sudden feeling of a cold metallic surface beneath his hands. He recoiled back in shock only to push into Iverissa. She gasped and swung at the air, having lost her grip on him. The frantic nature of her swinging only became clear to him when her arms mercilessly found his neck. He choked for a moment as she locked her arms around him. He managed to cough out the reassurance that everything was okay, and only then did her hold loosen.

'It's okay now,' he insisted confidently through his now unobstructed airway, having realised where he stood. Several clumsy moments of blindly feeling the surface had ended when Acalan's hand found a simple metallic handle. Relief swept over him as he twisted it and the door popped open. Moonlight flooded into the tunnel as the metal of the door screeched against the floor. After swinging the door open without a thought, Acalan's eyes took a moment to adjust to the view from the platform. Although it was late, the dim moonlight still came as a shock after the pitch-dark tunnel they had stumbled through.

A perfect moon crept over the watery horizon and illuminated the deep black of the night sky. Iverissa brushed him aside as she rushed out onto the platform and into the night air.

Acalan shuddered as a chilling breeze crawled in through the open doorway. As before on the promenade, his gaze fixated on the focal point of this new scene. Iverissa stood hunched over a stone barrier at the perimeter of the platform. Her stunning dress still clung to her figure as flatteringly as before, but this time, she clutched the fabric at her knees as it fluttered in the wind.

Acalan noticed that her ornate jade heels pointed inwards. He watched the shimmer of her unruly white hair as it trembled in the wind. She had flung her satchel to the floor at her feet. It sat still as if disciplined by the thick tome that sat within it. Acalan approached her and placed a hand on the small of her back. She jolted upright in surprise but did not turn to look, realising he was still there with her.

'I can't believe we're doing this,' she said softly.

'We're going to be okay,' he replied with a fresh surge of confidence, seeking contact with her eyes once more. Given a moment to reevaluate, he asked, 'Are you okay?'

Upon hearing this, Iverissa adjusted her stance and straightened up. Then, she began to tremble.

'It's so cold!' she complained, not answering his question.

It appeared that she was now regaining full control of her body and taking in her surroundings. In response to this, Acalan removed his jacket and placed it over her shoulders.

'Thanks.' Iverissa gave him the eye contact he sought, and her shivering stopped.

'Any time,' he answered sincerely, but did not question her any further. Instead, he looked outwards, giving her time to adjust.

He wasn't sure what he was observing in her. It unnerved him, but he wanted only to be supportive. When he reflected on what had driven him to this place, he realised it was his fear of ending up alone. He leaned on the stone barrier and peered downwards. Whether unable or unwilling, he didn't speak any more words at this moment. Instead, he began to scan his surroundings. It delighted him when he looked at the rocky cliff edge above and below. They were standing on one of many little escape hatch platforms, which indicated to him that the book bulging in Iverissa's satchel was accurate.

Bending down, he wrestled with the simple metallic buckle that held the satchel shut. While doing so, he noticed that Iverissa had flung her satchel down on top of what looked like an abandoned small brown paper packet of tobacco. This suspicion was confirmed when he lifted it open to peek in and found an unassuming box of matches. Acalan let out an exasperated yet controlled sigh as he held his face in his palm for a moment. This caught Iverissa's attention. She looked down to see him holding the box.

'Don't lose those,' she said sternly before letting a laugh slip out.

After producing the manual, Acalan flung it onto the concrete and flicked it open once more. It was the first time he was allowing himself to get excited about their escape attempt; it seemed to be working. Sitting on his knees, the chill of the cold floor coursed up his legs as he scanned for the right blueprint.

'So, we are…here!' he announced as he traced a digit down onto the page. 'That should mean…' He rocked his weight backwards onto his shins and peered back into the doorway.

The moonlight shone in and bounced off of a simple mesh fence that he now noticed for the first time. Hanging from the fence was a sheet of grey metal that was riveted in place at around head height. The sign displayed the three digits in a large pearl-white font: 374. With his updated perspective, he could also see steep concrete steps leading into deep black nothingness, one side ascending and one descending. He gestured towards the sign.

'Oh,' Iverissa commented.

'I would have guessed we were nearer one-seven-four,' he joked upon the realisation that they still had a long way to go.

'No, three hundred and seventy-four would be about right,' she said calmly. 'What? I worked that out too.'

IX

A Secret Lies Below

Upon closer inspection, Acalan noticed the sheen of a shining cord wrapped around the fencing. It dropped and climbed between each corner of the barrier, extending up and down to other levels. Baffled by this, he stepped back into the dim tunnel. As he left the chilly night air, he noticed a familiar damp smell that he was no longer attuned to after his break in fresh air.

The cord of mysterious substance ran between a series of lamps affixed to each corner of the dull iron rails. The fixtures themselves featured no decorative markings, seeming purely functional. Acalan squinted at them but saw nowhere to put his match. When he peered into the tiny windows, there was no oil, wax or wicks. There was only a wire that passed through before coiling in the centre of the lamp around a metallic loop. Each lamp housed a small ball of the mysterious cord that trailed out the side and onwards to the next in the chain.

Unsure how to light these lamps, Acalan attempted to tug on the slackened cord. Upon grasping it at the lowest point, he felt it warm up in his hands. A soft glow began to emit under and around his hands. The cord burned several inches outwards from his knuckles in each direction.

By this time, Iverissa had followed him. She had slung her satchel back over her gown and was holding the worker's matchbox. Now, she leaned in, interrupting his solo observation.

Her eyes widened, a faint gasp escaping her lips. 'No way... This can't be real,' she murmured, disbelief evident in her tone.

'What do you know that I don't?' Acalan quizzed her.

'Let me take a look,' she replied as she kneeled beside him.

Leaning forward, she motioned for Acalan to step aside, and he complied. With a confident touch, she lifted the slack cord gently, using the palm of her empty hand to guide it upwards. As with Acalan, it began to emit a harmless hue. She then released the wire and allowed it to swing against the fencing. Iverissa's dress draped onto the concrete as she crouched down on one knee, flaring her nostrils for an investigatory sniff.

'Yep. I've read about this,' she bragged with a blatant aura of self-satisfaction.

'Give me the short version,' Acalan pressed, refusing to encourage her.

'What do you smell?' she asked in response, thrusting the wire towards him.

Acalan hesitated but did not refuse. Without a word, he leaned inwards for a sniff of his own. A distinct scent contested with the earthy stench of the grimy tunnel walls. It was a smoky smell, with uncanny artificial notes. He fixated on it with intention, trying to place the familiar odour, and his mind made an association. It smelled like victory, and it was triumphant over the damp sewer stink. For a moment, he forgot about the crime that they were committing; its serious nature turned trivial. Anxiety made way for other sensations in his mind, and the roar of the crowd rolled into his imagination. Acalan slumped as the smell transported him back.

'It smells like the arena,' he said under his breath, without commitment to his words. 'I don't understand.'

'No, it smells like the victor's arrow,' she corrected him, speaking at full volume.

The association his memories had latched onto was the end of the trials, the moment after he won. The crowd would watch the council present the arrow to him and celebrate as he fired it upwards, tearing the sky. Whatever this mysterious cord was, Acalan agreed that it seemed to be of a similar composition. Iverissa waited patiently throughout his silence.

'I don't understand,' he repeated. 'Only the Titans can create this energy?'

'That depends on who you ask,' she explained smugly. 'I've read some conflicting stuff about the origins of this material,' Iverissa whispered, her voice filled with a hint of intrigue. 'But you know how it is, all that juicy information gets hidden away.'

'I went through an inventing phase, and those arrows they'd give you were fascinating,' she continued. 'I never actually invented anything that worked, and I stopped after the kitchen incident, but I learned a lot.'

'What did you do to your kitchen?' Acalan asked in shock.

'Doesn't matter!' She brushed the question aside, disregarding his concern and heightening his suspicion. 'My point is that it exists!'

'So…?' he pressed her.

'You can use it for anything.' She ran a match along the concrete floor, taking care to keep it clear of her gown. 'If you know how.'

After the spark grew into a minor flame, she presented it to the cable. In an instant, the flame was snuffed out from the matchstick, but it had escaped onto the cord. A fresh draft came in through the door and wafted at the resulting smoke. The rope crackled, and a blinding light burst outwards. Acalan jumped back, shocked by the sudden reaction, but Iverissa remained in place.

The spark sped along the cord in opposite directions, like a fuse burning from the inside out, tearing into two streams of light. The brightness climbed up and flowed down, illuminating the bowels of the city. After the flaring reaction, the cord returned to its initial state, but the light remained in the lamps. The staircase was now lit from all sides at once, courtesy of a single match.

Acalan didn't see Iverissa's celebratory dance as he craned his head over the fencing. An endless spiral descended into a portal of bright white dots, with no clear end in sight. When he turned to look upwards, the same view greeted him. It was an infinite stairway; the effect was jarring.

'I knew they were hiding things from us,' Iverissa stated.

She had stopped dancing before he looked at her, but he did notice that she didn't look to him for agreement. Her attention was on the stairs, so he presented her with a hand to help her to her feet.

Grabbing his hand, she hoisted herself up and then led him forwards with renewed confidence in her stride. Acalan didn't share her confidence in this moment. He didn't expect to find any secrets in this sewer but never mind that. One other thought in the back of his mind unnerved him: Where was everyone? Still, he continued down with her.

There is a set number of stairs a person can walk down before they begin to wonder if the descent will ever end. For Acalan, this came sometime after he lost count of the steps he had taken, yet still long before he could see the bottom. Each floor they passed was identical. Every level featured a cast iron door on the right-hand side and a tunnel to nothingness on the left. This didn't seem right to Acalan either; he had anticipated more complexity – or at least more than he could see. This place was supposed to be sophisticated, to support the entire city, but all he found with each passing moment was more stairs. Iverissa stopped in front of him briefly, interrupting the monotony by returning his jacket to him.

As they descended into the core of the sewage system, an increasingly foul smell began to assail them. Perhaps they were nearing a waste repository that was full and ready to be blasted by the Elemental Titan ritual, he thought.

'Now what?' Iverissa's words snapped Acalan out of the automatic stepping that he had settled into, bringing his attention to the abrupt stop ahead. There were no more stairs. It was a dead end.

'It's supposed to go the whole way down?' Acalan responded in disbelief, staring at the door in front of them. 'This is only…three-zero-four.'

On this level, there was no tunnel, just a single door. It was consistent with the others in its cast iron design, but it stood inside a much thicker frame. Acalan pulled at its handle, but it didn't budge. He then pushed and felt it bend through his arms, but it remained sealed. This came as an invitation for a shoulder barge that he readily accepted.

In doing so, he learned two things about level three hundred and four. The first thing came as a fright. As he barged through the door, the floor in front of him was not to be found. Instead, there was a steep and immediate drop downwards. In a moment of panic, he was able to clutch the door frame with his right arm. He teetered on the precipice as the door slammed out of his reach, and his stomach dropped as he felt his balance leave him.

Suddenly, he felt pain ignite in his chest and shoulders. His suit collar tightened around his neck as Iverissa grabbed it from behind, and his sleeves jolted as she yanked him back. It was she who suffered the brunt of the force when they tumbled backwards onto the unforgiving concrete steps.

Acalan learned the second thing when he rolled onto the floor and groaned in pain. Breaking open the tight seal of the door allowed air to flood in from beyond and assault their senses. The door had concealed a stench so disgusting that it was unimaginable to him before this exposure.

Acalan coughed at the taste of the foul air and pressed his sleeve over his mouth, but this had a trivial effect on the revolting stink. He retched and gagged, clawing at the cold stone around him. The discomfort paralysed him until he managed to contain the desire to puke without doing so. He looked to Iverissa, who also appeared disturbed by the smell, her eyes swimming with tears as she choked on the thick air. She quickly shifted her position when he looked at her, but he still saw what she had tried to conceal. A small, lumpy brownish puddle of vomit had been ejected into the corner of the step upon which she sat. It unsettled him to see it before he smelled it since she had been sick at his feet. Nevertheless, his nostrils had no chance of distinguishing its scent from the overwhelming stench coming from below.

The putrid room ahead remained intensely nauseating after its initial impression. Their bodies continued to resist the revolting air, and it seemed that they would never adjust to it. Realising that he should give Iverissa a moment of privacy, Acalan moved towards the dim light diffusing over the edge of the doorway. The formidable forewarning of sensory clues did nothing to prepare him for the revelation below.

As he peered downwards, he discovered that level three hundred and four was a misnomer. The room ahead was, in fact, not a room at all. Behind the cold steel door, at around head height, a deep black rocky ceiling stretched into the distance. The craggy canopy stretched into a cavernous horizon that loomed over the enormous underground chamber below.

'What is that?!' Iverissa spluttered, stumbling towards him.

Having found her feet, she leaned around Acalan. The blueprints had led them to expect a twisting matrix of tunnels and pipes intricately woven into a perfectly planned system. Instead, before them stretched a wasteland of rotting food and discarded canvas. A vast range of excess waste formed mountains throughout the expansive pit. Valleys of decay stretched between peaks below round openings in the rock above. Lakes of dark, grimy sewage water sat still, disturbed only by whatever vermin could call this home. All this was at least several hundred meters below Acalan and Iverissa's perch. They sat like a pair of judgemental crows, overlooking decades' worth of cans kicked down the road. There was no waste disposal network. *This* was the waste disposal network.

Words evaded them; it did not make any sense. Acalan wondered how something like this could happen. Iverissa wondered how it had been kept a secret.

Looking from side to side, Acalan saw nothing on his left but identified the distant light source on his right. Moonlight was leaking in through a great opening. The mouth of what he now understood to be a cavern stretched from the rough rock ceiling to the bottom of the dump. Waves rolled into the steep hills of rubbish; this stockpile of waste was on the coast, forming a beach without sand. From his vantage point, he could see it spilling into the sea and discolouring the otherwise clean water. The moon's luminescence bathed the behemoth of trash accusingly. A splash in the distance caught Acalan's attention; a waste bag bobbed in a pool of sludge, dropped from far above by an unsuspecting citizen.

At their feet was a rusted steel ladder fixed into the wall. Upon evaluation, it appeared to Acalan that if they were brave enough, it would take them right down. He looked to Iverissa, gesturing towards the first rung. Her eyes widened and her brow furrowed as she gave a minor shake of her head, her sleeve still pressed against her mouth. She broke eye contact without speaking a word. After scanning their surroundings desperately, her head drooped in acceptance.

'Can I go first?' Acalan asked in his least sincere tone. He hoped only to make her laugh, mindful that there was only one way forward.

'Just…don't…slip…' she managed to say between coughs, choking on the offensive air that lingered relentlessly. '…and if you do, don't take me down with you!'

It took only a few tarry rungs to blacken his hands. A thick layer of filth coated each iron bar of the ladder, making each step down more difficult. Since the climbers were so well dressed, the descent was already challenging enough.

A cool wind blew on Acalan's face as the night's sea breeze blew into the cavern. He was not afraid of heights, at least not particularly, but peering down still caught him off guard. Distracted by this, Acalan lost focus on his steps, and his feet shot off of the ladder and into thin air. The downwards momentum ripped one of his hands-free from the ladder and spun him around in the same movement. His back thrashed against the unforgiving rock. He hung facing outwards by his fingers, which burned as they clung desperately to the metal. The sole of his fine black dress shoe searched frantically for a rung to stand on but only found gravel to kick at. His fingers screamed as stones dislodged by his foot plummeted down.

Acalan let out an involuntary cry as he kicked away from the wall to swing himself back towards the ladder. He snatched at another rung with his free hand. A relieved exhale left his lungs as he clutched the metal underhand. He pulled himself closer and closer to the wall as he caught his breath.

'I told you not to slip!' Iverissa exclaimed.

Although her words were chiding, her tone indicated relief. Acalan composed himself before responding, allowing several moments of uncomfortable silence to pass.

'I didn't want to take you down with me,' he joked.

'Ack!' she shouted down at him, failing to see the humour. 'Please be careful!'

The pair continued the remainder of the descent in uncomfortable silence. Eventually, Acalan's shoe found the top of the pile. He froze for a moment. Although they had reached what they assumed to be the surface, the ladder didn't stop. Instead, it vanished down into the sludge.

Clinging to the ladder, Acalan tested his footing on the pile and found that it was like stepping into deep snow. As he released his grip on the bars and put his full weight onto his foot, it sank several feet into the sludge-like substance. He groaned when he pulled his leg back out, his suit trousers coated in dirt and dregs.

Iverissa surprised Acalan with how well she handled herself here. While the distance to the water wasn't so far, it was still almost a kilometer-long trek in unfavourable terrain. Her bare legs were exposed to the muck that stretched out ahead of them, and neither knew what it actually was. It was also extremely challenging to walk through; it felt like walking with weighted boots, as each step took great effort. As they trudged forwards, they did notice that they were able to find their footing on more solid pieces of waste. While small pieces of wood or foodstuff had mostly rotted and decomposed, there were some larger objects that sat on the surface and were still intact.

As they reached the peak of the final hill, Acalan looked down the slope and towards the water with contentment. Then, the hairs on his neck stood on end as he heard Iverissa yelp in pain.

He turned as she cursed in an enraged tone and clutched her leg. A stream of deep crimson stood in sharp contrast to her pale skin. She continued cursing while she pulled her shin out of the waste, but her tone now shifted towards one of fear.

A large glass shard from a broken bottle was lodged deep in Iverissa's leg, just below her knee. It had slashed into her as she had taken a step, with the tear starting near her foot. The worst of the gash was up at her knee, where the glass had anchored.

As Acalan rushed over to assist her, he caught sight of an old outhouse door that could be used as a stretcher, even if it was missing some chunks from one corner. He threw himself at it, dragging and sliding the large piece of wood along the surface towards Iverissa, drenching himself in muck without hesitation.

Iverissa laid down on the door, facing upwards, and writhed around in pain.

'Am I going to die?!' she sobbed as blood streamed down her leg and onto the filthy door beneath her.

Acalan pulled himself out of the sludge and removed his jacket with urgency.

'You're not going to die here!' he shouted at her. 'This is going to hurt, but you're going to be fine!'

There was no way for him to be sure of that, but the adrenaline coursing through his veins fuelled his words while he acted. Lifting the suit jacket in front of him with the collar to the floor, he tore at the seam in the back, pulling the coat into two halves. Tearing again, he liberated several more pieces of black fabric from the jacket. After placing these to one side, he wrapped a sleeve of the coat around the glass shard, which was roughly the size of his palm at its widest point.

'I need you to be brave for me,' he said evenly, concealing his fear as he spoke. He had no real idea of how to treat her wound properly.

'Okay,' she agreed immediately.

Even though she had agreed, her bloodcurdling scream when he ripped the shard free sent guilt rushing through Acalan. Iverissa struck her head back into the wood underneath her and arched her back. Her hands slammed repeatedly into the door before clinging onto it as the agony coursed through her. She took only shallow breaths and gasped when he tossed the glass aside.

Acalan lifted a long strip of fabric from the floor beside him and pressed it firmly on the wound, attempting to slow the bleeding. He struggled to hold her leg as she kicked and writhed against him, but he was able to maintain pressure until she tired. This didn't take long, and Acalan began to fear that removing the glass had been a mistake. Using a second piece of torn fabric, he knotted it tightly over the first to hold it in place. Iverissa was still conscious, as was clear from her weeping. Acalan dared not look at her face, as he had not yet composed his own.

After some time, Iverissa grew still, though she continued to weep softly. Acalan lay beside her and pulled her close, cradling her in his arms.

'You're not going to die here,' he repeated, failing to find the words to comfort her. Although it remained inescapable, the smell didn't seem so bad anymore.

X

Time to Go

Acalan's improvised bandage appeared to be helping with the bleeding, but Iverissa lay motionless on the door. Her blood covered his white dress shirt, having sprayed him when he ripped the glass free. Although he recognised that as a mistake in hindsight, he knew she couldn't walk with it embedded in her leg; it had to be removed. Iverissa's breathing steadied, but she remained still.

'Do you think you can sit up?' he asked, in denial of the situation, unwilling to accept her incapacitated state.

'It hurts, Ack,' she slurred, forcing the words out. 'I want to rest.'

'What do you think we would have found?' she asked him after a moment. 'On the other side.'

'I don't know.' He dismissed her pretence, still preoccupied with damage control.

'There's only danger out there,' she went on. 'That's what you said, right?'

'Whatever is out there, Iverissa, it has to be better than this.' He appealed to her curiosity in a desperate attempt to keep her awake. 'You're going to come with me and find that out for yourself.'

'I can't get there now.' She avoided his eyes and continued to stare upwards. 'I can't get there. You still can.'

'I'm not leaving you here. You're going to be fine.'

His lips quivered as reality set in. Blood coated her, and his improvised suit jacket bandage was slightly helpful at best. This was a promise that he could not keep, but as empty as it was, making it was all he could do. He kneeled beside her, bending over her and pressing his forehead against hers as he held her neck in his open palms.

'When you get to Jasebelle, don't forget me, okay?' She put a hand on his cheek and smiled warmly.

'It's okay. Lie back. Don't worry.' Acalan forced out reassurances as he struggled to maintain his composure. He needed to act but had no resources.

Iverissa lay back again, and her deep green eyes fell shut. To get clean water or medicine, he would need to go back up to the city and turn himself in. Even if he could get her back up there, they wouldn't treat her, since they would both be charged with trial evasion. Iverissa was unconscious, and he was alone. She was vulnerable, but this time, there was nothing he could do.

Over the sound of waves rolling in against the heap, Acalan began to hear a faint skittering sound. A clicking behind him, tapping away. Alerted by this, he became aware of a cat-sized creature on the edge of his peripheral vision. It was a plump grey rat, its muck-slick hairs unkempt and raggedy. He recoiled when he realised it was clutching the shard of bloody glass in its little paws. When he turned to catch it licking at the residue on the shard, it froze, caught red-handed.

For a second, Acalan and the vermin stared each other down. Its bulging red eyes glared at him with an insatiable hunger. Then, it screeched, bearing foul teeth that dripped with rancid saliva. It leapt towards Acalan, flinging the glass backwards into a puddle of slimy waste where it disappeared with a small plop.

Panicking, Acalan fell onto his rear before swiping the rat out of the air with a swift backhand. Its matted fur squelched against his hand, spraying out a greenish mist upon impact. As it spun through the air, he swung his bow off his shoulder and nocked an arrow in one fluid motion. The rat screeched once more, rolling in another puddle of viscous sewage before emerging again, baring its gangly teeth. When it thrust itself forwards this time, Acalan was ready. He released the bowstring, and his arrow burst into the rodent's skull, plucking it out of the vile air.

Having prepared another arrow, he scanned his surroundings. Another of these creatures was approaching. This one was smaller but still launched itself at him after he picked it out of its surroundings. Having identified it while it was still some distance away, it was simple for him to dispatch it. Experience then came into play as he nocked arrows at speed to defend them against several more. He earned himself a moment of safety but could see in the distance that he had attracted attention. A swarm of these beasts was rushing over the piles of waste towards them, due to feast on him and Iverissa within seconds. It was tricky to tell from a distance, but these rats looked larger, forming an army of what looked like medium-sized dogs.

Acalan reached back into his quiver, and his hand grasped his last arrow. He cursed silently to himself as Iverissa was still sound asleep on the door, a contented smile on her lips.

Swarm or not, he wasn't going to leave her behind. He slid off the door and scrambled to push it towards the ridge by the sea. Since the surface of this place consisted of non-solid material, he was pleasantly surprised when the door slid across it smoothly. He choked during the frantic dash through the sludge but didn't falter upon approaching the edge of the pile. It was a steep drop down the mound, and the pair loomed over the waves down below.

'Time to go,' Acalan said to himself before hopping back onto the board beside Iverissa.

As they tipped over, another of the grotesque rodents dove at them but missed and flew overhead to land face-first in the muck.

They gathered speed rapidly as the door plunged down the slope towards the water. Acalan held onto Iverissa as they rocked down the uneven ramp and crashed into the sea. The bitter sea water splashed over them as waves rolled inland, each one submerging the door a little more than the last. When Acalan rocked backwards in a bid to stabilise them, Iverissa slid out of place, and her unscathed leg dangled into the sea.

Clambering to gain control of the vessel, Acalan hooked Iverissa under her arms. A fresh wave caught him mid-breath and flooded his mouth with salt water as he clung to her like a backpack. Coughing and spluttering, he continued to hold onto her, moving with the waves as she did. Utilising their combined weight enabled him to prevent them from capsizing. They continued to float outwards until the waves graciously began to calm down.

Acalan's dress shirt and suit trousers clung to his skin, weighing him down. His legs were spread across the door, with his ankles hooked under it, and he cradled Iverissa upright over them. Her cheek was pressed against his chest, and she still lay motionless. Shakily, Acalan released one arm and raised a hand to her face. He held a finger below her nostrils until he felt the gentle flow of her breath over it. He rolled back onto the board in relief, and his head knocked against it with a clumsy thud. Acalan closed his eyes and shook his head. The dull pain in his skull faded into obscurity as they floated out onto the open sea.

When he opened his eyes once more, an endless sky stretched above him. A smattering of stars peppered the black canvas of the night, yet he was unable to identify any constellations among them. He smiled to himself upon noticing this. If Iverissa had been awake, she would have been pointing them out and explaining their lore in agonising detail. Alone, though, he found himself puzzled by these tiny white dots flashing at him. Each seemed to be screaming for his attention, but not one of them earned it. Instead, he scanned the inoffensive grey clouds that formed a misty haze rather than any particular shape or image.

Acalan struggled for clarity; what was he supposed to think? The Titans were not answering him, but he didn't know what to ask.

While drifting on the night sea and dwelling on this feeling of isolation, he felt a general sense of incapability. The raft started to spin ever so slowly, adding an unwelcome dizzying sensation. The silent clouds lingered above him mockingly. His heart thumped where Iverissa's temple weighed on his chest, a silent reminder that he had to keep moving. While unconscious, she had no way of voicing any discomfort, and this was exactly what made her vulnerable. He was the only one who knew she was there and that she needed medical attention.

Acalan slid off the makeshift wooden craft once more. This time, the chilling embrace of the Synnor-Jasebelle Sea met him as he plunged downwards. He felt his limbs tense and his torso tightens as he submerged himself. The water that had soaked his clothes before had warmed up with his body, so dropping back into the chilly depths was a fresh shock. Digging his nails into the wood helped him to pull his head back above water while he flailed his legs. He gasped at the night air and continued to kick, feeling his chest tighten with each short breath. After the initial shock subsided, he was able to regain control of his breathing. He inhaled through his nose and exhaled through pursed lips as he treaded water.

Once he had regained control, he had his first opportunity to look back towards Synnor. His exclusive perspective allowed him to see the dark chasm below the city proper. Above it, the city's rocky façade spiralled upwards into the sky, with several rings decorating its peak. Each district emanated a faint glow from its street lanterns. The brightest area was the city promenade in the Lower District, which ran around the bottom of Synnor. From here, it looked like a belt holding the city's overhanging gut in place over a steep drop. It was much too cold to enjoy the view, but it did occur to him that he was the first to see it all from the outside. It also struck him as a shame to steal that feat from Iverissa. Nobody living above the city knew of the behemoth that hid below, and she deserved the discovery. From sea level, it was so obvious. But up in the city, every person contributed to the pollution below obliviously. They had heard of the unimaginable complexity below the streets to deal with this; they had no reason to believe otherwise.

Turning his back to it all, Acalan continued to kick, but with renewed purpose. He remembered standing with Iverissa on the promenade as her explanation echoed imperfectly. It would take at least seven hours to swim across to Jasebelle - or was it eight? Frustrated at his inability to recall this detail, he continued his movement away from Synnor. He had no way of tracking their progress, and at this early stage, there was no end in sight. He pushed these thoughts aside and pressed on. He knew which way was forwards, and that was all he needed to know.

As the time crawled forwards, so did the Synnori fugitives. The night remained dark, so

Acalan knew he was still in the initial stages of the swim. It alarmed him that he was already beginning to struggle. His muscles were sore, and his breathing was out of control. He wasn't as fit as he needed to be – as fit as he used to be. If this were a few years ago, he would still be gliding along right now. Yet this detail was irrelevant, as the difficulty he faced only increased. Acalan reflected on his complacency: He used to exercise daily, used to push himself. Somewhere along the line, he had let it slip. In recent years, he would simply arrive for a trial, win it and return home to wash down the guilt with drink. He longed for a bottle at this moment, somewhere to curl up and hide, liberation from the need to tolerate this situation any longer.

When he submerged his head to refresh himself before popping back up with a shake, he thought of how long it had been since he had felt challenged in this way. It reminded him of the training he used to do, back before his first trials.

Alone with his thoughts, memories flooded him. Life had been much easier when nobody knew his face. Sprinting along the promenade and crashing through the crowds, he would dart around couples enjoying the morning air and dodge traders rolling their carts into the cobbles.

Joyful and nostalgic endorphins coursed through him as he continued to progress through the sea. He had found a sense of euphoria rooted in clarity, and the fog in his mind was clearing. The fear and guilt that usually drowned him were beginning to dissipate and make way for buoyancy. He reflected on his unaccountability. Before the fame, he had felt freedom from expectation. For the first time, he realised that under the dark night sky, there was no audience. He didn't need one; isolation could actually liberate him if he let it.

Acalan remained mindful of the strain on his body, but he felt capable nonetheless. Giving up was no longer an option to be considered, not even for a moment. He only wished that the stakes were lower.

By the time the sky began to brighten, Acalan had grown accustomed to the intense strain in his legs. They were numb but continued to kick defiantly. The sky was turning from black to grey, and Acalan recognised the start of tomorrow. As the early morning crept in, it provided enough light for him to see the Jasebelle shoreline on the horizon. He couldn't make out any specific details, only a long straight line of land ahead, but it was a clear destination that continued to drive him onwards.

A dull, smouldering red ball peeked over the horizon before brightening into the glow of a Jasebelle sunrise. The orange hues painted the sky with streaks of warmth. Clouds remained, but a deeper tone than the backdrop filled them.

The sun had initially presented as a distant orange-tinged white sphere, but over time, it expanded into a large burning yellow disc that filled the sky. The distant stretch of beach was starting to look reachable. Sand stretched as far as the eye could see, framed by a backdrop of grassy rolling hills.

'Nearly there.' Acalan spoke to himself for the first time after a night of silently pushing against the odds. The adrenaline of the past hours had worn thin and was now being replaced with exhaustion. He was trying to encourage himself because his body was beginning to fail. The shore appeared to be within reach as if he could extend an arm to feel the sand. When he reached outwards and slapped a hand into the water, he snapped back to reality. He was dazed and confused as he looked towards the shore, which was still some distance away. Acalan blinked tightly and pulled down on the door, unintentionally wetting Iverissa's dry and matted hair. Still unconscious, she fussed, and her hand rubbed at her face.

Now, Acalan was no longer making progress; rather, he was struggling to tread water. As minutes passed, he found it increasingly difficult to keep his head up and above the waves. His previously controlled circular arm movements turned frantic, but without the energy to produce any force. Acalan was climbing an invisible ladder without rungs as his vision of the bright sky began to fade.

Acalan rocked back, the wood slipped from his grasp and he floated away from Iverissa.

'Am I going to die?' Iverissa's voice echoed in his mind. A fresh wave of guilt choked him while he bobbed in the water, unmoving.

'Am I going to die?!' The voice repeated desperately, in a breathless tone.

Acalan's vision continued to fade until there was nothing left to see.

XI

Curiosity Killed the Cat

Acalan stood over the fencing, facing outwards as the early evening crowd moved past. A steady stream of people flowed in and out of the Grand Market, paying no notice to the teenager staring into the sea. After all, he wasn't causing any trouble. He produced a bundle of papers from an otherwise empty book bag that was slung over his left shoulder. Swinging the bag into the fence, he released the strap, allowing it to fall loose by his feet.

Glancing at his work, he tutted at the childish handwriting scrawled across the lined notebook sheets and into the margins. An old, browned paperclip held the pages together. Scores and strikethroughs decorated each line in red ink. Crimson question marks interrogated the misspelled quotations, highlighting their inaccuracies. His eyes fixated on a red circle around his writing, annotated with the accusatory question 'Why?!'. Acalan didn't even know why, nor could he identify any issue with the words he had chosen.

Losing patience, he flung the report out over the fencing. The sheets burst free from their flimsy clip and scattered outwards before spinning down over the barrier. One page caught the air and spun back towards him, catching against his chest before falling to his feet. Exasperated, he swiped it up from the ground without checking it. He tore the sheet into imperfect halves before laying them over each other and tearing them up again and again. Once he finished, little trace of his idiocy remained. When he threw the handful of tiny pieces of paper over the fencing, they floated gently around him like snow.

'Ack! Why?!' a voice scolded him from behind, causing his shoulders to shoot up. 'I would have helped you!' she added.

He looked over his shoulder to see her approaching with an identical satchel hung across her body. Hers was bulging, though, bouncing against her leg as she walked.

'I don't need your help, Iverissa,' he replied abruptly.

'Yes, you do. You throw like a girl...,' she teased, forcing eye contact, '...but you write like a boy.'

'No, really. I don't need help,' he emphasised. 'None of this will matter once I drop out.'

'You don't have to drop out, Ack. Your scores aren't that bad,' Iverissa lied. 'If you would just let me help you and stick with it, my dad will get you into the library.'

'It's easy for you,' Acalan deflected, his eyes clouded with shame. 'I can't keep up; I'm not cut out for it. I'm bottom of the class, is that not bad?'

'Ack.' Pity snuck into Iverissa's tone as her approach changed. 'Intelligence isn't just about test scores. It's about the ability to grow, adapt, persevere.'

'But what good is that without the scores?' Acalan's tone also changed, but his was tinged with defeat. 'You belong there. I don't.'

'You don't need the best scores to get in the front door, but you do need *some* scores,' she responded. 'Will you at least hang on for one more year and let me help you?'

'She makes me look like an idiot. It's a joke to her, you know!' Acalan changed the subject. He had a point. Some of his instructors did seem to enjoy making him look foolish in front of his classmates.

'You give as good as you get!' Iverissa objected. 'What about the chalkboard? The glue?'

Acalan's laughter was callous as she listed examples.

'Ack, you put a goldfish in her water. She could have died!'

'She doesn't even know that was me!' he protested. 'It wasn't even my idea, and she wasn't going to die.' His protests were met with a blank, unimpressed expression. 'Tainen thought it was funny,' he added with a shrug.

'Tainen is a prick.' Iverissa's demeanour shifted. She tilted her head to the side and crossed her arms. Her eyes wandered away before looking back at him once more.

'You are so weird about him. He's funny!' Acalan deflected. 'I don't know why you have such an issue with me making other friends.'

'He's a bully,' Iverissa stated, beginning to lose her patience. 'He excludes people who aren't part of his little club.'

Acalan rolled his eyes at her, spacing out while she lectured him. She didn't get it. Tainen was popular, and for good reason. His father was captain of the guards in the Upper District City Watch, so he was well off and had a bright future. After all, power and wealth went hand in hand.

Tainen lived in a mansion in Virrel Park near the palace, the most affluent area in Synnor. The area was so exclusive that money couldn't even buy the properties there. They were reserved for high-ranking government officials, as assigned directly by the crown. Acalan had never even been in Virrel Park and was heading there next.

'These people aren't your friends, you know,' Iverissa concluded, looking towards him expectantly.

'Whatever. I'll see you next week,' he brushed her off, snatching his bag from the ground and slinging it over a shoulder. He didn't look back as he meandered into the Grand Market and disappeared among the crowd.

As he approached Virrel Park, the cobbles of the main plaza continued. It was like any other street in the Upper District, flanked by strips of grass that ran parallel to it. The path wrapped uphill and around the back of the City Library. A short wall of fresh bricks ran along the side of the footpath. Before he had advanced far up the hill, he identified two brick columns separated by a tall, rounded wooden gate. The gate boasted a fancy metallic plaque reading '17 Virrel Park'. The gate had been left on the latch, as Tainen had promised.

Acalan lifted the ornate brass latch, and the gate swung open. As he stepped in, he could see a large iron padlock hanging on the inside of the barrier by its shackle. As he closed the gate, he flipped the shackle back into place and pressed it down. After confirming it was locked with a firm tug, he began to make his way up the wide stone pathway. The garden he was walking through would make a good park if it weren't private, he thought. Flowerbeds overflowing with vibrant plants he didn't recognise surrounded the vast lawn. The scent of freshly cut grass helped to ease his nerves as he approached the looming mansion.

Even from outside, he could hear faint laughter coming from a large bay window at the front of the house. A single pane stood partially open, hooked to the windowsill. From here, Acalan could not see into the house. When he reached the porch, the scent of fresh grass clippings was overpowered by a dingy smell that Acalan did not recognise. Puzzled by this, he stepped towards the door. An ornate '17' in plated brass was affixed to it, surrounding an identically stylised knocker that drooped temptingly. His first knock was almost silent, so he followed it with two harsh knocks to compensate.

The laughter stopped, followed by an unintelligible drone from the window. Acalan stood with his hands buried in the deep pockets of his blazer, unsure what else to do. The noise repeated once more without further clarification, followed by renewed laughter. Then, he heard shuffling on the other side of the door, and the tiny peephole in the middle of the knocker lit up.

The door swung open to reveal Tainen. His vacant expression stared Acalan up and down for a moment too long. Acalan took a step back before adjusting himself. He had to look down slightly to meet Tainen's eyeline. Tainen was standing against the doorway holding a simple glass bottle. Liquid sloshed in it; it appeared to be around three-quarters full.

'I said, it's open!' he announced patronisingly, which encouraged further laughter from the room behind him.

Acalan clawed at a non-existent itch on his neck without responding.

'What did you bring?' Tainen asked, breaking the silence.

Acalan tried to escape Tainen's gaze but failed. When he looked back, Tainen was pressing his weight into the door, like a council guard with a palace to protect. The moment ended with a sigh from Tainen, who got the hint that Acalan was empty-handed. Tainen pushed himself upright and away from the door, leaving it ajar.

'You can come in if you want,' Tainen mumbled over his shoulder.

Acalan made to speak but was heard only by himself. Tainen had already left him outside, so he followed him in and into a grand lounge area. Columned archways supported a lofty ceiling, forming a square in the middle of the room. A fine chandelier held a ring of candles far above the marble floor. A huge scarlet rug covered the floor, filling the majority of the space. Plush seating was arranged around the rug, consisting of two spotless white velvet couches facing inwards. Matching chairs with painted wooden arms and legs completed the circle. The early evening light shone in through the giant bay window and flooded over the teenagers sitting there. Acalan didn't know everyone in the room but recognised some of the faces.

Tainen threw himself onto the empty couch and put his feet up on the glass table, pushing empty bottles aside with the sole of his shoe. The silence was deafening as Tainen took a swig from the bottle he held by its neck.

'He finally managed to find the door,' Tainen joked, failing to introduce Acalan to the party.

Acalan stood awkwardly without commenting before taking a seat in an empty chair. Unwilling to say the wrong thing, he observed the room with his back pressed into the seat. Sitting on the sofa next to him was a pair of older students, a boy and a girl. They sat close to one another, paying no attention to him. He felt a nudge against his elbow from the other direction. A thin boy with short brown hair raised an eyebrow at Acalan, his extended arm offering him one of the mysterious green bottles. Taking the drink, Acalan nodded at him and received a smile of recognition in return.

It seemed that his arrival had interrupted an ongoing debate about Ms Maxtla, Acalan's literature teacher. The topic of the debate was how unreasonable she was. Tainen ranted about her most recent assignment to the class, which was due the next morning.

'She marks me down because I'm rich,' Tainen drawled to the room. 'It's because she's jealous.'

'When I was in her class, my scores were bad too,' the girl sitting opposite cut in. This was the first time she had looked away from her boyfriend since Acalan had arrived. 'I barely scraped a pass,' she pointed out.

'Yes, but you're as dumb as a sack of rocks,' Tainen jibed back without hesitation.

'Whatever.' She rolled her eyes and moved them back towards her boyfriend, ignoring the laughter around her.

Acalan's mind wandered to the realisation that his work for this assignment was floating in the Synnor-Jasebelle sea. With a subtle shake of the head, he took a sip from his bottle. The bitter taste caught him off guard, and he choked a little as it burned his throat. When he scanned the room, it relieved him to see that nobody seemed to have noticed. Tainen had distracted the group by swiping aside some books on the translucent glass table and revealing a dented metallic tin and a tiny matchbox. He cracked the little tin open and tapped its contents out onto the table. When he was done, there was a small mound of a leafy substance before him.

'You'll need to hide it better than that if your Dad actually does come back!' the brown-haired boy next to Acalan commented.

'I'm sorry, Zuma, but I don't remember asking for your opinion.' Tainen disregarded his concern and pinched a small amount of the substance between his fingers.

A sense of dread crept over Acalan as he watched Tainen sprinkle it into a small piece of paper. This was when he recognised the substance as flister. Acalan had never seen it in person since having even the tiniest amount on your person was highly illegal. He had only ever seen it in pictures featured in workbooks that had insisted on going nowhere near the stuff. It wasn't the side effects he was concerned about; it caused only mild hallucinations when smoked. His real concern was what happened to people who were caught with it. The house he was in amplified this concern. Tainen, however, seemed completely unconcerned as he struck a match and lit the end of the makeshift cigarette before inhaling deeply. He then rocked backwards into his seat as if sedated and exhaled a cloud of black smoke.

The makeshift cigarette made its way around the circle, with each person taking a casual puff. Acalan watched closely as they relaxed, leaning backwards into their seats, their shoulders dropping in turn. Eventually, it was passed to Acalan by the older couple beside him. He hesitated for a moment, staring at the burning ember at its tip. Even though he remained paranoid about being caught, he was curious. He looked up to see Tainen moments away from making a snide remark and elected to buckle rather than give him the opportunity. Upon inhaling, he noticed a bewilderingly sweet taste. He had always imagined that smoking flister was some sort of bitter and sickening experience, but this was far from the case. As he exhaled a black plume of smoke, the clouds of insecurity crowding around him dissipated almost immediately.

Acalan lost track of time. The sunset was outside, and he became increasingly relaxed as the room began to grow dim. Eventually, he was able to speak with confidence around these people and felt foolish for worrying earlier in the evening. The side effects of flister must have been exaggerated by his instructors, he thought. He wasn't experiencing any hallucinations, although it wasn't clear how he would identify them if he was. As time went on, he began to experience some nausea, but it wasn't overwhelming. He tolerated the feeling for a while as he watched Tainen climb onto the table.

'In the name of Eden!' Tainen hiccupped, startling himself. 'In the name of Eden,' he repeated, performing an obnoxious imitation of his father.

Acalan was about to laugh when he felt the contents of his stomach begin to twist. Only after he stood up did it occur to him that he might have made a mistake. The room spun, and he adjusted his feet in time to avoid falling before staggering towards the edge of the room. He searched the wall for the handle to a bathroom, but the more he searched, the more impossible the task seemed. Eventually, his hand wrapped around a door handle, and he stumbled forwards into an unlit side room. Satisfied with this, he swung the door shut with a grin, nodding at his own glory. He then sat on the floor, oblivious to his surroundings. It took some semi-critical thinking for it to occur to Acalan that he wasn't actually sure where he was, nor how long he had been sitting there for. He began to feel overwhelmed as he felt around. Drowsily, he tugged at the fur and velvet of the expensive coats that hung around him. His chest tightened, and his breathing became somewhat laboured. Controlling his limbs became an additional challenge. Soon, Acalan was rolling around on the floor of the unfamiliar cupboard.

A bright ray of light burst through slits in the cupboard door, and the sound of smashing glass followed. Acalan wrestled himself free of the jackets and crawled towards the slits. Peering out, he could see Tainen standing beside a towering male figure, his head hanging low. Acalan froze, taking only shallow breaths. The lights all around shone on the man's plate armour when he turned and barked orders to the room. Acalan squinted, now seeing several more men dragging his new friends out of the house. They struggled and screamed in desperate yet feeble resistance.

Acalan's legs grew numb; he couldn't guess how long he had sat in this confused yoga pose. He tried to maintain his faltering focus on the blurry scene ahead, but flashing colours and shapes were starting to obstruct it. He saw and heard the two figures that remained in the room speaking to one another. The tall one was shouting and gesticulating, which went unmatched by the smaller one. The taller individual reached down and grabbed the smaller one by his robes, effortlessly yanked him up and struck him with the back of a firm hand.

Acalan dared not peek any longer and forced himself back against a wall. Still unsure how to control his limbs or where he even was, he continued to be subjected to the scene that played out in the room. He curled into a ball and pulled a thick coat over himself. Despite this, the sounds and colours continued. Acalan sobbed meekly and waited for it to stop.

XII

The Other Side

With blurred vision, he lay motionless. The heat of the morning sun made the sand warm, but not hot. Distant shouts broke through his trance-like state. Everything was hazy, and he existed somewhere between sleep and awareness. Silhouettes shuffled around against the blurry background, but he couldn't identify them. They shouted around a cart, oblivious to his presence. As he approached consciousness, he became aware of a dull soreness in his chest every time he drew in a breath. His tongue licked at his cracked lips but could not shift the salty taste in his mouth. His clothes were damp, and the body they covered was spent; his muscles wouldn't have let him move even if he wanted to. Acalan didn't know who or what these shapes were. He didn't know what they might do to him if they saw him. So, he remained curled up in what remained of his tattered suit and watched from several hundred feet away.

They surrounded her in eerie coordination, like a pack of predators moving in on their prey. Then, they lifted her. The sun shone through tears in her dress as it dangled beneath her before she was placed onto a cart.

Iverissa! Acalan's eyes widened at the realisation but remained unfocused. He tried to shout but only choked up seawater. His nails dug into the sand, but he had no strength to drag himself out of the ditch. Like a marionette without strings, his limp body remained motionless in a wet patch of sand. They were the danger he had been warned about, and they were taking her. Despite his struggling, he succumbed to his weariness, and his eyelids drooped shut again.

When he finally awoke, the sun was beaming down from its zenith. He had agency in his muscles this time, but he grimaced at the ache that was triggered when he rolled over. He managed to sit upright, and his eyes adjusted to the brightness, allowing him to scan his surroundings. The beach was clean and deserted: he was alone. The sand was pure and stretched endlessly in both directions. The sky above him was a clear blue and didn't contain a single cloud. Had it not been for his searing headache and the relentless scratch in his throat, he might have thought he had passed into the afterlife.

A jarring click resonated through his neck as he turned his head to look back. What he saw removed any idea of paradise he might have had left. When he looked out at the water, it was still, but he could see the cliffs in the distance. Picking out Synnor itself was possible, but only barely; from here, it was a mere speck against the rocky backdrop. Looking at his home alerted him to the fact that he was outside of it. He swiped up his bow and brushed the sand off it, though he had no arrows to use. Then, he forced himself to his feet. His first steps were awkward, like those of a baby deer learning to walk. His feet struggled to find traction in the sand, and his aching legs escaped him before he found his balance and moved towards the grassy verge.

He came to a halt when he noticed it at his feet: a small leather satchel lying upside down. When he stopped to lift it, the strap emerged and dangled in front of him, but the buckle held its contents within. As he turned it upright, the shine of a small emerald rock caught his eye, and he lifted it by its silver chain. Seeing her necklace brought a lump to his throat, so he didn't stop to look any longer. Instead, he shook as much sand as he could from the satchel and swung it over his shoulder. Then, he slipped the necklace under its flap and out of sight. There was no time to consider the worst; she still needed him.

Having left the beach, it surprised Acalan to see open fields of long grass. There was a dirt road covered with gravel running into the distance. Vibrant purples and deep reds dotted the fields where countless wildflowers burst through the grass. Wary of thorns or poison, Acalan dared not touch them and left them swaying in the breeze. A steel wire fence ran alongside the path for as far as he could see. None of this made sense to him; Jasebelle was supposed to be a barren wasteland. As far as he could see, everything looked fine, nice even.

He anticipated danger with each step, looking over his shoulder as he moved. Time passed as he walked alone, but he remained undisturbed. There was no way to be sure how long he had been walking on this path; his legs had ached before he even started. The sun above was his best indicator of time, and it didn't seem to have moved very much. It had stayed above him and continued to warm him up against his will. Clammy sweat built up at the nape of his neck, so he found himself constantly adjusting his shirt. At least his trouser legs were dry.

In the distance ahead, an adult cow craned its neck over the fence. This struck Acalan as a particularly bizarre mirage since it was another impossibility. He approached the cow with caution, but it ignored his presence, turning away to snack on the grass. This movement revealed a group of calves lying in a circle, enjoying the sunshine. Acalan positioned himself on the fence and looked as close as his nerves allowed. One of the calves sprang up at his approach and hobbled over to its mother.

Acalan began to test this foreign place. He snatched up a clump of grass from the ground by his shoes. Gingerly, he offered this over the fence to the two remaining calves. Innocently enough, they both sprang forwards in his direction. He gasped at the sudden movement and dropped the grass in front of him, pulling back swiftly. They bumped into each other playfully as grass sprinkled in front of them before stepping upright with a synchronous shake. Having lost interest in him, they skipped over towards their mother.

He felt foolish as he watched them playing; his heart was racing, yet everything was completely safe. He shrugged this embarrassment off and pressed on. There was no one around to see him, and the Titans weren't on speaking terms with him anyway.

His eyes widened in awe and his breath caught in his throat when he discovered the hidden cityscape. A wide range of cottages were dotted around the outskirts, each with its own design. Fenced-off plots surrounded them, containing either crops or livestock. Wide roads cut through the lattice of these plots, and each led towards the city proper. Imposing structures stretched high above, their architectural grandeur giving them an almost ethereal quality. The towering spires were adorned with intricate carvings and metallic embellishments. They pierced the sky in a way Acalan had never seen before. He had anticipated a camp in the wasteland if anything, but this place was bigger than Synnor. The feeling of awe swelled within him, and two thoughts wrestled for priority in his mind: 'What is this place?' and 'Where have they taken her?'.

On his approach to the outskirts of the city, the smell of farmland was foreign to him but not uncomfortable. He also detected a faint burning smell but couldn't see the source of the flame. The smell seemed artificial but familiar. Upon flaring his nostrils, he was reminded of his escape from Synnor. There were more of these strange lamps here, dangling from cords overhead to light the stone roads. Once again, he was constantly looking around himself and over his shoulder, but each time he checked, there was nobody behind him. There were plenty of people in sight, but they were busy working on their land. Some of the people looked completely different from anyone he had ever known, with a variety of heights and builds among them.

'A strange place,' he thought. Although strange, it seemed like nobody was looking to hurt him. In all actuality, nobody was even paying attention to him.

The closer he came to the city centre, the more he noticed the intricate details that decorated the structures ahead. Delicate brass filigree adorned the facades of buildings and bizarre mechanisms adorned balconies, each piece a testament to the craftsmanship of an era he had never experienced. He felt as though he was stepping into a different time, one where Iverissa's daydreams could be a reality. The boundaries between imagination and reality blurred.

The first thing that stood out to him as the streets assaulted his senses was the noise. It was as if he were standing in the Grand Market, hearing the commotion of people rushing around. The difference here, though, was the various decibels of unfamiliar droning sounds from machinery around him. The burning scent intensified with each step he took. It was more than just lamps or ceremonial arrows. What was the mysterious substance being used for here?

There was no patrol or guard ahead; people were coming and going as they pleased. A steady stream of people passed from place to place, without any one person staying still for even a moment. As Acalan took his first step into this unfamiliar place, he expected a hand on his shoulder to stop him in his tracks. Instead, the world around him remained disinterested in his presence. Still, his heart raced in his chest; he knew he was not where he belonged. He focused on taking a deep breath before joining the crowd. The attire he was familiar with was made from simple fabrics and came in bland colours, but the people around him were dressed like royalty. He didn't even recognise some of the vibrantly coloured fabrics that passed him. By contrast, his filthy shirt and tattered trousers stood out, though the looks he received from passersby weren't ones of concern. There was a sadness present on some of the faces that glanced at him, guilt even. It took Acalan several minutes to put his finger on it; these people pitied him.

Spinning through the crowd, Acalan searched for the artificial light source. Wherever it was, it wasn't clear to him. As he looked around, he stumbled out of the flow of people onto a paved surface, which was almost completely flat. It was unlike the cobbled streets he was used to, and the people moved alongside it without stepping onto it. He crouched for a moment to take a closer look, wondering how it was built.

It was not long after Acalan had dropped his guard that a sudden impact connected with his spine, and he looked up in shock as he was tackled to the ground.

XIII

Accident or Emergency?

A great metallic box whirred past him and his assailant at high speed, missing them by a hair's breadth. Acalan rolled across the ground, having taken a particularly rough knock to the elbow.

'Have you lost your mind?' the stranger chided him while getting up.

Acalan looked at him to see that he had been pulled to the ground by a male wearing a long leaf-green overcoat. He found it surprising that the man was unarmed and making no attempt to restrain him. Instead, he straightened his coat, adjusting it on his shoulders.

Acalan scrambled around on the ground and took the opportunity to reassess his surroundings. A small group of bystanders had stopped for a moment but were already moving away when Acalan directed his gaze at them.

'Hello?' the voice prompted, trying to reach Acalan, who was clutching his elbow and looking all around.

They had tumbled onto the central reservation between two roads. Acalan realised this, but he had never seen anything that size move so fast. The closest comparison he could make was a horse-drawn cart, but this had been much quicker, and there hadn't been any horses.

'Are you hurt?' the man shouted over the noise of more traffic around them.

'I'm fine,' Acalan lied.

His elbow continued to scream for attention, and his grip upon it tightened. He grimaced as he attempted to find his feet before rolling back onto the ground once more. The gentleman appeared well dressed. Under a long coat was a formal waistcoat that remained buttoned even after the tumble. Its gold-tinted buttons matched others that ran up the lapels of his overcoat. When he made eye contact with the man for the first time, an expression of concern met him. The man was clean-shaven, and Acalan noticed that his short black hair was undisturbed by the fall, slicked aside in a neat left parting. The stranger offered him a hand from a rolled-up sleeve as machines continued to whizz past them.

'Do you need to go to the hospital?' the man pressed.

This question caused Acalan's ears to prick up. He took the offered hand, and the man helped him to his feet. Balance evaded him briefly before he could steady his gait.

'Yes, the hospital,' Acalan agreed, fishing around for information, Iverissa at the front of his mind. 'I need to go to the hospital.'

'I think so too,' the man concurred, but then looked through him as if distracted by something.

Suddenly, he threw an arm out into the road, causing another one of the machines to screech to a halt next to the pair. Acalan watched the stranger lean into the window and speak to a man sitting within, but he was unable to hear the words. A small velvet pouch changed hands, and both men looked at him expectantly as he approached. It had made him uneasy when they were speaking about him, but he was even more so when they stopped.

'Let me get the door.' The stranger gripped a handle on the side of the machine and swung it open.

A fresh whiff of the fake burning smell hit Acalan when he stepped towards the open door. When he looked into the cabin, there was seating behind the driver, and it seemed this was where he was to go. If this was a trap, then he was about to climb into it, but he needed to find her. He clambered into place on the seat and continued cradling his arm. The door startled him as it closed with a thud, narrowly missing his leg.

'Arthur, by the way,' the kind stranger introduced himself through a gap that ran along the top of the window.

The hum of the machine intensified when the driver cranked a lever.

'Be a little more careful…,' he trailed off, awaiting a name.

It took Acalan several moments to give this ground, but he failed to see how it could hurt at that point.

'…Acalan.'

Arthur's eyes widened at the given name, and his jaw dropped.

The atmosphere changed in an instant: Arthur lunged at the door but missed the handle. The driver didn't seem to notice this over the sound of the machine as he pulled away. Acalan peered back over his seat and out another window as they sped away. He caught a glance of the man waving frantically to no avail. The machine cart turned sharply out of view, and Acalan sat back in his seat. He rested his arm across his legs and let it hang freely for the first time since the fall. Aware of his deep breathing, he placed a palm on his heart and felt it pounding back at him. It seemed that he had been recognised, and he wondered what this man might have done to him had he known sooner.

There was a hand-sized window in the barrier between him and the driver. On his left and right, however, an overwhelming number of citizens kept filling his view. It was only when the vehicle turned once more that just how many people were packed into this place set in for Acalan. Almost none of the houses he saw had gaps between them, and from his position, he was unable to see their tops. Any spaces he was able to notice were narrow lanes that ran away from the bustle and into darkness. The city streets flew past, and the driver did not speak. Gratefully, Acalan sunk into the seat in silence and watched the colours rush past.

The vehicle turned onto a narrow path in the shape of a widened-out horseshoe and came to a sudden stop. It had only been a few minutes, but given their speed, they had travelled an enormous distance. Acalan could barely see into the building they stopped at, only able to make out some seating with a man sleeping across it.

'You're prepaid!' Acalan barely heard the driver grunt through the barrier.

This came as a relief to Acalan. Even if Iverissa's satchel had coins in it, he doubted they would suffice. In any case, he wanted out of this machine, so he grabbed the door handle and tugged it meekly with his injured arm. Failing this, he then shuffled around in his seat to pull once more with his good arm, albeit from an awkward angle. Mercifully, there was a clunk before it opened a few inches. It was heavier than he expected, which added extra clumsiness to an already tricky clamber out. Not a moment after he slammed the door shut, the contraption started up once more, and the driver was gone.

Acalan stepped cautiously towards the doorway into the hospital, eventually peering in to scan the room. He knew that Arthur had noticed something about his name, so he took some confidence from this. As long as he was in and out quickly and didn't speak to anyone for too long, nobody would recognise him. Acalan also noted that people seemed to be far more concerned with themselves, with this Arthur individual being an exception.

The bland room he looked into appeared designed with some expense spared. An inoffensive mint colour covered the walls down into plain, solid flooring. Acalan checked for anyone with a long green coat like Arthur's but saw no one with a similar sense of style. Nobody he saw seemed especially interested in him at all. A range of characters filled his view, though, the majority visibly injured and awaiting help. For many, their symptoms were something obvious, like bleeding. Others showed something more subtle, like an unusual sitting position. The patients were scattered across rows of simple seats. No one in the room even made eye contact with him as he walked in; they were too busy tolerating their own injuries.

At the back of the room sat a woman at a desk, shuffling papers around absentmindedly. Round spectacles magnified her wide eyes, and this was what exposed her, highlighting that they weren't looking at the documents at all. Acalan deduced that she was hospital staff, as she was certainly wearing some form of uniform. He didn't recognise the tunic but found some novelty in the fact that it matched the walls almost exactly. She placed the papers into a pile at her side upon noticing his approach and blew a strand of hair out of her face.

'What brings you here today, sweetie?' she asked in a cheerful voice, despite the fact he was clutching his arm. 'Handstand gone wrong?' She waited for a reply without blinking, letting the moment stretch on before breaking the silence to laugh at her own joke. 'If you're hurt, take a ticket, and a doctor will be with you as soon as they can', she said robotically, her tone dropping, as if reading from a script.

'No, I'm fine', Acalan lied, completely missing the joke. 'My friend cut her leg…'

'Wrong ward!' she interrupted. 'Only emergencies down here, Cupid.'

This was exasperating for Acalan, but he managed to remain calm; he was keen to get through this interaction as efficiently as possible.

'She was cut severely; I think she lost a lot of blood,' he added, still feeling that he was failing to be taken seriously.

'Yes, so she's probably in minor injuries,' she insisted, confusing Acalan.

It wasn't a minor injury; it was profoundly serious, he thought.

'All the way upstairs! What's the name, darling?' the receptionist asked, resulting in another unbearable pause from Acalan.

'Iverissa?' Acalan responded, almost as if seeking approval. He wasn't sure how honest he could be but needed some indication of where to start.

'That's a lovely name!' she remarked, seeming to sense some of his discomfort and attempting to distract him. 'Very strange, though. Not from around here?'

'Eh, yes. Well, no. She's not from here.' Acalan refused to pick up any conversational thread and attempted to skip through the dialogue to avoid making any mistakes.

The receptionist's shoulders dropped upon taking this hint, but she continued to help. A large binder emerged from under the desk, and she placed it on the surface with a thud. She opened it precisely and started to scan down the page with an index finger.

'Well... Wherever she's travelling from, she didn't pass through here.' She looked up from the page in time to see Acalan's shoulders dip. 'You should try upstairs, though!'

'Upstairs?' He jumped at the suggestion.

'Like I said, minor injuries. Floor seventy-three.' She nodded back at him, directing Acalan towards a cubicle behind her with a pointed finger.

Acalan stepped into the metal cupboard but did not understand why she had directed him there. He stood for a moment, unsure what to do, before turning back to see her watching him.

'Seventy-three,' she repeated slowly and loudly, noticeably attempting to enunciate more clearly.

Without enough knowledge to feel patronised by this, Acalan peered around the box he stood in. He noticed a panel with a varnished wooden border on the wall of the metal cubicle. There was a range of numbers in a grid, each with its own round button. It started with ninety-nine at eye level and decreased down to one at waist level. Aware of the eyes on him, he flung a hand forward and selected floor seventy-three. The button sank about half an inch into the panel and lit up reassuringly with a soft glow. Then, there was a clunk. Acalan jumped at the sound and backed into the corner. Two iron fences began to protrude from the entrance, meeting each other in the centre with a click, sealing him in. The last thing he saw as the box ascended was the receptionist kicking back and rolling away in her chair.

After transporting him to a new floor, the cage opened and Acalan stumbled up the narrow corridor. He found that the same bland green paint from downstairs stretched ahead, coating the walls here too. Doorways ran ahead asynchronously, each one inviting him in as no doors blocked his vision. Upon peering into the first one he approached, he saw an empty ward. The freshly made beds that filled the room had their plain blue sheets tucked in tightly. Each had a thick white pillow propped upright on it, awaiting a patient.

Unsatisfied by this, he stepped towards the next room. Here, plenty of the beds had occupants, although the atmosphere of the room was bewildering to Acalan. The general sense of discomfort that he had noticed downstairs was not present. Instead of lingering sadness, he was surprised by the reaction when he made eye contact with a little girl. She raised her right hand to wave with a triumphant grin, revealing an arm wrapped in a spotless white cloth. Moving her wrist seemed to cause her no pain since the innocent smile persisted. Another member of hospital staff, dressed in the same standard mint tunic, then emerged from behind her. The nurse seemed to be tending to the little girl's bandage, and most bizarrely of all, she continued not to fuss.

Acalan reciprocated with a half-hearted wave back but remained focused on finding Iverissa.

After wandering the halls for some time, Acalan's eyes fixated on a lone figure within one of the wards. She stood at the window, partially leaning against the plain white windowsill, staring out of the long glass window.

She wore a teal dress that sat imperfectly over her curves. The hemline was raggedy and harshly stained with a deep black ring. A brilliant white bandage clung to one of the legs that peeked out from this contrasting muck, and her feet wore socks that were similarly spotless. A folded basic blue blanket covered her shoulders and dangled over her upper back. Her usually perfectly arranged white hair was somewhat matted and unkempt.

Acalan's breath escaped him for a moment; his chest tightened with a burst of anxiety that vanished as suddenly as it arrived.

'You forgot your bag,' he forced a teasing remark through glassy eyes, holding the satchel out towards her with his good arm.

XIV

Visiting Hours

Iverissa turned sharply in place, revealing pupils that swam in pools of jade. Acalan approached and placed the bag at the foot of her bed as he passed it. He didn't stop to notice that it had been stripped of its sheets, which were wrapped around her. The silence was broken when she flung the blanket onto the windowsill and threw herself at him. Acalan locked up, his frame tensing as her hug squeezed his injured arm.

'I thought I'd lost you, Ack!' she exclaimed. 'Oh no. Are you okay?' she asked, noticing his discomfort and jumping off of him onto the balls of her feet. 'What's wrong?' she raced through her words like a panicked mother.

'I'm okay…,' he replied, brushing aside his injury in the sheer disbelief that she was standing. 'You look amazing!' he continued, realising he had chosen the wrong words and quickly correcting himself, 'Your leg, I mean.'

'This place, Ack. You won't believe it,' Iverissa rambled as she wandered over towards her bed and bent over.

She explained to him as she pressed a button on a little white box, which responded with a chirp. 'The medicine here… *Everything* here,' she emphasised. 'I'd suspected there'd be something, but these people are so far ahead.' Iverissa failed to coherently convey her point through her excitement.

Acalan's vacant expression caused her to stop mid-explanation. 'Come and look.' She hurried back to the window and waved him over, visibly unable to contain her excitement.

Acalan stepped forwards and leaned beside her, resting his weight on his good arm. The new world took him aback, and he was in the heart of it.

The hospital was one of the tallest towers in a dense web of skyscrapers that stretched as far as he could see. Many buildings were linked together by gravity-defying arches in their architecture. It seemed impossible that these shapes were designed by people; they were so alien to him. Artificial light ran along the streets below. The illuminated grid pulsed as the miniscule vehicles sped around it like insects.

'It was all a lie, Ack.' The pitch in her voice shifted downwards, causing her tone to change from excitable to solemn. 'It's not dangerous over here. Just look at all these people living their lives.'

Iverissa stopped to take a deep breath, and Acalan continued to stare downwards. She looked at him with a knowing smirk, but he didn't notice.

'I was the same at first. Even now, I can barely look away; I've been watching them all morning.'

The moment hung without interruption as Acalan continued to take it all in. He couldn't believe it; it seemed like Iverissa was right.

'They call it bellum. The nurses told me.' Iverissa broke the silence, noticing Acalan's eyes tracking cars on the ground. 'The whole place seems to run on the stuff. It's behind all their industry, and they're generations ahead of us, Acalan. Look at the carts,' Iverissa continued to ramble as she pointed out the window offhandedly. 'Machines like this are impossible puzzles without this stuff, I've already tried.'

Acalan nodded in disbelief. 'I can still smell it,' he commented, nostrils flared.

'The lights,' she explained, pointing to lanterns dotted around the room. 'Less of a fire hazard, or so I'm told.' She paused her explanation and paced over to one of the light fittings. She calmly removed the blanket from her shoulder before beginning to dip the corner of the fabric into the open top of the glass fixture.

'Look!' She pointed excitedly. The flame within the fixture danced around the cotton as if repelled by it. 'It doesn't consume anything!'

Iverissa's expression of childlike joy and curiosity was swept away by a knock at the door behind them.

'Hi Iverissa! Is everything okay?' A woman asked as she let herself into the room. 'Oh! You have a visitor – what a relief!'

'Wait until you hear this,' Iverissa muttered to Acalan before answering the nurse. 'Hi Gladys! I'm great actually, but my friend is hurt. Can you help him too?' Iverissa smiled at the nurse, seeming completely at ease.

'Oh, of course! What's the problem, dear?' Gladys addressed Acalan with a warm demeanour, making direct eye contact with him.

She was a middle-aged woman, wearing a mint-coloured tunic identical to those Acalan had already seen and was about a foot shorter than him. Her greying chestnut hair was pulled back into a bun. A pair of thin-rimmed glasses rested on the bridge of her nose, adding an intellectual air to her appearance.

Unsure of himself, Acalan took another look at Iverissa, whose head bobbed with quick, sharp nods.

'I fell over. My arm is very painful,' he said vaguely, clutching the offending elbow underhand.

'Don't be shy now! We have lots of people who *fell over*,' she teased with raised eyebrows, making Acalan feel somewhat embarrassed.

With a friendly laugh, Gladys turned her back to him and stepped over to a locked cabinet by the door.

'What's your name, dear?' she asked, making polite conversation while fumbling with a set of tiny keys attached to her tunic.

'I'm Acalan,' he responded, feeling comfortable enough to answer this honestly. They already knew Iverissa after all.

'Oh, another lovely name! The both of you have such worldly names!' Gladys complimented them genuinely.

Despite her smaller stature, Gladys emanated an assuring aura. Her collected poise and articulate speech gave the impression of someone with experience.

'Aha!' She interrupted herself by sliding a key into the lock and turning it swiftly.

A cloud of steam escaped the cabinet and dissipated around her as she yanked its door open. Gladys then reached in and pulled out a small vial before shutting the door once more.

'Would you like to come and lie down for me Acalan?' she asked, patting the bed. 'Only for a minute, I promise!' she added, sensing discomfort in his silence.

Acalan complied, the new posture forcing him to look up at the plain white ceiling panels above. His alertness sharpened when he heard the pop of Gladys removing a stopper from the top of the vial before blocking it with her thumb.

'Roll up your sleeve for me, dear,' she requested, her calming voice inviting him to comply.

Acalan hesitated, fumbling with the cuff on his shirt. He felt a hand on his good shoulder and looked to see Iverissa smiling at him on the other side of the bed. Her sparkling emerald eyes twinkled with understanding, reflecting the deep connection they shared. These new things terrified him, and there was no way of hiding it from her, but her smile conveyed an unspoken reassurance. When he managed to fold back the sleeve, it was revealed that his arm sported a prominent black bruise.

'I'd like you to let me know if you feel any pain at all.' Gladys said, waiting for consent from Acalan, which she received in the form of one slow nod. She then placed the tip of her index finger onto the back of Acalan's wrist. When she applied a small amount of pressure to his wrist, his immediate concern became the pain that he was supposed to feel. He was more worried about saving face than anything, so he chose to look up at the ceiling once more. She then began to trail her finger up his arm, maintaining the pressure as she did so. This was a very strange interaction; as far as Acalan was concerned, she didn't appear to be doing anything.

'Agh!' Acalan suddenly yelped as his entire arm locked up. He looked to see Gladys hovering a finger over the centre of the bruise.

'Always worth checking!' She laughed to herself. 'It isn't always this obvious,' she added, allowing Acalan to relax his arm once more and look back upwards.

He then felt a sudden but very intense cold localised on his bruise. Moments later, his entire elbow was numb. Gladys had poured the solution from inside the vial onto him, and it was bubbling away. When he looked again, she produced a mini roll of white bandage from a concealed pocket and began to wrap it tightly around the injury.

'When it's cooled down, it works like medicine!' Iverissa interrupted the moment, squeezing his shoulder in her hand. 'It's the same stuff! Bellum.'

'Yes, but remember, in moderation,' Gladys insisted. 'You can't go overboard!'

'Why not?' Acalan queried, already regaining the feeling in his arm, but not the pain. 'It's amazing,' he added.

'I'll let your friend explain,' Gladys sighed and looked at Iverissa. 'I've already answered enough questions for one day.' Gladys smiled at her, indicating a joke that Acalan was not in on.

'It's dangerous to use too much; eventually, your body will depend on it to function,' Iverissa explained in a cynical tone.

'Well, it's been nice to meet you, but now that someone has come to collect you, I hope not to see you again.' Gladys chuckled to herself one last time, got up and was gone as abruptly as she had arrived.

Acalan was in disbelief as he lay partially upright on the hospital bed. He was already able to bend his arm again without any pain. Although initially enthralled by this, he continued to use it as an excuse to avoid Iverissa's eyes.

'I'm sorry,' he whispered, unable to choose the rest of his sentence.

'Wait, what?' She approached the bed. 'Why would you be sorry? You saved my life.'

'I didn't know what to do and I put you in danger,' he rambled. The sudden feeling of her fingertips on his temples surprised him into silence.

Iverissa entered his space, locking eyes with him and allowing him to see deep into her pupils.

'I would have died if you went back. And if I hadn't, they'd have probably killed me anyway.' She allowed her palms to fall onto his cheeks. 'It isn't about forgiving you; I owe my life to you.'

Acalan looked downwards, avoiding her praise. She pulled his face lightly with her fingertips, and he was sure that she was leaning closer. He allowed his eyes to fall shut and flowed with the moment.

'I can't believe it!' A familiar voice startled them.

They snapped back to reality, bolting upright like children caught with their hands in the cookie jar.

'I mean, you're here! How are you here?'

Upon recognising the man by his distinctive long green coat, Acalan rolled back and swiped up his bow. Why had this strange man followed him all this way? He wondered as he held the bow defensively, although he still had no arrows to fire.

'It's okay, I don't want to hurt you.' Arthur said. 'Please, you should rest that arm.'

'We are leaving. Get out of the way,' Acalan ordered, attempting to take charge of the interaction.

'Listen. You must be so scared right now. This is a little scary for me too.' The man's polished shoes squeaked on the hospital floor as he continued to take slow steps into the room, eyeing the bow as he approached. 'You're from Synnor, aren't you?'

'What if we are?' Iverissa responded without hesitation, causing him to stop in his tracks.

'Well, if you were, then you'd be modern history,' he stated. 'You'd be the first to escape.' Arthur grinned and hid his hands in the deep pockets of his coat. 'You've come so far. You're safe here if you let me help,' Arthur continued, trying to bargain with the harmless bowman.

'I like it here...' Iverissa switched sides with a shrug. '...and I don't want to run anymore.'

This came as a shock to Acalan, who still felt lost. It wasn't even clear to him that this was real life, and he blinked through a moment of confusion. His arm shook as he bluffed with an arrowless bow, unable to defend her if she so needed. She didn't speak any words out loud, but he heard her through the softness of her skin as she took his empty hand in her own. He had thought he'd lost her, and his lip quivered when it finally sank in that she was safe. This was all that mattered, and Acalan began to gradually lower the empty bow.

'Thank you,' Arthur said solemnly. He then walked over to one of the vacant beds opposite Acalan's and brushed his coat under his legs as he lifted himself onto the bed.

The pair watched as a moment passed and Arthur lay on his back with a deep sigh.

'Right then!' he began. 'Unofficially, welcome to Jasebelle!' The charismatic announcement was incongruent with the motionless man whose legs hung off the bedside. 'Officially, I think it might be illegal for you to be here, or anywhere other than Synnor for that matter.' He sat upright again, ruffling his hair while scratching his scalp. 'It isn't easy for me to say this, but officially speaking, you have nowhere to go.'

'We can't go back! They'll kill us,' Iverissa protested, but Arthur responded with another calm exhale. His collected demeanour still failed to match the situation.

'Actually, she'll be furious that this has happened. If you were to go back, what they'd do would be much worse than killing you, but I don't want that to happen,' he said straightforwardly, and Iverissa sank back inwards. 'If you walk out there alone, you might be fine at first. You can leave the city if you like, travel the continent even, but this will follow you everywhere you go.'

'Sorry, what do you mean by "she"?' Acalan asked, unsure which Titan Arthur was referring to.

'Virrel?' he answered with an upwards inflection, as if the answer was obvious.

The two men exchanged looks of confusion, neither sure how to proceed.

'Listen, it seems like there's a lot to explain,' Arthur broke the silence. 'You are welcome to stay with me until we figure it out.'

'Fine. Thank you,' Iverissa cut in before Acalan could respond, setting off a creeping sense of unease in him. He didn't know what to do, and it seemed Iverissa had decided without him. To him, they were safest when they were alone.

Acalan's indecision left him feeling exposed for several seconds. This place was strange and overwhelming; he couldn't say for certain which way was up. Acalan couldn't understand why this same feeling brought Iverissa joy when all he felt was fear.

'Let's go,' he agreed.

XV

Answers

Acalan found navigating the city significantly easier when he did it with guidance. He and Iverissa trailed behind Arthur, who led the way to his home. Acalan was mindful that people were all around him, yet the trend of nobody being especially interested in him or his party remained. In contrast, Iverissa's jaw hung open as she took in her surroundings, this being her first time in the street. Her first few steps in Jasebelle were different from Acalan's; she didn't seem anxious about the flurry of passersby as they brushed up close. Instead, her wide eyes scanned around, absorbing all the differences from her home. Acalan had at least become more comfortable with the smell of the bellum-based machines around them. It wasn't an especially intrusive smell now that he was used to it.

Arthur led them through a small plot of land occupied by trees, grass and a little pond. The tiny park occupied the same area of space that one of the towering buildings would. It was refreshing to cut through, as it contained the only greenery

Acalan had seen since leaving the hospital. There was an empty wooden bench on one side of the stony pathway, looking across to a quaint little pond on the opposite side. Acalan caught a glimpse of a feathery creature as they walked through, just before it vanished below the surface.

'Almost there!' Arthur said, reassuring them as they emerged back into the busy street. 'Try to keep your heads down, though,' he added, having noticed Iverissa's tourist-like awe at the architecture. Her head drooped, her excitement trodden on by an undisclosed threat.

Arthur stopped and gestured towards a stone stairway that was identical to countless others they had passed. He fumbled in his inside coat pocket and readjusted himself, producing a small set of keys to open the door. The entryway was a darkened corridor with an unlit bellum lantern hanging inside the plain green door. Acalan didn't register the darkness until he noticed Iverissa inching closer towards him, brushing his arm.

Arthur grasped at a coil that hung from the lantern and pulled downwards. The resulting crackle at the top of the rope lit the lantern above them. The spark then fled along an endless string and into the building. As they had seen before, it lit more lanterns to reveal the end of a short corridor before curling up a stairway and out of sight. As the darkness was illuminated, Acalan heard a breath of relief from his immediate right and sympathised with one of his own.

Just like in the hospital, this housing building had a lift machine, but this one was fenced off, its door jammed halfway open. Arthur disregarded it, bursting into a brisk climb up a concrete stairway. He tugged himself up using the varnished dark wood banister held up by black iron bars. The bellum lamps were affixed to the railing and dotted the flights of stairs that looped upwards in a triangle.

Having ascended a few floors, Acalan couldn't help but notice the monotony of the place; its walls were plain grey concrete, as were the steps. He peered over the banister while Arthur rattled his keys at one of the bland doors. The lanterns below circled the few floors they had climbed, but the ones above continued upwards endlessly.

'I know,' Arthur agreed with a point that nobody had made. 'I'd like to be a bit higher, but this is what I've got,' he said as he turned his back on them once more.

Iverissa and Acalan shared a look, agreeing with shrugs that they didn't know what he meant. They didn't interrupt him to ask before the door swung open, allowing Arthur to invite them in.

'For legal reasons, I can't tell you to make yourselves at home…' He smirked as he stepped into the flat and occupied its space. 'But please, come in.'

When Acalan and Iverissa stepped into the flat, they were pleasantly surprised by the warmth that met them. Unlike the cold and unnerving stairs and hallways, Arthur's living room was a cosy place to be. Wood panels ran along the floor towards a large bay window in the back of the room. The wallpaper surrounding them was a spotless cream, clearly painted with care. Around the room, there was a series of certificates hanging in pristine frames. The qualifications they announced meant nothing to Acalan as he examined them. The rightmost wall of the room consisted entirely of an enormous bookshelf, with books filling the shelves from floor to ceiling. A large desk occupied the centre of the room, with a small fabric couch squeezed in at the side as an apparent afterthought.

Arthur flung his keys onto the desk, but the sound of them hitting the surface was muted by the papers that were strewn across it. Realising the mess, he started to gather the papers into a neat pile and place them in a thin, unmarked file.

'Actually, sorry. You shouldn't be looking at these,' Arthur confessed as he cleared up, drawing a look of suspicious judgment from Acalan. 'Look, don't panic. Let me explain.' He placed the file in a drawer by the window. 'I'm a lawyer. These papers relate to my clients.'

Acalan felt a creeping sense of embarrassment; he didn't recognise these words. He was equal parts surprised and relieved to see that Iverissa's eyes were also darting around.

'We don't have lawyers back home. What is that?' she asked innocently.

'Really? I suppose not,' he commented vaguely and exhaled forcefully with full cheeks. As he moved around the desk, he removed his jacket and slung it over the tall, padded chair behind the desk. 'Please make yourselves comfortable.' He offered seats to them as he sat behind the desk as if preparing to interview them, and they sat opposite him.

Iverissa's hand lifted slightly as she prepared to press him for an explanation, but she was halted with only a moment to spare.

'So, when someone breaks the law, they get punished, right?' Arthur asked, and both of his new clients nodded in agreement. 'We do this because people don't break the law if there is a deterrent in place, yes?' They nodded once more. 'Right. Well, how do we know when someone has committed a crime?'

'They get caught?' Acalan took the bait.

'Exactly. But when they're accused, do they get to defend themselves?'

Arthur's question poked at Acalan's conscience. The unpleasant memory of the party from his childhood came back to haunt him. It occurred to him that he had never spoken to Tainen again after that night. He was fine with that, but the part that made him uneasy was that he had never seen the other attendees again.

'Should they?' Iverissa interrupted Acalan's reflection by indulging in Arthur's conversational explanation.

'Should they?!' Arthur pushed himself back into his chair, lifting one foot from the floor and onto the front of the seat. He crossed his arms on his raised knee and rested his chin on them. 'That's what I do!' His proud smile appeared from behind his crossed arms when he rocked back.

'You stand up for criminals?' she asked in disbelief.

'I represent people who are accused of crimes, but suspicion and guilt are very different things.' he responded. 'I stand up for the people who have nobody else in their corner and do everything I can to make sure they get heard.' Arthur's voice faltered as he completed his point, 'I stand up for people like you, Iverissa – you *both* – that need defence.'

Iverissa shuffled around in her seat awkwardly, offering up no rebuttal. It struck Acalan that she had been enjoying a fragile state of denial until this point. He had just watched it shatter into tiny shards around her. Her silence indicated that she seemed, perhaps for the first time, to appreciate the gravity of the situation. In turn, he checked in with himself, still finding it difficult to place trust in these outsiders. This man could betray them at any moment, although he hadn't done so yet.

'So, what now?' Acalan suppressed his suspicions and allowed the interaction to continue.

'Well, now that is a good question. This has never happened, so there is no precedent,' Arthur said, sending a cursory glance over towards the books that lined his wall. 'I'm going to level with you here. Like most people, I don't know much about your home. We all have a rough idea of how difficult it might be for you…'

'Synnor isn't a bad place!' Acalan raised his voice. 'It's our home!'

He leaned forward sharply, steadying himself with his hands on the desk. Iverissa's hand shot down onto his thigh, resting there for barely a second before retreating suddenly. Two emotions rushed through Acalan, one after the other. At first, he felt insulted, but as his gaze darted between them, this feeling was quickly replaced by shame and embarrassment.

'I was happy.' Acalan struggled to get the short sentence out while also controlling his lower lip, which had begun to quiver disobediently.

'Acalan, I mean no offense. All I'm trying to explain here is that we enjoy certain freedoms here in Jasebelle,' Arthur said in a bid to deescalate the situation. 'One of my clients is an activist. She and her faction campaign for action in Synnor.' Arthur smirked to himself, looking over Acalan's head. 'They get themselves into trouble constantly, but all they want is those same rights for you back home.'

Acalan's head was spinning. A sizable chunk of Arthur's explanation made little sense since Acalan had never even heard some of the words mentioned. He struggled to understand why people would endanger themselves for his benefit.

I never asked for any of this, he thought to himself as Arthur spoke.

'Either way, I know she will want to help us. Perhaps we can speak with her in the morning. I'm sorry, Acalan, I don't mean to…,' Arthur trailed off as he attempted to address the elephant in the room.

'It's fine. I'm fine.' Acalan brushed aside the awkwardness.

The afternoon rolled into the evening. Arthur prepared a simple meal for the party, which was dominated by conversation. Iverissa and Acalan shared parts of the story of how they had escaped Synnor, although Iverissa did most of the talking. She excitedly recapped their journey, but she did so in exact detail and without embellishment. Eventually, though, she ran out of things to tell.

'I remember shaking so much. I couldn't control it.' Iverissa was glassy-eyed by the end of her story. Her voice trembled, but she paused and controlled her tone with a deep breath. 'I was dizzy, and that's all I remember.'

'What then?' Arthur leaned forward with both elbows on the table and stared at Acalan.

'Well, I pushed her into the water.' Acalan omitted details and got straight to the point. It was clear then, more than ever, that he was not half the storyteller that Iverissa was. 'We just got lucky to wash up here.'

As they ate, they spoke about their leaders. Arthur grimaced while Iverissa spoke about Virrel, but he didn't justify his reaction. He then changed the topic to Chancellor Wilson, the head of the Jasebelle Government. Acalan found it particularly difficult to wrap his head around the idea that they picked leadership by popular vote. It didn't make sense to him that the gods weren't involved. Attempting to unpack this reminded him that the Titans didn't seem to be protecting Synnor from anything dangerous on the outside.

If they didn't do that, then what purpose did they serve? He thought as he ate. Then, having cleared his plate, he zoned out fully. Were they even doing anything? He wondered for the first time in his life.

Once everyone had eaten, Arthur was quick to gather up their plates and exit the room, leaving his guests together. Acalan looked at Iverissa, who was slouching absentmindedly and looking around. He wasn't used to seeing her like this; she looked content. Her eyes explored the bookshelves beside them for a few moments before finding Acalan. At that moment, her posture stiffened. She shifted around in her chair before locking into a calculated sitting position and adjusting her hair. There had been a range of answers given over dinner, and this was what she had always needed. In his mind, however, there were more questions than ever. He had left behind the only place he had ever known, lost everything he had ever had. Yet when he looked at her smile, it all felt worthwhile. He shook his head and exhaled through the grin of an idiot with nothing but a bow and the clothes on his back. Seeing her sitting tranquility and out of harm's way was what made it clear to him: he would do it all over again.

'Are you allowed this in Synnor?' Arthur asked as he re-entered the room with his hands full. From one hand he slid three basic goblets onto the table, one of which spun on its base shakily before coming to rest.

Acalan caught a glimpse of Iverissa rolling her eyes when Arthur revealed a large green bottle. He poured wine into the three goblets before setting the bottle down in the middle of the table.

'I've never seen this! What flavour is it?' Iverissa asked, playing dumb. Her sarcastic tone was completely lost on Arthur, who began explaining alcohol to them.

'Yes, we have this back home,' Acalan intervened, without taking offense this time. He realised that Arthur didn't know any better, and both sides were just trying to learn about the other.

Acalan had never encountered the awkwardness of meeting someone foreign before and was trying his best. Until that day, he didn't even know it was possible to do so. He lifted a goblet to his lips and took a mouthful. The wine was vibrant and sweet, with fruity notes. He didn't allow his reaction to reflect in his expression, but this was much better than anything he had ever gotten his hands on at home.

'Good, right?' Arthur waited eagerly.

'It is good. Thanks,' Acalan confirmed reservedly, and a slight smile escaped onto his face when the warm aftertaste settled in.

Iverissa also took a sip but was far more enthusiastic.

'This is amazing! Wait, is this expensive?! Please don't waste the good stuff on us!' she insisted.

'No, it's pretty cheap actually. Hang on, let me show you something.' Arthur left the room to return moments later with another bottle. After he blew a layer of dust off of it, it was clear that it was of noticeably higher quality, with a shiny but slightly faded label. He rubbed it clean with his sleeve and sat it in the middle of the table. Acalan raised a hand to investigate closer.

'Sorry, we can't open it.' Arthur's words stopped him, and he lifted the bottle off the table once more. 'It's an old tradition; when you qualify as a lawyer, your parents are supposed to mark the occasion with a bottle of fine wine.' He laughed awkwardly before retreating towards the kitchen, holding the bottle closely. 'It's silly. You're supposed to drink it when you win the greatest case of your career.'

'How are you meant to know?' Iverissa asked.

'Well, that's a very good question.' He leaned against the door frame. 'If I'm honest, I had hoped to do it while Mum and Dad were still here. They would have known.' He smiled and allowed the arm that cradled the bottle to fall to his side as he gripped it by the neck.

'I'm sorry,' Iverissa said sincerely.

'Don't be. I was raised in a happy family, and we valued the time we had.'

The moment stretched into silence. Acalan was unsure what to say, so instead, he said nothing. Arthur was still smiling, so he didn't seem visibly upset.

'I hear a lot of lawyers never open their bottles,' he said with a shrug. 'Apparently, when the time comes, you *just know*.' Arthur vanished into the kitchen to return the bottle, leaving the echo of a sombre tone in the room.

XVI

After Dark

The wine helped the conversation flow back and forth as the evening progressed. As the contents of the bottle depleted, conversation became increasingly more natural. It was clear from Iverissa's relaxed posture that she had no real doubt about their host, but Acalan took some time to reach that state of confidence.

The conversation ranged from big-picture questions about the world to small personal details. Arthur shared stories of some of the cases he had worked on. Even though most would see them as petty in the grand scheme of things, they fascinated Acalan and Iverissa. After all, everything here was new to them.

'So, what do you do for a living?' Arthur asked them.

'I make bows and repair them,' Acalan answered honestly. 'I get plenty of practice, so sometimes I do it for people and they pay me.'

'I work in the library,' Iverissa jumped in. 'Well, I worked in the library,' she quickly corrected herself.

'She's always been the smart one,' Acalan snuck in a compliment, causing her to choke on her drink. 'That's what got her exemption.'

'Sorry, I don't follow. Exemption from what exactly?' Arthur interrupted.

'The trials,' Acalan responded calmly, but Arthur's eyes widened at these words, and he shifted backwards in his seat. 'Wait, you don't do that here?' he asked, attempting to clarify.

'No,' Arthur asserted. 'We don't do that here.'

Acalan and Iverissa looked at each other with wide, bewildered eyes. Neither understood the reason for the silence that followed. Arthur did not expand, and the atmosphere in the room shifted uncomfortably.

'Anyway, the library…' Acalan attempted to move the conversation past this, hoping that Iverissa would expand.

Graciously, she took the opportunity to give a detailed breakdown of the responsibilities that made her so important to the city.

'Without me, everything will fall apart…,' she trailed off, resulting in another moment of silence, but with a far less intense atmosphere.

'Right! I need to sleep.' Arthur placed his hands on his knees to stumblingly hoist himself upright. 'The couch will only fit one, I'm afraid, so one of you is on the floor,' he said, gesturing towards the little couch. 'Let me at least give you some sheets.'

After a brief moment, Arthur returned with a small stack of spotless white sheets and placed them into Acalan's open arms. 'Look. Please stay here tonight,' he requested. 'We can go first thing in the morning if you wish, but please try your best to get some rest until then.'

Acalan nodded. For Iverissa's sake, he wasn't running away this time.

After Arthur had left the room and his bedroom door clicked shut, Acalan wrestled with a bed sheet. Once he was able to grip the edges, he whipped it upwards and allowed it to droop over the sofa. He nodded to himself with contentment.

'You can take the sofa,' Acalan said quietly. 'I'll sleep on the floor.'

'Thanks,' Iverissa said, without turning to look. 'Are you tired?' She was perched on the windowsill, looking down onto the street.

'Exhausted, but I doubt I'll sleep.' He wandered over to her and climbed onto the window sill to sit opposite her. He looked straight into her eyes, catching her attention. 'Are you?'

'Nope, wide awake,' she answered. Her eyes wandered for a moment, and she scrunched up her face but said nothing. She looked out the window once more as if the words she wanted to find were written on the street below.

'What?' Acalan pressed. 'You clearly want to tell me something!'

'Why don't we go for a walk?' she asked gingerly.

'Iverissa!' Acalan groaned. 'That is one thing we aren't supposed to do right now.'

'Look, Ack, nobody is around.' She pointed at the empty street down below. 'Doesn't it drive you crazy knowing there's a whole new city out there? I just want to look around.'

When he looked out into the night, he could see that she was right. The scene below was motionless. He didn't share her excitement about exploring it, though; he was happy where he was sitting.

'All he asked was that we wait until the morning!' Acalan insisted, avoiding her point.

'So now we trust strangers, do we?' Iverissa teased in a cheeky tone, prodding him with an outstretched leg.

Acalan scowled. It took him a moment to realise she was pushing his buttons. He closed his eyes and rocked back, leaning his head against the wall.

'A short walk,' he conceded.

'A *really* short walk,' she added cautiously.

Having snuck out of the flat and made their way downstairs, they stepped out into the cool night air. Acalan was trailing behind as Iverissa skipped out onto the street before walking back to him with an innocent grin.

'Just to the park and back,' she whispered before strolling away from him.

Acalan laughed to himself. If it wasn't for her, they wouldn't still be together, yet here she was, pushing him out of his box once again. Still, he was unable to understand her relentless curiosity as he watched her wander ahead. This snapped him out of his thought paralysis, and he broke into a light jog to catch up.

Once he was alongside her, they walked together at a carefree pace. They were the only actors on an empty stage, illuminated by a series of bellum lamps that ran asynchronously along both sides of the street. Acalan's mind wandered with each step. If he was a performer, then his audience was in another auditorium. He was oddly at peace with this; he didn't feel like it was a performance when he was with her, so why would there be a crowd? It was when his mind wandered onto this unfamiliar turf that he caught himself. He thought of the wine he had drunk and noted its effect on his thought patterns.

When they stepped into the fenced-off park, they occupied an otherwise tranquil plot. Acalan recognised the pond from earlier, although it was completely still now, like a window built into the grass.

'Can we stay a while?' Iverissa pushed her luck. 'It's nice,' she added, lowering herself onto a bench.

'It is nice,' Acalan admitted as he joined her.

He spread his arms along the back of the bench and then rolled his head backwards to look up at the dark sky. He noticed when Iverissa slid towards him, but he made no mention of it. The gap between them closed, and she was now pressing into him slightly. Acalan shuffled around on the bench, trying to get comfortable, and his arm slipped down to rest on her back. Embarrassed by this, he retracted his arm briskly. However, it seemed that she had mistaken the movement for an invitation as she then rested her head on his shoulder. Acalan smiled, finding humour in his own awkwardness. It seemed right, so he cuddled her back.

A sudden rustle in the bushes caused Acalan to jump. Iverissa also got a fright, albeit from Acalan, and with a slight delay. A narrow yellow bill then appeared from within the leaves, and Iverissa giggled when the rest of the duck's head emerged from its camouflage. The curious bird peered at them, tilting its head slightly and freezing in place.

'You big baby!' Iverissa kept laughing and pushed his chest gently.

'What?!' he protested playfully.

'You jumped out of your skin!' she teased. 'I almost fell on the ground!'

'Oh yeah? Well, you must be scared of something.'

She stopped laughing immediately. 'You're not telling me you're scared of ducks, are you?'

'I'm not scared of ducks!' he argued back, only then noticing that she was still stifling a giggle. Regardless, it exasperated him that she was still missing his point. 'I feel like I've been so worried all day like I can't relax. Whenever I look at you, it all makes you seem so brave.'

Iverissa stopped laughing, but her silence seemed genuine this time, and she rested her head on him once more.

'You have to promise not to laugh,' she said in a calm and controlled tone.

'You were laughing at me!' he protested once more.

'Ack!' she pleaded.

'I'm not going to laugh at you, Iverissa,' he assured her.

'Since I was very little, I've been scared of the dark,' she confessed, still not moving her head from his shoulder. 'When they were still with us, it was only my parents who knew. Now, nobody does,' she explained. 'Well, not nobody.' She laughed awkwardly. 'Now, you do too."

Acalan breathed a stifled sigh of relief and pulled her close. In doing so, he could feel her starting to tremble reluctantly.

'You don't need to be embarrassed.' He felt out of his depth in his attempt to comfort her and fell silent. He considered her perspective with fresh context while they sat together. This was the first time he had noticed the full moon, which cast generous amounts of silvery light on the scene. There was also residual light leaking in from the lamps on the main road. The light shone over the innocent little duck, which had fully emerged from the bushes.

When Acalan directed his attention back to Iverissa, he began to understand his own discomfort at this moment. This sort of interaction almost always went the other way. It shamed him to realise that he couldn't remember the last time he had listened to her. He tried to think what Iverissa might say to him but grew frustrated when his mind came up blank. His only purpose here was to make her feel comfortable, yet he couldn't even do that.

Hopelessly speechless, Acalan placed a hand on the nape of her neck and eased her head from his shoulder and onto his chest.

To help calm Iverissa, he managed to spark a conversation. Although he struggled at first, Acalan saw no reason to rush it. Over time, it grew easier and easier, and eventually, it was like they were sitting back up on that hill by the arena. It wasn't so difficult. For the most part, he was letting her speak and only listening. After some time, Iverissa had stopped shaking and was laying calmly against him.

'He looks happy! I bet he isn't scared of the dark,' she sniffed, acknowledging the duck, which had since made its way into the water and was floating happily on the pond.

'He isn't even scared of us anymore!' Acalan joined in with her joke. 'I'd have shot him if I had the bow with me!' he said, causing her to laugh quietly while it swam in circles, indifferent to their presence.

'When I was young, I'd stay up late and read.' She spoke more about her fear, understanding that it was illogical but frustrated by her inability to shake it. 'I didn't want to sleep until I was too tired to stay up.'

'Is that why you've dragged me out here?' he joked cautiously.

'No, I grew out of that.' She smiled. 'They told me I'd grow out of it all, which would have been nice, but at a certain point, I realised it wasn't going to happen,' she explained.

When she grew up, she did the only thing she could do to manage her fear: she learned how to live with it as an adult.

The more Acalan listened, the more it became clear why it was a secret. She seemed deeply ashamed of this part of herself, and he couldn't think of a reason that she would have needed to bring it up. It was completely understandable to him that she had chosen never to mention it, but it explained a lot. It explained her unease in the library, for starters.

'Those tunnels must have been so hard,' Acalan said out loud as the realisation hit him, shining a spotlight onto the achievement. 'I didn't even know, you could have locked up and stopped, but you didn't!'

'I didn't really have a choice in the matter.' She avoided the compliment. 'It was bearable, perhaps more so than I would have known,' she said, her tone surprised. 'Don't get me wrong,' she continued, recognising the discomfort. 'I'm not saying it was fun. I was brave enough to cope,' she completed her thought with a tone of apparent disbelief.

'It was never going to stop you,' Acalan piled on clumsily, still struggling to provide suitable support. Still, he realised that she needed it less with each word that she spoke. Even though it scared her, she was in control.

'It's funny. I was so scared, but I felt brave enough because you were there with me,' she tried to explain.

At first, he protested, but to an extent, he understood. Acalan reflected on the challenges that they had faced getting to Jasebelle. He didn't think that he could have done any of it without her; he wouldn't even have wanted to. He had left his place in the world, his responsibility to the Titans, and everything he had ever known, all for her. He looked back down at Iverissa, who was still resting on his chest, eyes closed contentedly. What if it was all thanks to her?

The duck broke the silence with a quack. Acalan felt Iverissa giggling, her body wobbling against him. Although words evaded him, this was the moment that Acalan realised he was in love with Iverissa Zyrel.

XVII

Captain of the Watch

The toilet facilities in the palace were not as luxurious as one might expect, and one certainly wouldn't find Virrel using them. Most halls were restricted and only used by the Queen and her key advisors. These were for the staff. A stocky man burst in, disrupting the silence in the vacant stalls. The man leaned over one of the basic sinks, which groaned under him when he rested his weight on it. The sink retracted into the wall when he stood; it appeared to have gotten dislodged over time and was on its last legs.

He flicked the black tap open but received no water. When he rattled it, he found that the entire tap spun in its fixture. Frustrated by this, he stepped to the left, over to the next sink, in search of a working tap. Here, a murky stream trickled out and down the plughole in front of him. The man cupped his hands, collecting a small pool of water before closing his eyes and submerging his face. Then, he splashed the water up his face and over the top of his shaved head. With a shake of the head, he stared at his reflection in the cracked mirror before him. The narrow face that looked back still had water running down it, dripping from his pointed moustache and goatee. His father had always emphasised the importance of the city guard, so Tainen had expected more. The reflection that looked back at him didn't look successful; he just looked tired.

It was only because he had seen them that he was being so hard on himself. He was fairly sure it was them anyway. It wasn't easy to tell from so far, he reassured himself, but he couldn't stop replaying the moment in his head.

There he was, standing at the gates of his estate, looking down the hill and over towards the library. His property boasted a splendid view over both the library and the main square in the Upper District. Tainen scoffed at the view, dissatisfied with what he had. He couldn't see the palace, which was behind him, further up the hill. Even though he felt that he should be staying in the palace by then, he was still in his father's old house, near the bottom of Virrel Park. The night was silent, as it almost always was. Tainen inhaled deeply, taking the quiet for granted until it was interrupted by a clattering in the distance. He squinted; the scene ahead of him remained the same. As he exhaled a cloud into the chilly night air, it cleared to reveal a well-dressed couple, bolting out of the back of the library. He froze as they darted around the building and skittered across the cobbles.

He sensed immediately that something wasn't right since they had left the door ajar. Yet he remained where he was, watching as they left his field of vision. Something within him rendered him unable to act. Maybe it was because the council had passed him over too many times, and this was a subtle way of getting back at them. He snapped himself out of this thought pattern, realising that he didn't have the manpower to act anyway. His cigarette expired, and he flicked the butt onto the cobbles. They looked like a couple of partygoers, he lied to himself and turned to go inside. Not worth chasing.

A sharp sting bit at his knuckles and the broken fragments of glass rattled around the sink. He cursed as he retracted his arm and flicked it, only then aware that rage had gotten the better of him again. He pinched at a shard lodged between his fingers and winced when it slid free. Flicking the shard down the plughole, he investigated his reflection. Teary eyes stared back meekly from within a dangling shard. A week had passed, and he still couldn't hold his head high. Even if he had someone to tell, he wouldn't dare. One thing was for sure, though, he wouldn't make the same mistake twice.

In contrast to the vacant bathroom that he stepped out of, the palace lobby was still teeming with the frantic activity of workers and guards as they dashed around urgently. Without meaning to, he met the eyes of another guard across the polished floor. Realising his mistake, he pivoted on the spot and made his way in the opposite direction. He had an appointment with Virrel's key advisors and intended to be punctual.

'Sir?' The other guard had caught up with him and looked expectant.

'Excuse me?' Tainen responded, towering over his subordinate as he continued to stride ahead.

'Another demonstration this evening, sir. The Grand Market this time,' he explained, keeping up with him. 'Should we assign more resources to the area?'

Tainen halted when the guard said this, catching him off balance.

'We're already leaving the Upper District exposed enough,' Tainen stated firmly. The Lower District wasn't strictly his responsibility, and he had to put his people first.

'They are getting restless, sir,' the guard protested, frustrating Tainen.

'I don't remember asking your opinion on the matter,' he replied. 'Inform the Lower District guard to continue their containment operations and carry on as usual.' He took several steps forwards. 'If people are gathering, wait for someone to give you an excuse, and then, I want you to start making arrests.'

The Lower District guard stood speechless as Tainen stormed off. The chaos continued as he progressed through the palace; damage control was still underway.

Without a clear sense of where he was in the building, he eventually sought guidance. He stuck an arm out in front of a particularly scrawny-looking individual. The clerical assistant jumped back, dropping several binders that slid across the polished floor.

'I don't have time for this!' He exclaimed while scrambling to collect his documents from around Tainen's feet.

'I'm looking for the roundtable,' Tainen stated monotonously, ignoring the man's comment. He then noticed an immediate shift in the man's demeanour as he stood upright.

'My apologies. This way, sir,' he said robotically, taking the lead without elaborating further.

Tainen wasn't sure who he was meeting, but he had never been allowed this far into the palace. He was confident that it was in some way related to the evasion, but he couldn't be sure what that meant for him. Most likely it would be a call for his involvement in the official response, but he was still anxious that it had happened on his watch. Since the evasion had gone undiscovered until they were due to appear in front of the crowd, it had left a somewhat red-faced Virrel to explain. Word had then spread after she was unable to do so, and the people were beginning to ask tough questions.

When they reached the roundtable, Tainen's guide rushed off, and he stood alone before the closed door. He gave several confident knocks but received no response. The door squeaked as he opened it slowly, announcing his entrance. The dimly lit room contained a massive roundtable, which had a maze-like pattern expertly engraved into it. Wooden chairs with tall, straight backs surrounded the table. Each seat had its own detailed pattern carved into the backrest, none of which he recognised. The exception was a much wider golden throne that sat on the opposite side of the room. The backrest of this seat curved inwards and had several ornate decorations that burst out from the centre. A deep black mantle was draped over it, obscuring his view of the pattern.

Sitting on the cushioned black fabric was an elegant woman that Tainen recognised. She sat with one leg crossed over the other, comfortable in the space, yet her upright posture seemed calculated. The black fabric of her dress matched that of the cape that she had set aside. The dress was layered under a delicate bodice-like garment consisting entirely of a thin gold chain. Each loop of the chain linked to a metallic shoulder piece that enveloped her upper frame. The golden shine matched the ornate circlet that sat upon her long red locks.

'Please, don't be shy. We don't have time for shyness,' Virrel said, inviting him in. Her speech was slow and measured with great intention.

Although his heart was racing in her immediate presence, her soothing tone of voice surprised him.

'You're probably wondering why I've personally asked for you to come here today?' she asked with raised eyebrows.

Tainen nodded gingerly and stepped into the room, allowing the door to swing shut behind him.

'Well, it's been a busy day! Has it not?' her words poked at him knowingly. She bit her lower lip for a moment, appearing to find joy in the tension. 'Has it not?' she repeated, her expression feigning confusion.

'Yes, your highness,' Tainen answered briefly. 'It has.'

'And why might that be?' she spoke with full control over the awkward tone in the room but elected to maintain it.

Tainen started to feel a thin layer of sweat forming on his brow. *She doesn't know that he saw them, does she?*

'Because of the evaders?' he attempted.

'The evaders!' she raised her voice and lunged forwards in her seat, causing him to jump. 'But…' she sat back once more, lowering her voice back to the unnerving register she had opened with. '… it's a little more complicated than that.' She placed both feet on the floor with intention before gracefully standing upright.

Tainen focused on controlling his breath when she wandered around the table. He shuffled his armour around with his shoulders, the clammy heat of the room adding to his discomfort. A similarly warm breath crawled up his neck as she stepped into his personal space, allowing the silence to linger. *She knows,* he thought but remained silent.

Mercifully, she then stepped away, allowing him a moment to breathe. She raised her shoulders slightly and placed her palms on the round table. In one fluid motion, she lifted her slender frame effortlessly and slid backwards to perch comfortably on the table.

'You seem nervous,' she pointed out with a wry smile. 'What are you not telling me, Captain?' she asked upfront, forcing engagement from him.

'We have been overwhelmed; all my men are in the Lower District…' he answered, trying to misdirect her.

'Well, it's interesting that you'd mention that,' she cut him off. 'That's why I wanted you here tonight.'

Tainen was disarmed by this remark; she wasn't making any sense. If she understood the challenges his men were facing, then surely, he should be out there leading them. Although he was confused, he still felt relieved. She didn't seem to know about what he had seen.

'I'm going to tell you a secret, Captain,' she whispered to him as she bent forwards before pressing one finger against her deep crimson lips, shushing him. 'When the people in this city see things that they aren't supposed to, they get the wrong idea.' She looked to him for confirmation, which she received in the form of a slight nod. 'They start to think that they might be better off elsewhere.' She shook her head at him, lending physicality to her rambling. 'Sometimes, they need a reminder of what sort of danger this city protects them from.' Her gaze wandered around behind him, as if he wasn't there, before returning to focus on him once more. She then lifted a basic goblet from beside her on the table and sniffed at its contents. She scrunched her face up in apparent disgust before looking back at him.

'Do you know what this room is for?' she asked politely, ignoring his discomfort. He shook his head. 'Don't worry! I know you don't, none of you do!' she said excitedly, rolling back to lie flat on the table. 'This is my council! Well, they aren't here now.'

Tainen was surprised to hear the queen speak in such an offhand manner. When she appeared in public, she seemed much more reserved.

Virrel continued to ramble as she floated a hand over her head and pointed around the empty seats. 'Only very important people get to sit in here. They help me make very important decisions.' Her patronising tone continued when she pushed herself into a half-upright position and met his eyes once more. 'I'm going to be candid with you, Captain.' She adjusted her hair with one hand while propping herself up with the other. She then lifted her leg upwards towards the chair between them, touching it with the tip of her toes. 'We've had a bit of a reshuffle.' She stretched her leg fully, pushing her foot into the seat and causing it to tumble towards him, revealing an unconscious man, who tumbled onto the floor.

Tainen jumped back urgently as the chair and body crashed to the floor. The deafening thud echoed around the room. Dread overwhelmed him when he looked at the pale skin of the motionless corpse in fine robes sprawled out on the marble floor. Whoever this man once was, Tainen did not recognise him.

'Not a good start, Captain!' Virrel scolded him. 'You were supposed to catch him!' She laughed at her own joke, causing yet another dramatic shift in tone.

Tainen watched the dust settle around the empty chair, noticing then that there was no engraving on its back. 'We have a new vacancy,' she added. 'The chair is for you, Captain! You'll even get to choose the picture on the front if you like.'

Tainen's blank expression kept his cards close to his chest. Getting the recognition that he deserved overjoyed him, but one thing didn't add up.

'What about the Lower District?' he asked meekly.

Queen Virrel let herself fall back once more, cackling as she pulled her leg back onto the table, arching her knee.

'That's the best part!' she forced through her laughter before collecting herself in an unnervingly short amount of time. 'We won't need to worry about them anymore. Don't look so nervous – you're going to love it!'

XVIII

Not From Around Here

Acalan smiled to himself while Iverissa spoke to him. Although he remained speechless, he was content in this moment. They were still alone together, except for their new feathered friend, who continued to glide around in circles. Iverissa was excitedly explaining to him that she had read some restricted text about the law but hadn't understood the context at the time. She was stumbling through terminology that Acalan had never even heard before. The long words held no meaning to him, yet they seemed to fascinate her. Her wide eyes refused to focus on anything in particular, looking towards him and away in quick succession.

His attention wavered; he was unable to determine when to say something to her. It certainly seemed like the best time, he thought. They had put everything on the line to earn this moment together. Yet, he found himself unable to find either the courage or the words. There would be nobody to witness his humiliation if he got it wrong, though. Nobody except this judgemental little duck. The duck splashed away happily. It was carefree and uninterested in him or his dilemmas.

'Ack?' Iverissa interrupted, having noticed his attention on the ripples in the pond.

Uh-oh, he thought, what was she saying?!

She continued to look at him expectantly, tilting her head slightly.

'Yes?' He attempted to guess his way out of the situation.

'Great!' She jumped onto him, locking him in a tight hug.

Acalan reciprocated, although he was immediately confused about what he had agreed to.

'You'll need to carry him back!' she stated. 'Oh! We'll need to train him, okay?' she added.

Acalan looked back at her but dared not agree to anything else.

'I'm messing with you, Ack. You seemed so attached like you were about to wade in there and bring him with us.' She gestured with a nod towards the disinterested duck, which stepped out of the water with a wiggle and wandered back into the bushes.

Acalan was relieved, albeit a little embarrassed. Still speechless, he recognised that he didn't need to speak. He simply laughed with her.

The ambience was then interrupted. They both shared a confused expression and shrugged simultaneously at the sound of distant shouts. They couldn't pick out any words, and the shouting grew louder over the next few moments.

'Should we move?' Iverissa asked.

'Probably just drunks,' he replied, shaking his head in response. 'They'll come and go.'

She nodded back to him, and they sat together in uncomfortable silence, waiting for the moment to pass. Eventually, a tall man stumbled into the pool of light in front of them, confirming Acalan's suspicion.

The man stepped towards them, leaning inwards onto the fence and burping. Acalan made eye contact, raising his eyebrows, and regretted it immediately. Realising his mistake, he adjusted his gaze.

'What?!' the man demanded, before stopping to cough.

Acalan remained silent.

The man stumbled into the park, kicking aside stones with each step. 'Something to say?'

Acalan continued to ignore him, hoping that he would get distracted and move on.

'You think you're…' The drunk hiccupped, causing a pocket of boozy air to assault Acalan's senses. 'You think you're better than me?' he accused.

Acalan still said nothing, scanning for the best place to stare. He avoided the man's eyes but noticed a large scar on his right cheek. As he continued to look around, the man's face leaned closer, occupying his field of vision almost entirely. He noticed bushes of overgrown nostril hair poking out of the crooked nose that housed them. Acalan was paralysed.

The sound of hurried footsteps suddenly resounded in the space as several more people ran in.

'Nobody wants to fight you, you moron!' a joyful voice called out.

Both Acalan and the aggressor turned to look at a shorter man with spiked red hair. This other man also slurred his speech, but he was standing upright with much more confidence and appeared to be more in control. 'I hope he wasn't bothering you; he gets like this when he drinks.'

'Nobody is bothering anyone,' Acalan said, having assessed the situation.

Two friends accompanied the red-haired man: a man and a woman. The couple swayed together, the man's arms wrapped around the woman. They seemed far more interested in each other than in Acalan. Ignoring them, the red-haired man stepped towards him and placed a hand on the shoulder of his brutish drunken friend.

'Come on, mate, it's past your bedtime,' he teased in a chipper tone, receiving an absent-minded nod from the huge man.

Acalan was only able to breathe comfortably again when they exited his personal space. It seemed that the altercation had ended as quickly as it had started; the drunken man no longer acknowledged Acalan.

'We're sorry,' the red-haired man insisted. 'He's sorry too, but he won't realise it until tomorrow morning.' He pointed towards his friend, who now seemed almost completely oblivious to what was happening.

It was almost as if a symptom of his drinking was a distinct lack of object permanence, causing Acalan to vanish into the bench.

'Didn't catch your name, mate.' The red-haired man extended a short arm around the lumbering liability that he accompanied.

Acalan's shoulders relaxed, and he accepted the handshake. For such a small person, this man had a respectable grip.

With a firm up-down motion, Acalan introduced himself. 'Acalan. I'm Acalan,' he said, noticing the grip on his hand tightening as he spoke.

'You're not from around here, Acalan, are you?' he interrogated, the fun tone of moments ago replaced by a more sinister one.

Acalan's eyes widened, and he looked towards Iverissa for the first time to see that her mouth was open, though she said nothing. She seemed equally aware of the tension but unsure of what was happening.

It then felt like his arm was yanked out of its socket as it was pulled sharply away from him. There was a sudden whiplash as his chest lunged forwards, taking his neck with it, and his head followed. He then felt the shock of another skull connecting with his own. The red spikes did little to mitigate the searing pain that followed. Iverissa shrieked and lunged forward in a hopeless attempt to intervene. Despite his intoxication, the goliath subdued her effortlessly.

Dazed, Acalan fell backwards into the bench. He pressed a palm to his forehead to try and stop the ringing. His other hand scrambled for something to grab onto, but he was unable to find his balance even while seated. He closed his eyes tightly and cursed, shaking his head.

Suddenly, his shirt tightened, compressing his chest as his assailant clutched the fabric. Acalan palmed at the arm that gripped him but found no purchase. Instead, he was pulled off the bench and fell to the ground like a bag of sand. When he looked around, it enraged him to see a distressed Iverissa pushed to the ground by the brutish drunk, who then focused on him once again.

'You sound like you're from over there!' the red-haired man announced, grandstanding to his friends. 'I heard that Acalan likes to kill defenceless people.'

Desperately trying to get back up, Acalan pushed his palms into the stony ground. He then recoiled following a blow to his chest that came from a boot swinging into him from above. Rolling onto his back, he looked up at two figures. Seeing them allowed him to anticipate the kick that came from his other side. What he failed to expect was the crack that accompanied it. He gasped for air, experiencing severe pain in his chest.

'Let's show him what being defenceless feels like,' Acalan heard another voice add before the speaker rushed over to join in the assault.

Acalan had never endured a beating like this, had never even been in a serious fight. This was evident in his lack of technique as he tried and failed to grab any of the dirty boots that swung towards him. It was only after the first blow to the back of his head that he started to curl inwards and stopped trying to fight back. He couldn't understand why he was being attacked in this way, but he knew he was defenceless. Desperate screaming and crying came from Iverissa, although he wasn't sure where to look. Acalan didn't know what to do, but it wasn't his decision to make. His muscles spasmed as he absorbed hits from all angles. After everything he had survived on the last day, Acalan hadn't expected to die like this.

'Stop!' A final, hopeless plea came from Iverissa before Acalan blacked out.

There was silence as he tumbled through the darkness, which came as a shock. Acalan had thought that this would be where he would face the judgement of the Titans, yet he was all alone once again. Perhaps this was their judgement, and they wouldn't even let him into the afterlife. Acalan continued to fall backwards but felt no wind around him. He swung his arms around, desperate for something to clutch onto, but found nothing. A light source approached rapidly from below, and his muscles contracted painfully as he braced.

Acalan jolted awake in a dimly lit room. Chilling air crept in through a hole in the wall that also let in a stream of light. The shadows of the iron bars over the hole stretched over the grimy stone floor. Aside from himself, there was nothing in the room. Bare walls surrounded him. The low ceiling also contributed to a claustrophobic environment. A steel door sealed the tiny room shut. As he took his first conscious breath, the dreadful pain in his side was an immediate reminder of his beatdown.

Not ready to move, Acalan shivered in his cold corner. The only discernible movement was that of the tears that escaped and progressed down his face. He flinched at the intense sting when they ran into an open cut by his eye. While avoiding moving the rest of his body, he brought an arm up to wipe them away. When he relived the moment of assault in his mind, his eyes continued to form fresh pools. As much as his ribs ached, he was haunted more by the memory of Iverissa crying for help.

Acalan didn't pity himself, yet his lower lip quivered. 'I should have been able to protect her', he thought, dwelling on it, not even sure where Iverissa was. This was then followed by the realisation that he didn't know what this place was either. He forced himself upright, enduring the pain that accompanied the movement, but only long enough to sit up and lean against the wall. Acalan jumped at the sudden sound of metal hitting metal.

'Don't get comfy. You're going home today,' a deep, raspy voice spoke through a slot in the door.

The speaker then slid through a food tray, which immediately toppled over and onto the floor. The soup seeped into cracks in the floor, and the morsel of bread that accompanied it fell to the side. Although the soup could not be saved, Acalan crawled over and, after brushing most of the dirt off, forced himself to eat the bread.

Acalan was unable to track the passage of time while he lay there. Even if he could stand at the window, it would be too high for him to see out of. Although limited light came in from outside, it was definitely daytime. It seemed that Acalan had been right after all: the world was a nasty place that he wasn't welcome to be a part of. He would have taken no pleasure in explaining this to Iverissa had she been there. Despite how many times he had tried to tell her, there would be no vindication. It didn't matter anyway; he was returning to Synnor, to be held responsible for his actions.

'If you were to go back, what they'd do to you would be much worse than killing you.' Arthur's words echoed in his mind, forcing Acalan to assess his options once again. This assessment was fruitless; even if he were to take the coward's way out, he had no means. All he had were his clothes and an upturned food tray. Perhaps he could fight when the guards tried to move him, in the hope that one of them would panic. If he could scare them, they might release him from his responsibility with a blade to the throat. The tragedy of it all overwhelmed him, drawing out a weak laugh; he had thought they had made it. How naïve, he thought.

Thoughts like this kept Acalan company until he heard sounds from the opposite side of the door. The flap had been bolted shut, so he could only hear muffled speech between the two parties. He waited patiently as the conversation increased in volume. This was the plan he would commit to: once they came in, he would fight to the death. Of all the thoughts that passed through his utterly defeated mind, this one was particularly humbling: hopefully, he could fight hard enough to be worth killing. The door clunked, and Acalan forced himself to take a deep breath through the pain. He had no more time to prepare himself; it was happening.

'I want you to remember this!' a familiar voice shouted as the door was opened. 'This is the moment that ended your careers!' the voice scolded the two guards that stood in the doorway before its owner stormed past them, shoving one of them aside.

The long green coat caught the draft from the window as Arthur rushed into the room. Acalan's muscles relaxed again. He didn't need to fight, so his shoulders fell back and his arms lay flat on the cold floor. His head rested back against the wall, and his eyes fell shut for a moment.

'It's okay,' Arthur said in a paternal tone.

When Acalan opened his eyes again, he could see Arthur kneeling beside him. He had brought in a bundle of supplies cradled in his arms. He now allowed them to scatter onto the floor.

'Where does it hurt?' he asked.

'Everywhere.' Acalan laughed shakily. 'Here, mostly.' He clutched at his ribs.

'Okay. Let me help. Like these *incompetent cowards* should have done!' He raised his voice on purpose so he could be heard from outside the room.

Arthur began to unbutton Acalan's shirt, noticing Acalan's core tensing with apprehension as he did so.

'Don't worry, it's bellum. Same as the hospital uses.' He handed Acalan a small vial of clumpy powdered substance, identical to the one he had seen in the hospital. 'Put it on your cuts,' he instructed before tearing open a larger bag that Acalan didn't recognise.

Acalan complied, feeling an unpleasant stinging as he sprinkled the substance on his wounds.

'This is going to get worse before it gets better, okay?' Arthur asked though he didn't wait for Acalan to agree.

The crystalised substance that he rolled out onto a square piece of fabric had the same scent as the powder, although this was the strongest Acalan had smelled. It looked like the same substance in a different form.

'Three... Two...' Arthur pushed the compress down onto Acalan's ribcage, causing Acalan to yelp involuntarily as the intense cold tore through his core.

'Agh!' Acalan began to struggle as Arthur shifted his body weight onto the fabric. He kicked his legs, attempting to lift Arthur off as the pain continued to build.

As Acalan cried out at full volume, he felt a click in his chest. He then fell quiet as the pain subsided immediately.

'Oh,' he said, stunned, before lunging forward to hug Arthur. 'Thank you.'

'You're welcome.' Arthur wrestled himself free from the embrace. 'Sorry, not a hugging person.'

'Right.' Reality began to set back in for Acalan, who had clung on at the edge of death. 'Neither am I,' he laughed.

'Listen, that hurt because your body can't really cope with that amount of bellum.' Arthur brushed aside any awkwardness, immediately getting back to business. 'It isn't magic. There's a limit to what it can help with, and you tested that limit this morning,' Arthur explained. 'We use it in moderation because, at one point, it starts to destroy rather than heal. Do you understand?'

Acalan nodded meekly.

'You'll need to avoid it from now on, at least for a few weeks. Now, let's see about getting you out of here, shall we?'

XIX

Refugee

The bellum on his cuts and bruises had warmed by the time it finished its work. Acalan wiped some bubbly residue from his cheek using the back of his hand. He then rubbed it into his skin, where it soaked in without leaving a trace.

'What about Iverissa?' Acalan asked.

'Don't worry, I've spoken to her already,' Arthur confirmed. 'She's a bit shaken up, but not hurt. She was more worried about you!' Arthur gathered up the discarded medical supplies he had rushed in with and deposited them into his deep coat pockets. 'You were brought here after the incident. You're looking at assault charges, but they're nonsense,' he explained in a chipper tone before his smile slipped away and he shifted to a sterner expression. 'The problem is that they know where you're from and they want to deport you.' Arthur went silent before acknowledging Acalan's vacant expression. 'Send you back,' he clarified.

'Can you stop them?' Acalan asked.

'I have an idea. This hasn't happened before, so it's just an idea,' Arthur rambled. 'I'll need your help for this to work.'

'Of course. I can help,' Acalan agreed without hesitation. 'What do you need?'

'I need you to ask for help,' Arthur stated. 'I can help, but it needs to come from you and Iverissa for this to work.'

'I'm not sure I understand what you mean.' Acalan shuffled backwards against the wall.

'You're a refugee, Acalan,' Arthur said, his lack of expression an indication of the solemnness of his words. 'You fled home because both your lives were at risk,' he went on. 'There isn't any legal precedent for this, so it will be based on emotion.'

'Oh.' Acalan's shoulders sank. Of all the challenges to give him, this struck him as a somewhat unfair test.

'I need you to be honest,' Arthur added. 'As much as I can try to tell them, I need them to believe you and want to help.'

'Right. Okay.' Acalan shook himself. 'Who's them?'

'Best case scenario, the warden,' Arthur said. 'I doubt they'll be alone, though. The entire government will be around a table at the moment, trying to figure out what to do with you.'

Arthur got to his feet, brushing down the bottom of his coat as he did so. He gripped the lapels of it between his thumbs and forefingers, flicking it swiftly. 'Try not to overthink it; it will only harm our chances. Come on.'

Arthur's posture stiffened when he stepped into the hallway outside the cell. Two guards stood in purple and black checkered uniforms that Acalan did not recognise. The uniforms were covered with various pieces of shiny metallic armour. The metal clinked tellingly as they stood to attention when Arthur approached.

'Listen here, gentlemen, here's what's going to happen. You are going to take us to the warden immediately. You will ensure that Miss Zyrel is also escorted there to meet us upon arrival.'

'The warden is very busy –' one of the guards began to respond before Arthur interrupted.

'Let me be clear, gents. This facility is already accountable for gross negligence. Such negligence relates to the treatment of my clients or rather, the lack thereof,' he stated, reaffirming his authority.

The two guards fell silent, sharing a befuddled look. Although Acalan knew Arthur to be a calm, soft-spoken individual, this tone was much more direct. This confidence demonstrated further to Acalan that he was in good hands, whether he deserved it or not.

'Sir...,' one of the guards attempted to reason with Arthur but was immediately shut down once more.

'This is not a request,' Arthur declared. The two guards looked back at each other once more, and one of them nodded before turning to walk away.

'Right this way, sir.' The remaining guard gestured in the opposite direction, walking around Arthur and past Acalan, who still stood in the cell's doorway.

As the guard led them up the corridor, he didn't turn back to face them at any point, nor did he make any conversation. A lack of windows limited the amount of light filtering in, and lamps were sparse. Acalan peered through the slits in the doors they passed, many of which were open. Part of him hoped to see his red-haired attacker rotting in here, but even a glimpse of one of his accomplices would suffice. Much to his disappointment, though, it seemed that these cells were vacant. The lack of criminals being held came as a surprise for Acalan, who had been a victim of assault on day one.

The guard stepped sideways into a lift and waited for them to join him before selecting a floor, all without speaking a word.

For the first time since he had regained consciousness, Acalan checked himself and saw that a mixture of dirt and blood stained his clothes all over. He looked to Arthur as they ascended in silence. Arthur's nod back offered some reassurance.

'It's fine,' Arthur mouthed to him.

Acalan scrunched his nose and shrugged back. It would have to do.

The doors opened to reveal a short corridor and two large wooden doors. Arthur took a deep breath in and stepped ahead of the others. The guard lifted a hand as if to stop him, but Arthur brushed it aside. He placed a hand onto each of the ornate golden handles and used the movement of his arms to twist them inwards. When he pushed them away, the doors swung inwards on their hinges and knocked against the walls.

'Donna!' he called out as he entered.

The high-ceilinged room contained a semi-circular bookshelf that ran around the back of a high, wide desk. Behind the desk sat a short woman with a precisely trimmed black bob. Another lady with straight blonde hair accompanied her, but she was facing away from them.

'You know I respect you. That's why I'm going to allow you to explain why you denied my client medical treatment,' Arthur challenged the warden, continuing to walk into the room as he did so.

Donna, the warden, pressed her fingers into the desk in front of her and leaned forwards out of the tall-backed chair that towered over her.

'This is bigger than you, Arthur,' she said, in a tone of apparent exasperation.

'We have rights in Jasebelle, Donna! Have you forgotten that?' Arthur continued his offensive.

The taller woman then turned. Her silvery cape revealed her slender figure when she spun. It was attached to a tight black dress that curled into an elegant flowery design at the top. Tight sleeves ran from her shoulders to her wrists, which she brought together, clasping her fingers.

Arthur halted halfway into the room and stumbled backwards.

'Hello Arthur!' she greeted him, her voice gentle. 'Are you representing the Synnorians?' she asked directly.

'Y-yes, that's right,' Arthur replied hesitantly, noticeably reigning in his tone, as if out of his depth.

This was a sudden cause for concern for Acalan, who stood a few paces behind. He did notice that the woman still smiled back regardless.

'That is appropriate; please don't feel uncomfortable.' She tilted her head, causing the light to reflect on one of two metallic clasps in her hair. The flowery shapes of the clasps were consistent with the patterns across her dress. 'Now, perhaps you would introduce me to your clients?' she asked.

'Right, yes. This is Acalan Izel,' he started shakily. 'And here is Iverissa Zyrel,' he added as Iverissa walked into the room hesitantly, waving upon her introduction.

'Hello, Acalan, Iverissa.' The woman disconnected from the moment to introduce herself. 'I'm Allie Wilson, the Chancellor of Jasebelle.'

'A pleasure to meet you, Your Majesty,' Acalan said, eliciting a raised brow from the chancellor.

'Please, Chancellor will suffice.' Her soft and welcoming tone didn't match her words but still struck Acalan as genuine.

Acalan cringed as he remembered what Arthur had explained to them last night. The chancellor was like the monarch but chosen by the people.

'Sorry, Chancellor,' Iverissa amended for him. 'We're here to ask for help,' she said, jumping straight to the matter at hand. It was evident by then that Arthur had briefed her too.

'Let's take this one step at a time, okay?' The chancellor smiled back. 'Right, Mr…'

'Tillman,' Donna jumped in from behind the desk when Arthur missed his prompt.

'Yes. Mr Tillman,' the chancellor continued. 'Am I right to understand that your clients were involved in an assault last night?'

'Yes, Chancellor, that's right.' Arthur made a point of responding quickly, so as not to be cut off again. In rushing this, he hadn't processed his own words.

'I see. In that case, I hardly think it is appropriate to continue welcoming them into our home.' The chancellor remained blunt but warm, her calm demeanour continuing to be at odds with the subject of her speech.

'No, Chancellor, you misunderstand. My clients were the victims of an assault,' Arthur explained.

Acalan looked at Iverissa for the first time since she had entered, smiling at her. He wanted her to know that he was okay. She smiled back and nodded in understanding.

'With respect, Mr Tillman, they look fine to me,' she argued politely.

'Yes, but that is no thanks to this facility. My client, Mr Izel, was beaten to within an inch of his life.' Arthur finally seemed to be finding his voice again. 'Malpractice by the staff here almost killed him. They denied him medical treatment until I arrived on site.' Although he did not raise his voice, he still exuded confidence, addressing the entire room as he spoke.

'I see.' The chancellor's intonation remained consistent. 'Is this true, Warden?'

Donna sunk back into her chair, and it seemed unlikely that she would interrupt Arthur again.

'Understood.' Chancellor Wilson didn't dwell on the moment, nor scold the warden. Instead, she opted to move past it procedurally. 'Then the issue here is citizenship,' Wilson concluded to a silent room.

The warden nodded in agreement, bringing a hand up to scratch at her round jawline.

'My clients are...,' Arthur began, before he noticed the raised finger of the chancellor, stopping him in his tracks.

'Mr Tillman, may I speak with your client directly?' she requested.

Arthur clasped his hands in front of himself before he swivelled to look at them. A single nod indicated to Acalan that it was time.

'Mr Izel, why are you here?' Chancellor Wilson asked sincerely.

'I'm a refugee?' he said with upwards inflection, looking to Arthur for approval.

'Are you?' Wilson asked, allowing a hint of emotion to slip into her speech in the form of surprise. 'There is no war to flee from; has there been a material change in circumstances overseas?' This was the first time the chancellor followed the conversation rather than led it.

'No war,' Acalan responded. 'Everything is normal back home.' He struggled to articulate himself. Having left everything behind, it was particularly difficult for him to express the need to be rescued from the world with which he was familiar. 'I'm a trials archer.' Acalan started to well up. He clenched his hands and forced the rest of his words out. 'That was my purpose.'

Iverissa noticed that he was getting overwhelmed, so she stepped over and gripped the tips of his fingers in her own. Acalan cleared his throat with a slight shake of the head.

'I am familiar with this Synnori tradition.' The chancellor seemed unaffected thus far, her blank expression staring back at him.

Acalan felt Iverissa's fingers tighten, her other hand reaching over to rest on his bicep. He could do this.

'Those men who attacked me, they said I like to make people feel defenceless. Nothing could ever be further from the truth.' His fingers pressed Iverissa's apart as he spoke, and he locked hands tightly with her. 'They were going to kill one of us, no matter what happened. There was nothing we could do.' His nostrils flared as a tear broke loose and fled down his unflinching cheek. 'If I'm not welcome here, then so be it, but we will be brutally murdered if we return home.' He clenched his teeth to reign in his emotions before forcing out a final sentence. 'Whether or not I deserve it, I'm asking for your help.'

'I see.' The moment stretched on unbearably while the chancellor calculated a response. 'I'm sure you understand that we are in an unprecedented situation here.' She paused once more, choosing her next words with care. 'Warden, I would like you to arrange immediate release.'

The warden leaned forward in shock, though she did not voice the disapproval that was evident on her face. Instead, she sought specifics on the procedure. 'They have no documentation; how should we process them?'

'You have my approval to release them under refugee status,' the chancellor responded. 'Paperwork will be required, but it doesn't sit with you,' she clarified.

Donna squinted then nodded in agreement.

Arthur pulled Acalan and Iverissa into a group hug, before stumbling away from them in a delayed attempt to maintain professionalism. He grinned, gripping Acalan's shoulder.

'Well done,' he said under his breath.

XX

A Normal Life

The smell from this machine was much fainter, only noticeable because it was foreign. The material was glossy, and its black finish blended nicely with the kitchen counter. A range of buttons presented themselves to Acalan, and he squinted at the symbols on them. The bizarre combination of hieroglyphics was meaningless to him. Iverissa shuffled him aside and pushed the bowl into place. It clunked as she locked it before straightening up beside him.

'What now?' she asked.

'I think this one is for the power,' Acalan suggested, pointing at a tiny lever on the side of the machine.

'That's all you've got?' she teased. 'How to start it?'

Iverissa reached out to fiddle with the buttons. Several of them didn't seem to do anything at all as she worked her way through them. It was stressful for Acalan to watch her mashing them down without knowing their purpose. He didn't get the chance to say anything before one of the buttons ejected the bowl towards her.

'Be careful!' Acalan finally said as he caught the bowl.

Iverissa laughed at the splatter across her apron and took the bowl from him once more.

'I'm learning,' she joked as she clicked it back into place once more. The machine purred as she surveyed the options once more.

Acalan didn't see exactly which button caused it, but the machine then roared into life. The beaters spun rapidly as they screeched and steamed. The mixture sprayed everywhere this time, covering Acalan, Iverissa and the kitchen worktop. Iverissa must have pressed every single button in her panicked attempt to make it stop, but the machine was relentless. Acalan squinted to keep the mixture out of his eyes and grabbed the lever. He thrust it down, and then, there was silence.

Both of them stood there for a moment, soaked and too stunned to speak. Then, the machine started up all over again, this time spinning in the opposite direction.

Iverissa cursed and ejected the bowl once more. It shot towards her this time, bounced against her chest and fell to the soft linoleum floor. The remaining mixture sloshed out of the bowl and splashed over her socks and shins. Her eyes widened and her mouth shrank as she first looked at Acalan and then assessed her mess.

Acalan looked towards the machine, which continued to whirr, but it had no more ammunition. This device was supposed to make his life easier, but using it properly seemed beyond him. A shadow then moved in the corner of his eye, and he turned slowly to find that they had been caught.

When he stepped over the threshold of the kitchen, Arthur saw it with fresh eyes. Acalan and Iverissa were covered in the white mixture, and so was his kitchen. The splash zone stretched up and down the cupboards and spread across the wallpaper. There was, of course, also a puddle on the floor from the overturned bowl that continued to grow. The machine still sprayed the remaining residue from its beaters, as the pair had given up trying to make it stop. Acalan could feel the heat growing in his cheeks from the embarrassment of the moment. Arthur's silence was intolerable until he burst into uproarious laughter at the scene.

Iverissa giggled as she wiped the mixture from her face. She then used the back of her hand to adjust her hair before leaning on the counter.

'How do we stop it?' she asked innocently. Arthur's laughter continued as he approached wordlessly and clicked a button on the back of the machine. There was a sizzling sound as the beaters came to a halt, and a compartment on the machine popped open at the top. In the box, and now on display, was a small pile of blue bellum powder. The whole thing felt so beyond Acalan, who was just relieved it was over. He looked at Iverissa, who was still full of wonder, poking at the powder with an outstretched finger. This was his insight into the sort of experiments that she ran at home; her wide eyes were windows that revealed joy rather than fear.

Although his heart continued to pound in his chest, and his forehead was sweaty, it seemed like things were going to be okay. They had fled for their lives, and the immediate problem they faced was cooking. This society was so far ahead of them, and they would need to catch up, but it was possible. Acalan couldn't help but imagine days when these things weren't a problem after they'd learned how it all worked. A happy life in Jasebelle was an option that was available to them. They were safe.

'Sorry,' Acalan uttered the only word he could think of.

'Don't worry about it,' Arthur brushed it aside as he ruffled through a drawer. 'Let's clean up.' He threw clothes at each of them, and they got to work.

'Can we try again?' Iverissa asked in a quiet, timid tone.

'Let's go out to get something,' Arthur suggested without looking up from the puddle. 'I want to introduce you to someone.'

***

Acalan was oblivious to the chatter around him in the bustling café. The aroma of the coffee blended with the murmurs of conversations and the clinking of teacups against saucers. He fussed at a hangnail on his thumb, struggling to remain present in the conversation. Arthur's laughter prompted him to look back up and see Iverissa gesturing expressively.

'It wasn't anything like bellum,' she laughed. 'It did stink though.'

'Weren't you worried that someone would find it?' Arthur asked.

'Well, not really. I just put it in the chute and then, it was gone,' Iverissa replied. 'Just like us in the end!'

It stumped Acalan to see her so at ease with it all. For him, there was still a lingering unease to tolerate, a sense that he didn't belong. Yet, when she spoke, there was a bubble of familiarity amidst the foreign ambiance. As the conversation flowed, he remained a spectator. His fingers drummed nervously on the edge of the table, the feel of the smooth fabric of the tablecloth a soothing distraction. The hum of voices around him faded into the background, making it much more tolerable, until a voice from over his shoulder addressed him directly.

'And you, sir?' the voice asked, snapping him back into the moment.

Acalan turned to peer up at the speaker, a lady with chestnut hair and a welcoming demeanour. She wore a checked pinafore, and light reflected towards him from the tray she held under her arm.

'Oh, no,' he mumbled, unsure what he was declining. 'Thank you.'

'You're very welcome, sir,' she responded politely before moving around him to pour more tea for Iverissa and Arthur. She leaned over the table to adjust a plate of cupcakes in its centre. Her fingers gripped the paper cases cautiously, avoiding the pretty pink frosting to place an overturned one back on top. 'Do let me know if I can get you anything else,' she added before making herself scarce once more.

'It actually happened!' Delight filled the new voice that came from the opposite direction.

'Elena, please.' Arthur gestured towards the speaker with his palms downwards, encouraging discretion.

'They won't believe it!' Elena failed to take the hint, rushing around the table to handle them like unopened Christmas presents. 'I'm not sure that I believe it!'

'Please, Elena,' Arthur interrupted. 'They've been through a lot,' he pointed out.

'My goodness, of course!' Elena stepped back and pressed down the waist of her coat, which had shuffled out of position. 'I hope not to overwhelm you, welcome to Jasebelle!' she said to them before turning back to Arthur. 'You've done amazing work here! A once-in-a-lifetime achievement,' she complimented Arthur sincerely, finally calming down.

Arthur sank his hands into his pockets and shifted his weight in the chair. 'It's nothing, much easier than getting you lot out of trouble!' he responded bashfully as the lady hurried around the table to sit beside him.

'I'm Elena, and it truly is a pleasure to meet you,' she introduced herself as she sat on her coat, extending a hand across the table.

'Iverissa,' said Iverissa, reciprocating first.

Elena's eyes widened, and she leaned forward to add an extra hand to the shake.

'That's a wonderful name!' Elena shot a look of wonder at Arthur before looking back. 'And you are…?' She tucked the loose black strands of her messy bun behind her ears as she blinked at Acalan.

'I'm...,' Acalan halted himself at the last moment, swallowing his name before it escaped. The beatdown he had received had been fully healed by bellum, but the memory remained.

It took Elena a moment to recognise his hesitation, and Arthur confirmed it non-verbally before she spoke again.

'I heard what those lowlifes did to you,' she leaned in closer to speak softly to him like he was a nervous child. 'That isn't who we are,' she said, ducking to meet his eyes and noticing him squirm. 'It's not who we *all* are.'

'Acalan,' he forced out.

'Hi Acalan.' She relaxed again, grabbing a cupcake from the table and putting an arm over the back of her chair. 'All these years of waiting, and now, I'm speechless,' she revelled, laughing to herself as she bit into the tiny cake.

'Elena is an activist,' Arthur explained as she took a few sips of tea, causing her to choke slightly. 'She wanted to make you an offer.'

'You want to help us?' The tone of Iverissa's question was uncharacteristically timid.

Elena nodded enthusiastically, forcing herself to swallow an unchewed mouthful.

'Exactly!' she swiped up a glass of water from the table and swigged at it. 'I wanted to offer you a home.'

'We need one of those,' Iverissa laughed.

Almost a week had passed since they were granted refugee status. When Acalan had been lying in his cell, contemplating the worst, it never occurred to him what the best might look like. As it turned out, several questions accompanied such an outcome. The first question that came to mind almost immediately was, where would they stay? Arthur had already done so much for them, but his flat was simply far too small. It was kind of him to offer accommodation until this point, but his home was a modest arrangement for one, never mind three. The second question followed naturally: how did a refugee pay for a house?

'Then come and live with us', Elena extended her invitation. 'Work with us.'

'Doing what?' Acalan spoke up.

'Well, look around you!' Elena pointed overtly at the people of Jasebelle, who surrounded them. They seemed to inhabit a world of their own, far removed from him. Each and every patron was draped in fabrics that shimmered with vibrancy, with Acalan's table being the exception. Having fixated on his own fear of these people, he had missed something that had been clear to him ever since he arrived. The passing glances that did take them in were not necessarily hostile but carried a sense of indifference. It could be mistaken for guilt, had he not identified it on day one. There wasn't an ounce of acknowledgement in their gaze; they pitied him.

'These people don't care,' Elena added wistfully.

'We can't make them care,' Acalan insisted, feeling a tug on his arm from Iverissa as he said so.

'I was hoping you'd try,' Elena responded with a half-laugh through her nostrils. 'You'll get free rooms if you do.'

'What can we do?' Iverissa asked without reservation.

'Just talk to us.' Elena shrugged. 'I want to get your story out there, and Arthur will get a break if we change our tactics.'

'I don't mind!' Arthur insisted. His teacup clinked as he placed it onto the saucer, only then noticing Elena's wry smile.

'You can have a normal life here,' Elena said, completing her offer. 'Maybe someday, all of Synnor can.'

XXI

Unexpected Guests

Reflecting on it after his week in Jasebelle, Acalan noticed how his anxiety had evolved. When he had first walked out onto the cobblestones as a free man, the thought of meeting any other new people scared him. Meeting Elena had calmed this fear, but it hadn't removed it. As he walked through the Jasebelle streets with Arthur and Iverissa, he couldn't help but relive the incident. People flowed around them as they walked, and he didn't know what any of these people might do. Although he was still alive, a part of him had died in that cell, the part that loved the crowd.

As they cut up a dingy back alley, his imagination had plenty of time to get creative. He didn't believe that these 'activists' would assault him, but a new concern filled his mind. They cared about improving life in Synnor; that was their purpose. So he wondered what their motivation could be. Why would they care? While he followed Arthur through the streets, he felt a looming sense of pressure. What if he wasn't everything that they hoped he was?

The narrow street widened into a vast courtyard with a simple fountain occupying the centre. A small group of children were playing hopscotch beside it, the squares etched haphazardly on the ground in white chalk. Small archways surrounded the walls of the courtyard, each with its own cute little door a few paces in.

When they reached the centre of the courtyard, Acalan could see a short man ahead, struggling on a shaky stepping stool. Colourful streamers decorated his archway, and it appeared that he was applying the finishing touches. When the group approached, he stumbled off the stool and folded it abruptly before dashing inside.

'Nobody saw that,' Arthur instructed them, laughing to himself.

'Sure…,' Acalan agreed.

Arthur stepped towards the wooden door that the man had rushed into, twisted the handle and pressed into the door. The door opened a fraction before pushing him back and slamming shut once more. Movement could be heard on the other side, although Acalan couldn't guess who or what was shuffling around in there.

Acalan looked at Iverissa for guidance. If she was still okay with this, then he would be too. Her head and face remained facing forwards, but her eyes moved to him. She smiled and gave a slight shrug.

Arthur groaned, dropping his head back for a moment. Exasperated, he paused before giving three firm knocks. The movement inside seemed to increase in speed before going quiet abruptly. Then, the door clicked and swung open.

'You're early!' Elena spoke around the door, her tone playful.

'We agreed on sunset, Elena.' Arthur looked from side to side and smirked slightly, failing to maintain a serious tone.

Elena swept aside several long strands of wispy black hair that dangled across her face; the rest was held back loosely in a messy bun. The loose strands curled forwards after she tucked them behind her rounded ears.

'Yes, I remember,' Elena responded in a strikingly disingenuous tone. She tilted her head, her fingers absentmindedly twirling a long strand of hair that still hung free. The flame from a bellum lamp that dangled inside flickered, shining over her neck. It illuminated a large tattoo that was partly concealed by the high collar of her tight overcoat. She stepped backwards before stretching up onto her toes, supporting her weight with an arm against the door frame and effectively blocking their view of the interior.

She wouldn't maintain eye contact with any one of the three for more than a second as she kept peering over her shoulder. It wasn't clear what she was looking for, though.

The space past the doorway appeared to be just like where they were standing. The same archway was present inside, and this led out into another identical courtyard. There was even a set of colourful party streamers dangling from the interior arch. As they all peered around Elena, the short individual passed by, carrying a table on his back.

'So, can we come in yet?' Arthur teased knowingly.

'Um…' Elena took a final look back over her shoulder.

A hand extended into view, giving a thumbs up from behind the wall.

'Yes, of course,' she responded, grinning with a sudden hint of confidence. 'Please, come in!' She waved them inside before turning and briskly stepping within.

The lighting in the inner courtyard was warm, provided by a grid of bellum lamps above. They illuminated arches right around the square, each with its own bespoke curtains. The curtains that were open revealed little bedrooms, with simple wooden nightstands next to single beds.

The moment they stepped into the inner courtyard, a cork fired into the sky with a loud pop, causing Acalan's shoulders to jolt up with it.

'Welcome home!' came a shout in unison, followed by cheers and applause.

There were only about fifty people present, forming several rows, yet they shouted with the conviction of five hundred. The group stood in front of a scrawled banner that stretched above them, the red paint on a white canvas reading the same. Elena had turned on the spot and was also clapping her fingers gently against an open palm.

'Sorry, it's not much!' she said, surveying the scene that they had walked into. As she said this, the banner fell down on one side, bringing an abrupt end to the applause as it drooped over the group.

Elena laughed to herself as the gathered people struggled to shuffle it off of themselves.

'Who hung that?' she barked sarcastically at the group before doubling over with laughter.

'So, a party then?' Arthur said loudly, addressing the group as a whole and resulting in another resounding cheer.

The well-dressed group raised their glasses in his direction.

The sparkling wine was unfamiliar to Acalan, but he found it quite palatable once he got used to the fizz. Through mingling around and struggling through small talk, he was able to familiarise himself with the group as a whole. Their objectives seemed to be generally in line with what Arthur had explained, that is to say, they were very interested in Synnor.

The people he spoke with each asked him a range of questions about his home. This became increasingly tedious for him as the night progressed. Several drinks were in his system, and they were all that was enabling him to interact. Speaking with these people reminded him of the fans he would meet on the streets back home. The man he was currently talking to, whose name Acalan had forgotten immediately, seemed to be trying to impress him, but surface-level conversation failed to hold Acalan's attention. As his mind drifted, Acalan looked over the man's shoulder towards Iverissa.

She was doing much better than him. Iverissa and the young lady she was standing with were both laughing heartily. A minor spill from Iverissa's glass soaked her fingers. Even this was no issue. She flicked them dry while pinching the stem of her glass in her empty hand, none of this halting the conversation. Acalan envied her confidence as he watched her from across the square. They were underdressed for the occasion, wearing cheap clothes that Arthur had sourced for them in the morning, but Iverissa didn't seem out of place.

Acalan shuffled his own shoulders at this thought. The itchy seams of his plain white cotton shirt were causing him continued discomfort. He took another sip from his glass, which provided some compensatory comfort in the moment.

Glancing over the man's other shoulder, Acalan could see that Arthur and Elena seemed similarly comfortable in each other's company. Elena looked down at her feet, causing loose strands of hair to escape from behind her ears. When she looked back to Arthur, she tucked them back once more, answering whatever question he had posed.

'I don't know why he does it,' the man said, changing the subject, finally noticing that he was losing Acalan.

'Sorry, what?' The sudden change of topic snapped Acalan back into the moment.

'Mr Tillman. He barely makes any money when he represents us,' the man explained, stepping beside Acalan to look over with him. 'They bang us up constantly for civil disobedience, but we don't have the funds to pay him for his time,' he went on. 'I never got the impression that he cared that much. About Synnor, that is.' He stopped to take a mouthful of wine. 'Whatever it is that keeps him with us, I'm thankful for it. We wouldn't be able to do what we do without him.'

'Hmm...' Acalan nodded, unsure what insight he might be able to add. He pictured the fine wine that sat sealed in Arthur's flat. Arthur had been upfront with them about his ambitious career goals, and free legal advice didn't seem to align with them. A sudden crash at the door as it was blown off its hinges interrupted this thought. Panic spread through the partygoers as a stream of guards marched through the smoke in twos before splitting up to surround the square.

Acalan was alert once more as he scanned the scene unfolding before him, but he was unable to figure out what was happening. He looked to Arthur and Elena, who had jumped backwards together and stood with their knees slightly bent. Arthur appeared equally panicked, also scanning the crowd until he met Acalan's eye. Acalan looked to him for some understanding but received only a bewildered shrug as the circle of guards sealed them in.

Through the smoke stepped a familiar figure. She emerged confidently, taking quick yet short strides. A long black cloak clung to the back of her legs when a stiff breeze followed her into the courtyard. Her red hair also lifted slightly, though it remained pinned in place by a shining gold circlet that sat undisturbed.

Acalan's thin wine flute escaped his grip, shattering onto the stone by his feet. *Virrel was in Jasebelle.*

A brutish male figure followed several paces behind her. There was something strangely familiar about his face, which was partly concealed by a pointed goatee and moustache. Acalan didn't focus on this man, as a third person stepped in with them.

Chancellor Wilson emerged from the smoke, still carrying herself without urgency. Virrel then made direct eye contact with Acalan. Her acknowledgement of his existence unnerved him to an extent; back in the arena, she would have been otherwise occupied with her speech. She grinned at him, as if she could sense his discomfort from across the square.

Virrel lifted a hand abruptly and pointed two fingers upwards, causing the gold colouring of her cloak to shine under the lamps above. In an equally sudden movement, as if conducting the guards behind her, she extended the arm out. Acalan followed her gesture, shocked to see that she was pointing at Iverissa. Before Acalan was able to process what was happening, two guards were already approaching Iverissa. They lifted her effortlessly by her arms. She resisted, kicking and screaming violently, but the faceless men brushed this off, their movements inevitable.

Acalan looked around for help as this scene unfolded before him, but everyone around him remained stunned and stood watching.

As they dragged Iverissa over towards Virrel, Acalan couldn't watch for a moment longer. He burst into a rapid sprint, rushing across the tiled floor towards her. He swung his arms, which had initially pushed him forwards, preparing to lunge at the closest guard.

He was blindsided by a fist cracking his jaw, plucking him out of the air and causing him to tumble forwards onto the floor. His mouth filled with a metallic flavour as he rolled across the stone. This was the only symptom of his burst lip as the adrenaline rushed through his body. He rocked backwards to look up, swiping a crimson stain from his mouth with the back of his hand. The towering bald figure looked down at him and scowled, warning Acalan to stay down.

'There is no need to be so dramatic,' Virrel talked down to him. 'I only need one of you,' she stated in a menacing tone.

Acalan rolled forward to stand, but a boot on his chest crushed him into the concrete.

'They're refugees!' Arthur called out as he emerged from the background. 'You can't take them!' he argued.

Virrel laughed uproariously before stopping with a deadpan expression. 'Oh, you're serious?' she asked knowingly before turning to Chancellor Wilson.

'There has been a material change in circumstance,' Wilson stated emotionlessly but did not look downwards to avoid the risk of making eye contact with Acalan.

Virrel clapped rapidly, giddily flaunting her glee.

'Then take me,' Acalan spluttered from under the boot.

'No!' Iverissa screamed, continuing to swing and kick against the guards with renewed vigour.

'Actually...' Virrel raised her index finger, dismissing this suggestion. 'It's Miss Zyrel that we require. We have no further use for the archer.' She stepped over towards Iverissa, leaning in to goad her. 'Was it worth it? You learned a little too much for your own good, didn't you?' she added patronisingly.

Iverissa swung her head forwards, attempting a headbutt, but found no purchase. The men holding her twisted her arms, causing her to bend forwards and yelp in submission.

'You're probably wondering what I mean.' She looked past Iverissa and down to the ground, where Acalan remained pinned. She was right, but he remained silent.

'Oh, come on! Grand archer of the Upper District, one of the best in Synnor. You must have *something* to say!' Virrel spun mockingly with arms wide, addressing a crowd that was not present.

'Unless you're not so grand after all?' she continued to prod him rhetorically but let out an exasperated sigh when he remained stubbornly silent.

'Fine.' She stepped over towards him and lifted up the bottom of her dress to sit down on the concrete by his head. With crossed legs, she rested her face in her hands. 'You think that you are important, that you are an impressive competitor, but you never have been,' she began, launching an all-out attack on his character. 'Oh no, take me instead!' She flailed her arms around, mimicking him cruelly. 'We don't *want* you anymore. You served one purpose to me: a distraction.'

'Shut up!' Iverissa called out as she continued to struggle, halting Virrel's monologue.

Acalan watched Virrel's fiery pupils light up and her jaw drop in apparent delight.

'No way! You didn't tell him?' Virrel shouted back to Iverissa before stopping herself, biting her bottom lip. 'This is perfect!' she announced, rubbing her hands together. 'Can I tell you a secret

Acalan?' she whispered to him with a hint of sarcasm. 'The Titans aren't proud of you; they don't even exist!' She leaned forward and prodded him with an outstretched finger. 'You were never competing in their name; you were killing in mine.' She paused. 'You were one of my best executioners, and you have a body count that could end a war!'

'Please stop!' Iverissa cried out in desperate protest, shaking an arm free only to be immediately restricted once more.

Acalan was shaking involuntarily against the ground, allowing Virrel to see that she was breaking him down in real-time.

'To be honest with you, Acalan, I don't know why she's playing dumb.' Virrel changed the topic and directed his attention towards Iverissa. 'I'm sure she's read all about it. The only thing I want to know is why she didn't tell you.'

'What?' Acalan uttered breathlessly while Iverissa cursed at her from the background.

Virrel opened her mouth wide before covering it with her fingertips, exaggerating a false expression of shock. With the addition of Virrel's mocking expression, her words sank in for Acalan. Iverissa had known about this all along. She could be heard sobbing, but Acalan couldn't look. His gaze remained locked on Virrel.

'What?!' he repeated, louder.

Virrel nodded slowly, pressing her lips together.

'Right, c'mon you!' Virrel sprung up to her feet and stepped away. 'Let's go!' she said excitedly. Acalan watched helplessly until the boot lifted from his chest. A tightly curled fist yanked his shirt upwards before another knocked him unconscious.

XXII

Alone

Acalan awoke in a sweaty haze. The darkened den was warm even though it was missing a wall. Rolling around unconsciously brought several moments of bliss, but they soon slipped away. Light bled in from under the curtains that dangled as a door leading back out into the square. When he turned onto his side, Acalan flinched at the soreness on his cheek. Upon realising where he was, his blissful ignorance faded as the memory rushed back.

As the moment came back to him, his breathing faltered. Rather than the sadness that he would have expected, he felt empty. An emotionless void yawned inside him, and there were no tears to be shed as he forced himself upright. Frustrated by this, he tensed his neck and flared his nostrils. Acalan swung his legs out of the bed, and they shook as his feet touched the floor. He wanted to cry but couldn't bring himself to.

'You were one of my best executioners.' Virrel's words haunted him.

Memories of standing in front of the crowd flooded back with a fresh, tragic context. Acalan ran through the people he had executed, struggling to process the length of the list. He couldn't even remember their names, only some of the faces, and many of them blended. Countless victims had been stripped from their loved ones, and they must have felt what he felt then. It was always purpose that he sought, but he had ended up with nothing and couldn't help but feel like his destiny was to end up alone. He stood up and straightened his back, enduring minor pain as he stretched his spine.

Acalan stepped over towards the curtains that kept the light out. He swept them aside without consideration for who might be on the other side. Squinting under the morning sun, he scanned the courtyard. His gaze passed over a lone woman with her back turned, sweeping away at the tiles. He then fixated on a table to his left, which he recognised from the previous night. Bottles of sparkling white wine remained, their role in the party cut short. Emerging out into the warm morning light, Acalan lumbered towards the table. The bottles clinked together as he clutched two around their necks and dragged them back to his hovel.

After allowing the curtains to droop shut over his shoulder, he took refuge once again in darkness. He stepped past the bed and flopped down on the floor, in the furthest corner of the arched room.

Anger crept in when he reflected on the chancellor's betrayal.

He twisted the cork violently, the pop and fizz of the wine inside somewhat out of place at his pity party. When he took a swig from the bottle, he knocked the other one onto its side, and it clinked against the stone. *It wasn't easy to ask for help.* He continued to chug at the bottle in an attempt to suppress these thoughts. *They promised to protect us.* The thought wouldn't die. Acalan pressed his head back into the curving stone roof, gritting his teeth and shaking uncontrollably. It didn't feel fair.

He sat there, forcing deep breaths through his ever-tightening chest. The desperation of this loss was unlike anything he knew, and it came bundled with anxiety about the control that he had conceded. As the minutes stretched, he revisited the decisions that had led him there.

She had wanted to stay in Jasebelle, and he knew they needed to flee, but he could have voiced his doubts. He remembered how she had looked at him and cursed his dumbfounded silence. The curious jade of her eyes longed to give these people a chance, but they also looked to him to agree. Acalan had allowed the vote to pass, but he had abstained by remaining silent. None of the notes in the warm wine were pleasant enough to offset his sickening feeling of regret.

Hopelessly emotionally blocked, he tried to vent his anger by throwing the open bottle overhand. The shattering of the glass did not release a fraction of the tension in his mind. Instead, it sprayed booze back over him. He deserved his fate, but Iverissa didn't deserve hers.

'You probably shouldn't be drinking alone.' Arthur peered nervously around the curtain. 'Mind if I join you?' he asked cautiously, and Acalan grunted with a shrug.

At first glance, Acalan saw Arthur as the personification of his mistake. He should have run from Arthur when he had the chance, Acalan thought, but it was no use now.

Arthur stepped in gingerly, closing the curtain behind himself before joining Acalan on the floor. The silence lingered for several minutes, as neither man was willing to speak first. There was a storm of grief buffeting Acalan's mind, and he was battening down the hatches. Arthur was a reverent onlooker, observing Acalan cuddling the second bottle between sips from a place of safety. Arthur's only movement was the raising of a hand towards the bottle, which caused Acalan to tighten his arms around it.

'I'll give it back,' Arthur promised, extending his open palm closer.

Reluctantly, Acalan handed it over. This allowed Arthur to take a generous swig, despite Acalan's frustration, before handing it back.

'So, now what?' Arthur prompted as he assessed the storm's damage.

Acalan remained silent and gulped down several mouthfuls.

'How long are we going to sit here and feel sorry for ourselves?' Arthur prodded around the wreckage brashly, not taking silence as an answer.

'What would you know about feeling sorry for yourself?' Acalan snapped back at him.

'To be honest, not as much as you,' Arthur replied, matching his tone. 'We all have something to dwell on, though. I thought that I was going to be rich and famous.' He smirked through his own ironic tone. 'If we are complaining about things, then protecting you both would have been historic. This is the thanks I get?' Arthur scolded him. 'I thought I'd be successful by now, yet here I am, sitting on the floor drinking this bathwater with you.' Arthur snatched the bottle from Acalan and took several mouthfuls of his own.

'Hey!' Acalan protested feebly, grasping for the bottle.

'I need you to understand that this isn't about either of us,' Arthur said, ignoring him and placing the bottle on the floor, just out of Acalan's reach. 'It's about her.'

'She's gone,' Acalan muttered with false indifference.

'So, what then? This is where you give up?!' Arthur lectured him. 'I've seen the way you look at her, Acalan. If you were ever going to let them take her, you wouldn't have come here in the first place.'

'I don't know what to do, okay?' Acalan shouted back at him. 'Is that what you wanted to hear?!'

'It is, actually,' Arthur responded in a calm tone, with a condescending sense of self-satisfaction. 'I'm trying to get you to see that it's okay not to know, but you need to be brave enough to find out.'

'I can't do it alone,' Acalan interrupted with a stammer. The intensity of it all finally broke through his façade as his words were punctuated by a choked sob.

'You're not alone, Acalan,' Arthur said as the curtain twitched and then opened once more.

Elena's loose bun shuffled upwards as she pressed her cheek against the wall. 'I heard shouting, is everything okay?' she asked but was already assessing the scene inside. 'Oh.' Her imagination filled in the context of the two men sitting by a bottle, one of them curled against a wall.

Acalan shielded his face, but his sniffling could still be heard by Arthur, who rubbed his shoulder gently.

'It's okay,' Arthur said softly, nodding towards Elena, inviting her in.

She entered cautiously, taking extra care to step around the shards of glass that were strewn across the floor. She did not speak, so it took several minutes for Acalan to notice that she was still there, sitting on his bed.

'Nobody is going to want to help me,' Acalan forced out, too ashamed to face them with his tears. 'They all know what I've done.'

'You're wrong.' Elena couldn't resist the urge to jump in. 'We already knew.'

'What?' Acalan peeked from behind his hand, meeting her eye.

'Synnor is barbaric,' her voice wavered, its passionate tone reflecting genuine concern. 'They keep you trapped there under this façade that there isn't anywhere better and that you must do what you did because their gods say so,' she continued.

Acalan swiped at his tears but did not interrupt.

'This is why we go onto the streets to shout about it!' She gestured towards the curtain. 'Yet no matter how much trouble we get ourselves into…,' she smirked at Arthur, '…people want to pretend that problems over there don't exist. Ignorance is bliss, right?' She rolled her eyes.

'I knew about it before I met you, but I still needed to help if I could convince you to let me,' Arthur added in a positive tone. 'I owe it to Elena and her team that I knew not to be afraid of you.' He looked towards Elena, and she smiled back at him with a nod. 'I still want to help if you'll still let me,' he concluded.

'Let us give you a minute to gather your thoughts,' Elena suggested. 'Have no doubt, though, my people are behind you even if Jasebelle is not.' Elena's tone was uncharacteristically solemn as she and Arthur exited. 'Come and find us when you're ready,' she added, leaving him alone again.

Acalan felt foolish as he sat alone in the dark with his dried tears and puffy eyes. It hadn't occurred to him that he was the last to know the truth. He felt embarrassed by his self-pity when he reflected on the journey he had been on. By the time he knew that the crying had been helpful, he only regretted showing it. Arthur was right, though, if he was ever going to give up, then he wouldn't have left Synnor in the first place. He sniffled one last time and squared his shoulders before clearing his throat and climbing to his feet.

When he pulled back the curtain this time, more than one person was standing out there. A group was gathering in a semi-circle around one of the rooms that had its curtains tied wide open. Faces from last night's party stepped alongside him as he approached, forming part of a growing crowd. He could hear a screech from the front as a small wooden crate was pushed along the stone floor. He then saw Elena's head bob shakily over the top of the crowd before she found confidence in her balance.

'Good morning, everyone!' she started. 'I hope we're all feeling bright and breezy; we have a busy day ahead.' She cleared her throat forcefully. An arm emerged from behind her back to reveal a folded newspaper clutched in her hand. 'Have we all had a chance to read the news this morning?' she asked, receiving deafening silence in response. 'Quite right!' She laughed to herself. 'Well, this morning, there is something very interesting in here.' She bent forward, stretching out her arm to a young man in the front of the crowd and dangled the paper in front of his face.

'Synnor joins Bellum Age – isolated no more!' he stammered through the headline. 'Wait, what?!' he followed up, having processed the words.

Murmurs rippled through the crowd. It seemed that for the first time, everyone else was as baffled as Acalan.

'Ahem!' Elena stood upright once more, twisting the paper back towards herself. 'In a historic trade deal that subverts centuries of avoidance…,' she began, exaggerating her public speaking voice cynically, '…Synnor opens its port to bellum. In a generation-defining moment for the two nations, large-scale shipments will begin to cross the waters. This represents an impossible handshake between leaders.' Elena stopped on this point, imitated vomiting and flung the paper over her shoulder.

Sheets fluttered out messily into her dwelling, but she did not turn to see this. A second wave of muttering spread through the crowd, and it suddenly dawned on Acalan. This was the material change in circumstances that the chancellor had spoken about.

'It's a lot of money coming into the city, but this is blood money. We act for Iverissa, but not for Iverissa alone. When we take our next actions, it is for generations of innocent Synnori lives lost,' Elena's voice cracked as she shouted over the increasing volume of the crowd to regain their attention. 'So, what's first?' Her tone shifted down as she opened the discussion to the floor.

Various protest suggestions from the crowd were then shouted back flippantly, some of them peaceful, some of them not.

'It won't work,' Acalan said quietly, his voice drowned out by the noise of the group around him barking about smashing windows and starting fires. 'It won't work!' he shouted, catching Elena's attention.

Meeting his eyes from her perch above, she raised a hand to him, waving him towards the front. He nodded to her before cutting through the crowd, placing a foot onto the shaky crate and hefting himself up. He looked out at the crowd. Though it was a small gathering, he struggled to speak and looked to Elena, who smiled reassuringly.

'It won't work,' he repeated once more, searching his mind for the right words to break the silence. 'They will ignore you.' Silence remained as the crowd awaited his point. 'People want to pretend that problems don't exist, right?' he asked rhetorically. 'They aren't going to care about my life, nor will they care for hers. Even if there were a hundred of us, I doubt anyone would lose sleep over it.' Passionate anger began to creep into his tone. 'Do a thousand bodies even qualify for your newspaper?' Acalan gesticulated frantically, pointing at the sheets strewn around the makeshift podium. 'How many of my people must be murdered needlessly for it to be put on the front page?' Acalan yelled at the top of his lungs, finally wearing his heart on his sleeve.

A pin drop would have been audible within the crowd, enthralled as they were by his speech.

'Ignorance is bliss, or so I hear,' he said softly, allowing the silence to lend itself to his charisma.

'I listened to some of you speak of "the dream" between sips of fizzy wine, uniting our societies and releasing my people from tyranny,' Acalan spoke on behalf of his silent nation. 'If this is the sort of civilisation that you ever want to become, then we must fight for every life, and we have to start today.' Acalan paused for a breath. He looked at Elena, who stared back expectantly, captivated by the voice he had found. 'We have to save her.

'My actions have facilitated more deaths than I could ever dare to count, and I never even asked any questions…,' he trailed off momentarily. 'I will carry that with me forever.' Acalan finally knew who he used to be, but he had left that behind. It wasn't up to Virrel to decide what sort of person he would become. 'If Jasebelle is sending bellum over there, then let's send a surprise over with it…

'Send me.'

XXIII

Atonement

Talmu sat upright as he looked downwards into the arena below. The seating wasn't designed for comfort, but his posture defied that entirely. He hadn't decided what he was hoping to achieve by attending since the damage was already done. Still, he wanted to see how it would play out. It was only certain that the council was in for a shock in the coming minutes. What was unclear to Talmu was how they would respond. The crowd waited uncomfortably for something to happen. In the vast expanse of the empty stadium, a palpable air of anticipation hung thickly in the silence. Rows upon rows of joyous witnesses awaited the impending competition without any idea of what was coming.

At first, whispers of uncertainty circulated among attentive members of the crowd. Some fidgeted, their eyes darting across the vacant stage, searching for any signs of activity or explanation. Time ticked by, with each passing minute exacerbating the atmosphere of bewilderment as more people noticed. It became clear to everyone, without any warning or announcement, that the trial had failed to commence. It was as if the stadium itself held its breath, uncertain of what was about to unfold. Murmurs then grew louder, spreading like wildfire through the stands as people tried to make sense of the unexpected delay.

Talmu had thought that his guilt would subside once she was gone, but this had not been the case. In reality, seeing her that night and hearing her escape plan had ignited a spark. It wasn't her fault that she wanted to know more; her curiosity was the root of her intelligence. She had been asking puzzling questions for many years, so it had only been a matter of time. Her desperation to understand was an element of her character that he saw in himself. There was no villainous motive for studying; he had never believed that, and this made his actions all the more sickening.

Gestures of frustration and impatience emerged as spectators tapped their feet anxiously. A collective restlessness began to grow, compelling some to rise from their seats and pace restlessly along the aisles. The once calm atmosphere morphed into a simmering sea of confusion. The absence of communication from the organisers deepened their uncertainty. It left them adrift with unanswered questions.

A sense of disarray permeated the echoing emptiness. The absence of any clear guidance or information fostered an atmosphere of doubt. The crowd's attention soon turned towards the council guards, who scurried around the empty stage. Whispers grew into frustrated exclamations, as speculation filled the void. Every passing moment without resolution added to the growing confusion. There were no visible signs of progress, and this heightened the increasing impatience of the audience.

Had he not reported it, she would have gotten herself killed, Talmu thought. He tried again to reason with himself, but there was still a fatal flaw in his justification. His satchel lay beside his feet, bulging with the presence of an ancient library book. It lay in repose, peeking slightly out of the bag, waiting patiently for its pages to be turned once again. Its cover, adorned with faded lettering, hinted at the wisdom and knowledge it contained. However, without readers to seek enlightenment within its pages, the book's spine was barely creased.

In the absence of information, imaginations ran wild, conjuring up potential reasons for the delay. Rumours swirled, theories clashed and the once-united audience fragmented into pockets of speculation. The atmosphere became charged with frustration, disappointment and a longing for clarity. As the competition's delay persisted, Talmu remained still in his seat. The confusion, thick like fog, hung heavy in the air.

The satchel, with its cherished book, still sat there. It was a silent reminder to him of the vast world that awaited exploration. Its presence beckoned to him after all these years, still urging him to go, but the time for that had long since passed. It would be Iverissa who would face this discovery, but without the choice he'd had at her age. Stealing the book all those years ago made him no better than her, and despite rejecting its contents, he never returned it. The words within constituted a forbidden journey of knowledge, and he could never part with it.

No cloaked individuals were assembling at the stairway below. Instead, Queen Virrel walked forwards alone and ascended. Her burning red hair was unkempt, neither brushed nor styled. She was still dressed extravagantly, though, in a dark dress cut just above the knee. Her usual robes that would trail down the stairs behind her were nowhere to be seen. Her steps were hurried and her posture was tense as she approached centre stage. Her progress seemed disorganised, and there was a great deal of uncertainty in her movements. There was no applause, only utter silence.

'People of Synnor, I thank you again for gathering here in honour of your Titans,' she spoke the same words as always but with a new fury. 'I am horrified to announce that no offering can be selected at this time.'

One united gasp came from every member in the audience, except Talmu.

'The founding principle of Synnor is simple.' Virrel silenced the crowd once more by going off script. 'Combatants are selected, and the defeated pass into the afterlife. It is only there that they can deliver our message to the Elemental Titans.' Not a single breath was audible in the arena when she paused. 'Trials evasion is the most serious crime that any individual can commit. They aren't just spitting in the faces of you, their fellow citizens, but defying the gods themselves.'

It might not have been clear to the rest of the audience, but Talmu noticed the signs of her mask slipping. It was normal for her voice to boom around the venue, but her tone was usually almost robotic. Now, the rage was clear in the words that erupted like fiery embers from her lips. Intensity laced them as they cut through the air. Virrel's once measured and composed tone was gone, replaced by a torrent of impassioned speech; the precision was gone. As she continued to ramble furiously, her gestures became increasingly animated.

'We live in worship of Eden Synn. We owe our existence to Synn, and we will always prosper under his watchful eye. It is this watchful eye that will find its tribute. Praise Eden.'

The crowd was not able to recognise their response to all of this when she dismissed them, but Talmu was. He had experienced these thoughts and feelings all those years ago, and he recognised the same doubt in those around him. Something about her words seemed dishonest in an intangible way, like when a child was hiding a mistake. He was also experiencing his own doubt, but that was separate. By the end of Virrel's rant, he had already stopped listening to her spin. The doubt in his case was about his actions. The one person he wanted to speak to was Iverissa, but he had sentenced her to exile. She was forced down a path that he had never been brave enough to choose.

As he exited the arena with his satchel bouncing against his leg, a question followed: Was he brave enough to make it right?

He produced the book from the satchel and brushed congealed dirt and dust off its cover with his hand. Those who flowed around him were oblivious to the lie. The events of the day had been the first sign that the Titans were a work of fiction. There had been no selection, but also, no wrath. It would have been noble if he had done it in the first place, but it could only be his atonement at this point. Talmu had to get the truth out there.

XXIV

The Diversion

There was an uncomfortable silence between Acalan and Arthur while they awaited Elena's return. She had already taken charge and laid plans where she could, but that morning's war room meeting hadn't been an especially tactical one since they lacked information. Without Iverissa there to ask the questions, Acalan was at a loss. He and Arthur were the only quiet ones in the courtyard, surrounded by members of their new group. Elena had told him that she and her people stood behind him, and she had meant it, so they had formed a task force that morning. These people weren't skilled cloak-and-dagger agents but troublemakers with a cause. Graciously, Elena brought an end to the discomfort by arriving with a large wooden crate.

The group rushed towards Elena, causing the crate to slip from her hands and thud onto the cobbles. A range of blunt weapons were pulled from the crate for inspection. Elena was like Father Christmas to these men; they swung at the air in delight. They didn't look worried about what was to come, but rather, excited. Acalan fixated on one of the men, who looked more like a boy. The fresh-faced activist was unintimidating with his new bat but seemed pleased nonetheless.

Acalan broke the silence. 'I have a question.'

'Ask away,' Arthur responded with a gentle smile.

'If you're so concerned about your career, why do you spend all of your time getting them out of jail?'

'Oh!' Arthur clawed at his neck while he calculated a response before laughing to himself. 'As you have already learned, we often surprise ourselves with the things we do for the women we love.' He grinned at Acalan knowingly, turned and strolled away to greet Elena.

When Acalan joined them, Elena handed him the first set of decent clothes he had worn in a while. The combination of black fabric and leather would be ideal for quick movement through the night.

'These were pricey, so bring them back in one piece,' she said as he took them from her.

Acalan didn't acknowledge the joke, still uneasy about what was to come. 'They don't look scared,' he commented under his breath.

'We're here to help, no matter what,' she said, disregarding his concern and disengaging from his point. 'You need to get changed; the shipment won't wait for you.'

'They know this is a suicide mission, right?' Acalan said tactlessly. 'Even if we make it there tomorrow, there's no way we get in.'

'These men have been in and out of jail their whole lives, so they want to try,' she replied. 'Disruption is their legacy, and this is their chance to be remembered for more than that.'

'I can go alone,' he stated outright. He had no interest in being remembered by anyone.

'I don't want to argue with you, Acalan,' her tone was warning. 'We've demonstrated at the port a number of times, so we know how to get you onto the ship.'

'Right.' Acalan was surprised, albeit relieved, to know that they truly wanted to help. 'How will we do that?'

'You'll need a diversion,' she responded. 'We'll make something happen. It's what we do.' Elena shrugged with a half-grin.

'What about the other side?' he asked cautiously.

'You've already escaped once, so find her and do it again.'

The mission was simple: get into Synnor undetected and extract Iverissa.

'Oh! One more thing!' She reached an arm over her shoulder to pull around an intricately crafted black metal bow.

Elena extended her arm, offering the bow to Acalan with a warm smile, yet Acalan's gaze was perplexed; he still had his own bow. Superstition aside, he favoured the rustic charm of his own wooden bow. With a gentle shake of his head and a polite smile, he respectfully declined Elena's gift, opting to stick with his trusted companion.

Having walked out of the city together, the group made their way towards the port. The walk was not as long as Acalan's initial approach to Jasebelle, although it was in the opposite direction and paved for most of the way. The light drizzle became a downpour as evening turned to night. Acalan's new clothes had fit closely, to begin with, but clung tighter now that they were soaked. Eventually, the group approached a ridge that looked down a winding road towards the port. Two distinct sections formed the fence that surrounded the docks: sturdy iron barriers surrounded the majority of the site, with an additional but flimsier arrangement added on. From this distance, it could be seen that the site was crawling with workers.

'That's new,' Elena commented, surveying the fence panels as they bent in the wind. It appeared that this extension of the site was as recent as the trade deal it serviced. Without waiting for a consensus, she then led the way downhill.

They peered over the solid iron fence, watching the workers rolling barrel after barrel along the wet ground. None of them rolled them the whole way, though. Instead, they utilised transporter machines partway.

The smell of burning bellum mixed with the sea spray to unlock a memory. Acalan's mind was cast back to Synnor when he had prepared to make his escape. He pictured Iverissa in her teal dress, leaning over the fencing and looking out at the horizon. In his memory, he saw the satchel on her back, bulging with stolen sewer blueprints. He hadn't recognised it as a weak moment for her at the time. It was only with his fresh perspective that he understood her struggle through the blacked-out tunnels. Nothing terrified her more, and he wouldn't have even known if she hadn't told him. The ongoing downpour lashed across his cold face, snapping him back into the moment. It was his turn. She needed him to be brave.

Ahead, he could see various large metallic containers, with men hauling their contents out into the stormy night. Acalan had never seen anything like the behemoth of an ocean freighter that rocked in the waves. The vessel stood several stories tall, and its length dwarfed the port that serviced it. A smattering of guards observed the operations within the port, ensuring progress despite the storm. A flash of light burst through the sky, causing Acalan and his cohort to duck out of sight once more.

'And to think, you wanted to come alone,' Elena pointed out as they hid. 'You wouldn't have lasted two seconds,' she remarked then smiled as Acalan rolled his eyes at her and flung his hood back up.

The fabric of the hood was soaked through at this point, but it helped to stop the rain from landing directly on him, which wasn't nothing.

'I thought it would be tighter,' Acalan said sarcastically. 'This looks easy.' He had anticipated some challenge to sneak into the hold with the high-value cargo but not so many eyes.

'Yes, well, it's a good thing we're with you then, isn't it?' Elena responded, matching his cynical tone with a self-righteous smile. Her smug moment was interrupted when the section of temporary fence which they stood by bent outwards in the wind. 'Give me ten minutes.'

'Ten minutes for what?' Acalan interrogated her through the fabric that he pulled up over his nose to keep the rain off his face.

'We'll do what we do best, just give us ten minutes!' she answered. 'When you see an opportunity, that's when you go.' She pulled him into an embrace and spoke into his ear over the storm, causing his muscles to tense. 'Good luck,' she said, her solemn tone a rare change from her usual optimism.

'Thanks,' he responded uncomfortably, shuffling her off.

She smiled back at him without comment, seemingly satisfied that she had found the right thing to do. Her group did not interrupt the moment as they awaited an order.

Another bolt of lightning filled the sky with a flash, and Elena turned on the spot to lead them away. In theory, Acalan had a few minutes to prepare himself, but in practice, he misused them. The anxiety of the moment was uncomfortable, so he fidgeted with his bowstring to distract himself. He knocked one of his new arrows and pulled the bowstring tight. It was in perfect order, as it had been in the morning. As Acalan stood with the bow drawn, he closed his eyes, keeping the rainwater out. Rain ran down his face and onto his makeshift mask, and he zoned out, hearing echoes of the arena in his mind.

The fabric of his mask concealed a smile, and the crowd chanted as he released the arrow into the darkened plains around him. Even after everything, there was still a part of the memory that brought him joy. When the energy from the bow reverberated in his arm, he opened his eyes and watched the arrow vanish into the darkness. There was no cheering. Instead, he heard Amara's screams. His heart pounded out of his chest, and he stumbled backwards, dropping the bow to the ground. The fence caught him as he fell, bending under his weight as he slid to the ground. Another flash from the sky illuminated the darkness ahead of him. This allowed him a glimpse of the Synnori guards dragging the feeble market trader past him, escorting him to his death as the crowd chanted. Acalan lay drenched in a puddle for several moments before he was able to control his hyperventilation.

It's not real, he reminded himself, taking several minutes to compose himself. The chanting was real, though, so he scrambled to his feet to find its source. While he couldn't make out the words, he assumed that this was Elena's doing; it must be time.

'What's that?' a voice shouted across the yard.

'North gate!' another responded.

Soon enough, the shouting men had made their way away from Acalan, allowing him to vault over the fence and into the dock. After landing on his feet, he surveyed the yard. Through the rain, it appeared that the coast was clear, with the remaining workers stepping off the gangplank.

Ahead of him, he saw his diversion. Elena was sitting cross-legged on the ground, and her comrades sat with her. Their clubs and bats littered the concrete yard as they held a peaceful demonstration. A swarm of guards circled around, while others fanned out to block the gate. Acalan couldn't tell what they were chanting, even as it grew louder, but it appeared to be doing the trick. Elena looked in his direction, noticing his head peeking out from behind a container. The guard nearest to her extended his hand towards her back. In his other hand, he held a truncheon down by his side and appeared to be barking instructions at her. With a distant smile to Acalan, she jumped to her feet and attempted a spin. The guard stumbled as she stood, but a swipe of the truncheon on her knee halted her before she could act. Lightning struck once more, and the thunder that rumbled after it drowned out her scream as she rolled around on the ground, resisting several guards who pounced on her at once. Chaos ensued when her men followed her lead. Acalan's eyes widened in shock at the guards' heavy-handedness. Bellum would cure their wounds, and Arthur would get them out of jail, but it still distressed him to watch them being beaten on his behalf. In the trials, one must suffer for the greater good, but there had never been one. Here, the rain washed away the blood of those who suffered for him still. This time, he had to make it mean something. The window of opportunity had opened, and he dashed across the yard.

When he approached the vessel, he slowed to a brisk walk upon noticing a figure standing at the top of the ramp, blocking his way. *Oh no*. He cursed to himself. *Too early*.

'I know you're scared, Ack. I would be too.' Echoes of Iverissa filled his mind, coaching him through it as if she were there. She had said the words before, but this was the first time he believed them. Acalan filled his lungs with a deep breath, causing his chest to grow and his shoulders to rise. Feigning more confidence with each stride, he took great care not to slip on the slimy wooden ramp as he approached the man at the top. The windy conditions battered the two men around, and they both hid under their hoods.

'You lost, mate?' the man raised his voice over the weather. 'Last barrels are on,' he added, raising an eyebrow at Acalan.

'They told me to come back on?' Acalan lied with an upwards inflexion, scanning the deck as he assessed his options.

There didn't appear to be anyone else among the rows of crates that were strapped down tightly against the metal deck.

'Nobody should be telling you anything except for me.' The man placed his clipboard to the side and stepped towards him.

Acalan stammered through another unconvincing attempt at deception as he looked back down at the dock. By then, the guards had restrained Elena's crew and were escorting them away. When he faced forwards again, a gust of wind passed over his shoulder and blew the other man's hood off. The rain lashed over the man's face, and he ran his hand through his spiked red hair.

Acalan's chest tightened as he felt his fight or flight response coming into play. A large and recent cut running down the man's forehead was visible before he pulled his hood back up. So this was what he did for a living when he wasn't assaulting foreigners on the street.

A flash illuminated them. The man stepped back but was unable to dodge when Acalan slammed his skull into the man's nose, returning the headbutt from before. The man dropped down to the deck immediately and rolled around in an attempt to find his feet. Acalan's vision blurred, and he held his head as it pulsed in pain. As it turned out, giving a headbutt still hurt, it just wasn't a surprise this time. After blinking tightly, he saw a fist approaching his face with just enough time to duck under it. He then threw his weight behind an uppercut into the man's stomach on his way back up.

The man stumbled backwards into the crates, and voices called across the deck. Acalan lunged at the man and gripped his soaking wet robe, causing it to tighten around the man's puffed-out chest.

'I'll get you down there.' One of the voices was much closer, a few paces away.

Acalan tightened his arms down against the man's chest, hugging his arms into his ribcage. He gasped in preparation before landing another headbutt. This time, the man fell limp, still standing upright against Acalan. Acalan then twisted his feet and purposely fell around the crate, taking the unconscious man with him.

Footsteps reverberated against the metal deck as the owner of the voice approached. Acalan held his breath and lay motionless, his chest pressed down tightly by the unconscious man. A hooded figure stepped into his vision and stood still, looking back for his colleague. Several unbearable seconds passed before he shook his head and stepped down the gangplank. Acalan's head rested on the cold wet metal of the deck, and he exhaled under the weight of the red-haired man.

His respite was cut short when a second set of footsteps thumped against the metal deck. This time, Acalan remained calm as they approached. Suddenly, the red-haired man tensed up on top of him and his arms began to move. In a panic, Acalan wrapped a hand across the man's face and clung on as tightly as he could. He then wrapped his remaining limbs around his prey, restricting his movement. With each moment that passed, his victim's desperation increased. Eventually, the approaching footsteps brought the other man into view. He stepped over towards the clipboard that the red-haired man had set aside, lifting it up and examining it. Right then, Acalan felt the fight drain out of the red-haired man, and his body fell limp, but he dared not release his hold on him. The man placed the clipboard back onto the crate, taking some care to place it out of the way beside a small satchel and then left the ship. Only then did Acalan notice that he was hyperventilating; the sounds of the storm had concealed it. Adrenaline had replaced rational thought, and he had acted.

He continued to cling to the corpse for several minutes for fear that it would somehow move. It haunted him how quickly he could take a life; he hadn't even decided to do it by the time it was over. Suddenly, the sound of the ship's horn blasted into the night, and the gangplank was pulled away from below.

Acalan rolled the body off of himself and shuffled back to sit upright against the crate. The lifeless body lay still, its vacant eyes staring at him accusingly while he fought for control of his breathing. Nothing he experienced in the arena could have prepared him for that. Despite Virrel's assessment of him, Acalan had never killed anyone before.

XXV

Home

Having set off, the ocean freighter crawled through the channel. Since Acalan was on the top deck, he was able to peer over the railing and watch as the ship's hull split the waves. As strange as it was to him, this was much better than his first trip through these waters. His only company as the rain subsided was the red-haired corpse. This reminded him of the satchel that was sitting off to the side. Upon lifting the soaked lip of the bag, he looked at the dry contents inside. There were a few items one might carry but no real treasure. First, he lifted out some cigarettes in a crushed red box. These were of no interest to him, so he flung them aside. He did feel that the associated matches may have some use, having been caught without them in the past. He then lifted two heavier items out, lightening the bag. The first was a large bottle of spirit that was almost completely empty. The second was a short but incredibly sharp blade sheathed in a leather belt strap. Acalan dropped the rest of his haul back into the satchel and affixed the knife to his waist. It was not as if its owner would miss it, he thought, justifying his actions as he swung the satchel over his shoulder.

Having fleeced the dead man for all he was worth, Acalan still found his presence haunting, so he wandered away and across the deck. After some searching, he found a gap between the rows of crates that was wide enough for him to fit into. Sheets of thin green material were pulled tight across the tops of the crates and strapped at each corner. When he inspected this closer, lifting one of the tarps with a finger, he discovered that the underside of the material was bone dry: the rainwater was running right off it. He grinned when an idea came to him, but he had nobody to impress with his genius. Producing the knife from his waist, he set about removing the straps and slid the sheet off.

After tugging the sheet free, he shook it like a freshly washed bedsheet, and the water sprinkled off. He then ran the sharp blade through the fabric, slicing it into two pieces. He carefully placed the first half of the sheet down on the deck between two crates, with the dry side up. Then, he suspended the second half over the top of the two crates, providing a makeshift roof for his fort. Impressed with himself, he crawled inside, curled up into a ball and forced himself to sleep.

Acalan slept the sort of night's sleep that leaves a person feeling robbed of the hours. He jolted awake, clutching his new blade before a distant clattering reminded him where he was. The early morning light broke through the front of his makeshift tent. When he moved, he dislodged the ceiling with the top of his head before pulling it down and out of sight. When he popped his head above the rim of one of the crates, it astonished him to see that many of the crates were open and missing a side. The horizon bled orange behind the men rolling barrels off the deck and down the gangplank.

Something was unnerving about watching these men. On the Jasebelle side, they would shout and bawl at each other while they worked. In Synnor, they worked in silence, without so much as a moment of eye contact. This was good for him, as it gave him an idea. He stepped out into the open and selected a barrel from a crate. His back clicked as he pushed; the weight startled him, yet the barrel tipped over. Confident that he remained unnoticed, he rolled it out and over the lip of the crate and towards the gangplank.

The scene at the bottom of the gangplank took him aback when he looked down upon it. This port was significantly smaller than Jasebelle's and eerie in its silence. No barrier surrounded it, nor did any guards patrol it. Apart from the labourers, it seemed completely unmanned. All that was down there was a cluster of barrels awaiting collection. This struck him as strange, but the more he thought about it, the more he realised that he wouldn't have known what to expect in the first place; it was a wonder to him that this place even existed. In any case, he couldn't see the city from here, only a dirt track that ran out of the dock and uphill into the trees. He made a point of avoiding any eye contact as another man approached him empty-handed, seeking another barrel.

Acalan felt the man's gaze upon him as his footsteps slowed. He had definitely been noticed. The man came to a standstill about four yards in front of him. Acalan's mind leapt to the blade at his waist, but he froze. Silence hung in the air as he instead prepared himself for interrogation, but then, his shoulders shot up at the sound of a deep, guttural scream from behind. The man barged past Acalan and towards the scream, no longer interested in him. Acalan turned to look back but couldn't see up onto the ship; he was halfway down the gangplank, with the waves crashing below him. His tongue pressed into the back of his teeth while he tried to decide his next move. This was when it occurred to him that he had left evidence. It sounded like someone had unexpectedly discovered the corpse of the red-haired man. With this happening, Acalan felt no need to keep up his charade any longer. He kicked his barrel over the side of the gangplank, allowing it to plummet down into the sea. Then, he burst into a sprint towards the trees ahead, vanishing into the forest and leaving astonishment and shouting in his wake.

Once he was alone again on the dirt track road, he felt a bizarre calmness. Two indentations ran parallel through the dirt, tracks left for him to follow. Birds were chirping, and the morning breeze rustled the leaves above. The overgrown trees were alive and well, undisturbed by human intervention. The burning in Acalan's legs began when the path started to rise steeply upwards. The sound of the forest around him was calming until an approaching sound drowned it out. Whatever the clinking and shuffling from uphill was, he couldn't let anyone see him.

Without time to think, Acalan immediately rushed over to the side of the road and trudged through the vines there. In this frantic moment, they clung to his clothes as high as knee level, halting his progress. He stumbled and became entangled as they wrapped around his boots. The sound of the approach was upon him, but he could not move further. The best he could do was throw himself into the vines' embrace, covering himself and lying motionless. As much as he wanted to see what was approaching, he dared not move an inch as the sound passed. As it faded, he sat upright, causing a bird to flap wildly as it flew off of the vines that he had thrown across himself.

After re-emerging onto the path with a renewed sense of urgency, Acalan hurried forwards for some time until it widened into a plain. Synnor's nature was not unlike Jasebelle's, except that the grass here was wild and overgrown. To his left, the grassy plain stretched ahead, climbing a hill that overlooked the road. Giant boulders covered in moss and weeds dotted the landscape. To his right, the grass stretched only a short distance before stopping at a sudden edge. The path ahead continued, eventually leading up to an enormous stone wall. The wall towered into the sky, casting a long shadow in his direction. Acalan approached in a crouch, obscured by tall grass as he made his way uphill to get a better look at the gate.

Standing on this side of the wall was jarring to him. After so many years believing that the city walls were in place to keep danger out, only now did he realise that they were there to keep people in. Upon this reflection, he became aware that the only thing they kept out was him. His scan of the top of the wall puzzled him; there was a range of gaps for archers to stand watch in, yet each and every one was empty. The small gate below was guarded, but only by two guards who leaned on their spears. They were not alert; instead, they appeared disinterested, waiting for something to happen.

Eventually, a cart emerged into his line of sight. Several horses drew it, and only one man was seated on it. With the load piled high, the horses dragged the cart sluggishly. A range of cords haphazardly tied the barrels that were its cargo down. Perhaps he could backtrack and then sneak onto the cart, he thought. It continued as he walked through this idea in his mind, stuck on one main issue. If the men posted at the gate were there for anything, they would surely cast at least a cursory glance over the cart's contents when it returned.

There was a sense of irony about the whole affair. So much effort was involved in hauling these barrels up the hill, yet the contents of one would drive a machine there and back many times over. Acalan watched as one of the guards from the gate stepped forward, produced a clipboard and scribbled onto his sheet. Did these men even know the power of the material they were transporting? he wondered, reflecting on the difference in possibilities outside these walls. They would have no way to know what they were delivering and how much power was on their cart. This was when the idea occurred to him.

Acalan swung the red-haired man's satchel from his shoulder and dropped it onto the grass. He then removed an arrow from his quiver and placed it beside the satchel. After rummaging around for a moment, he produced the spirit and set that down on the ground. Then, he unclipped the knife from his waist and sat himself down on the ground. He jabbed at the leg of his trousers with the knife to tear off the bottom a few inches. He did this without wondering what Elena would say if she were there to watch him rip the new clothes she had given him to shreds. After cutting off a small square, he popped open the bottle and tipped it over the fabric, dousing it in spirit. Satisfied with this, he wrapped it around the tip of his arrow and tied the loose ends tightly.

Acalan held the arrow close to his eyes for inspection while he took a match from the box with his empty hand. Upon examination, there was no way for him to know if the arrow would even fly straight with this modification. It would have to do, he thought, looking back down the hill. The two guards began to step away from the cart and vanished inside the gate. The driver of the cart wandered towards a large rock in the grass. The rising smoke from his cigarette signalled it was time for Acalan to act. He held the arrow at arm's length and struck the match against the rock he hid beside. The match crackled and then began to burn brightly.

The flame leapt onto the cloth on the arrow tip when Acalan brought it close, causing it to burst into flames. Although he had anticipated this, the size of the flame still caught him off guard when it licked several feet upwards. He took great care not to burn himself as he nocked the burning arrow and drew it back. He grimaced, unable to draw the bow back fully as the flames bit at his fingers. He attempted to adjust the bow upwards to compensate for this but soon ran out of time and released. His arrow sped upwards, its bright yellow flame contrasting with the blue above as it arced towards its mark.

XXVI

Clash on the Cobbles

A sudden breeze caught the arrow, causing it to flutter as it dropped. Acalan held his breath as it fishtailed for a moment and swooped downwards. He exhaled only when he heard the clunk of the arrowhead sinking into the side of a barrel. Dipping behind the rock, he anticipated an explosion that didn't come. Upon hearing confused utterances from the driver up ahead, Acalan took another look. The arrow was upright and crackling, having split the wood of the barrel it had sunk into. Suddenly, a loud boom resonated through the air as the contents of the barrel exploded outwards, followed by a chain of detonations.

The initial blast knocked the driver over the large rock, which protected him from what followed after the first few blasts began to merge into one and grew exponentially into an inferno. The flames licked at the city walls but were unable to cling to the stone surface. Fire leapt onto the gates, causing them to burn and fall, leaving behind an empty frame. By the time the explosion had subsided, all that was left of the cart and gates were charred remains.

Acalan stayed where he was as thick black smoke ascended into the sky, announcing his return. The driver sprang up and fled into the hole in the wall that had been the gate. Acalan waited for an emergency response to arrive, without a plan for when they did. Yet even as the plume of smoke continued to rise into the air, no response came. Acalan waited several minutes, but still, nothing happened. He began to shake with indecision, unable to see the cause of the delay. His window of opportunity, if he had one, was closing.

Forcing himself to act, he gathered his effects and made his way to the now gateless gateway. The smell of burnt bellum from the smoking wreckage filled his nostrils. His bow slackened as he looked into the city, unsettled by what he saw.

The streets of the Upper District were deserted. There should have been citizens going where they needed to as they pleased, but a chilling breeze was all that flowed over the cobblestones. This did at least calm his fear that he would be immediately apprehended; since there wasn't a single person around, he lowered his bow. *Where is everyone?* he wondered.

As he jogged lightly up the alleyway towards the main square, he could see that the surroundings were abandoned. The businesses he passed had their doors closed and lights off. A flicker from behind a window caused him to slow for a moment, but the light was snuffed out immediately. He was sure that he heard movement inside, but there was only silence when he approached. This added to his lingering sense of unease. Were these people scared of him?

Turning full circle, Acalan scanned the surrounding windows for movement, only to see that many were boarded over. Strips of wood in conflicting colours criss-crossed over the windows, providing trivial protection.

Stumped by this, Acalan continued onwards. He checked to the sides and back over his shoulders as he ran but was still unable to see concrete evidence of life. A draft then blew across his cheek as the street widened onto the main square.

Across the cobbles on his right was the towering library hall. Above the giant public entrance, the arches on the front of the building stood menacingly, detailed with titanic lore. However, there were giant gaping holes in the façade where ornate stained glass had once been. The morning sunlight refracted across countless shards of all colours that littered the square, causing a dazzling array of beams to reflect upwards, distracting the gaze from the bottles and bricks that were strewn about. Acalan couldn't make sense of the aftermath that he stood alone in. What had he missed?

Acalan stepped into the square, cautious not to trip on the debris. As he emerged into the open, he began to hear sounds in the distance. The noise was chaotic, although distant. The clanging and shouting sounded soft from so far away and barely got louder as he rushed through the square.

On the far side of the square, a small patch of grass with a bench served as a viewpoint down into the Lower Districts. He knew that from here, he would be able to see what was going on down there. Acalan caught his breath as he leaned against the iron barrier at the edge of the viewpoint. He couldn't believe the scene before his eyes. Plumes of smoke like the one he had created rose from all over the city. They didn't climb as high as the one that he had made, but there were so many.

Anarchy had torn through the city as the citizens had taken up arms and rampaged through the streets. Acalan scanned for the presence of guards in response to this but saw none in the Lower District, yet there were numerous guards on the bridges to the Upper District. However big or small the given bridge was, countless council guards manned it, standing in formation. Their shields formed a barricade with their spears extended outwards, sealing the Lower District off.

'Get back inside!' A deep voice barked an order at him.

Acalan spun on the spot, drawing an arrow as he moved. He recognised the brutish male figure by his pointed goatee and moustache. This was the man who had accompanied Virrel to Jasebelle.

'Where is she?' Acalan demanded with his bow drawn, attempting to intimidate him.

'You shouldn't have come back.' Tainen disregarded the question, drawing an enormous two-handed blade from a scabbard on his back. 'You aren't needed anymore.' With that, Tainen rushed towards him, swinging his blade.

This startled Acalan, who fired his arrow over the oncoming man and across the square. It harmlessly glided away into the distance. Tainen then trailed his sword behind him before swinging it upwards, narrowly missing Acalan, who rolled across the stone pathway. As Tainen corrected his footwork, Acalan scurried around the bench and nocked another arrow.

Even after his encounter with the rats below, Acalan was still not used to his target fighting back. Despite this, he was able to fire his second arrow swiftly and accurately. The arrow lodged into the brutish man's shoulder plate, causing him to pull back with an involuntary wince. Acalan could see that the arrow had drawn blood, causing a minor splatter of crimson.

Tainen cursed in frustration but continued to approach with his sword pointed downwards. Gritting his teeth, he exuded a sense of inevitability as he ripped the arrow out of his shoulder and tossed it aside. Upon getting the chance to look closer at the features of this man, Acalan finally recognised a face that had haunted his childhood. Behind the enraged and weary expression, Acalan recognised the bullied bully. This was what he had grown into.

Acalan unwillingly confronted the unpleasant memory. Until then, he had allowed the drugs to compartmentalise it in the back of his mind. No matter how much young Tainen's words might have bitten at his peers, the weedy child had had no way of defending himself from the violence of his father. Only then did Acalan understand what Tainen had become.

Tainen grunted, lifting the sword overhead with both arms. 'You're not welcome here!' he shouted, swinging the sword downwards with a roar. Acalan's realisation had him frozen in place for almost a moment too long. He hit the ground but managed to avoid the swing. When he rolled over to face upwards, he saw the blade smash into the stone bench and lodge there tightly, its tip only inches away from his nose. Rubble peppered his face as Tainen shook the hilt furiously to no avail.

'You've become your father, Tainen!' Acalan shouted from down on the ground.

He was still trying to find his feet when the brute rushed him and pinned him down. This was when Acalan learned that this giant of a man punched even harder when enraged. The first blow burst his lip once again, causing a familiar metallic taste to gush into his mouth. A flurry of blows followed without respite. Acalan raised his hands to protect his face, but his weakening arms were brushed aside. Becoming increasingly dazed by each blow to his face, Acalan reached for the knife that he carried in desperation. Iverissa's scream echoed in his mind as he groped helplessly at the blade through his robe, but Tainen's knee pinned the fabric in place, and there was no hope of shuffling into a better position. The memory of the beatdown he had received in Jasebelle reared its unpleasant head. Acalan realised that the blows would not stop until he was dead.

'You know nothing about my father,' Tainen said, still gripping him tightly but allowing him to respond.

'I remember,' Acalan answered vaguely as he spat blood onto the cobbles, causing Tainen to halt his raised fist. 'He had power and he abused it,' Acalan expanded.

Tainen's grip loosened.

'He was wrong to hurt you,' Acalan concluded, feeling that a breakthrough was imminent. Yet upon saying this, he felt Tainen's grip tighten once more.

The next punch resulted in a crack in Acalan's nose. Stunned by the blow, Acalan's eyes watered, blinding him almost entirely.

'You don't understand.' Tainen pulled Acalan upright by the neck of his robes, lifting him off the ground. In doing so, the fabric of Acalan's robe moved, exposing the knife. In a swift movement, Acalan unsheathed the blade, slipping it through a space in Tainen's armour and into his abdomen.

Tainen's body seized up as he gasped for air.

'I'm sorry,' Acalan said as he twisted the blade. 'But I understand completely,' he insisted.

Tainen tumbled to the floor with Acalan, landing on the knife before Acalan was able to roll him off. The distant clattering continued in the district below as the two men lay incapacitated. Both were breathing heavily, but neither continued the fight. Acalan clung to the bloodied dagger when his arm fell to the side, even though the danger had passed.

'You never told anyone.' Tainen pressed hopelessly on the wound as his blood escaped onto the cobbles.

Acalan sat upright, running the full length of his sleeve under his nose in an attempt to clean his face. Blood smeared across his upper lip, as he couldn't bear the pain of applying enough pressure to wipe it away.

'Those kids never went home,' Tainen added without moving from the ground, his voice struggling through emotion.

'How could I?' Acalan answered, making eye contact with him. 'I was supposed to be among them.'

'Some of the parents never stopped searching.' Tainen sniffed as his breathing faltered. 'I couldn't bear it.'

'Neither could I, Tainen.' Acalan found common ground and lay on it alongside him. 'It was wrong.'

'I'm sorry.' Tainen broke eye contact to look up to the sky. His apology did little to address the searing pain all over Acalan's face, nor did it change the past. Nevertheless, it was spoken from his deathbed, with no clear ulterior motive in sight.

'Where have they taken Iverissa?' Acalan asked, noticing his opportunity.

'Virrel wants to make an example out of her. They're in the Palace,' Tainen said, causing Acalan to sit upright and clamber to his feet. 'Wait!' Tainen pleaded, holding Acalan's attention. 'The bellum,' he said breathlessly, his eyes shifting towards the sound of the Lower District.

'What about it?' Acalan rushed him.

'You have to stop her...,' Tainen trailed off.

'Stop her doing what?' Acalan pressed, only then recognising the vacant expression of Tainen's lifeless eyes.

Acalan's nostrils flared as he gathered his bow from the ground. He shook with rage; there was no time for guilt anymore. Acalan was choking on blood but left another victim in his wake. The bench behind him was a crumbled headstone, with a great sword lodged in it.

Even though he ran clumsily after his beating, the Palace was mere minutes away. When Acalan left the square, he jogged up the base of the hill in Virrel Park. As he progressed upwards, the destruction lessened. The quality of the barricades increased alongside the size of the mansions. Acalan did not stop when he passed number seventeen, Tainen's home. He couldn't even look at the building as he bolted past, pushing through the pain in his chest and starting to sprint. If Acalan had been a pawn, then Tainen was a knight. They had both taken orders from their queen but never could have known that they were just pieces being moved within a game. The time for guilt was past; now was the time for action. Acalan was going to kill Alanis Virrel.

XXVII

Grand Finale

After continuing up the winding path for some time, Acalan's perspective widened at the final bend. The ramp ahead led towards two short towers with a lowered drawbridge. Through the middle, the slope continued into the palace grounds. Raised from the rocky hilltop underneath it, the stone walls ensured only one point of entry. The main site itself consisted of the main palace building and several smaller buildings that he couldn't see clearly.

Bursting out from the back of the grounds was the main tower, an enormous column that protruded into the sky menacingly. Seagulls surrounded it, flying in circles around its pointed steeple. Acalan found that as he approached the gates with his bow at the ready, it seemed smaller than he remembered. Although Virrel Park was open to the public, Acalan hadn't been there since he was a teenager.

Only two guards stood by the drawbridge, leaning absentmindedly onto the towers at their backs. They righted themselves upon hearing his approach. The parapets above them were unmanned, the guards most likely diverted to the Lower District. As Acalan advanced, the guard on the left dropped his spear amateurishly. When he bent over to pick it up, having failed to catch it, his colleague stepped forward.

'Halt! The district is locked down,' he spoke in a nervous tone that didn't match the order he barked.

Disobeying his order, Acalan continued to approach, drawing an arrow as he did so. Without a moment of thought, Acalan released the arrow from his bow. Before it had even hit his target, Acalan had already begun to knock another. As the second guard finally looked up with his spear back in hand, it was too late. The second arrow dropped him to the ground. Both guards writhed on the stone, each clutching an arrow in their leg.

Acalan received no applause, yet he was in a state of complete focus. Although the setting was entirely different from the arena, he still found the same state of mind as he entered the palace grounds. He stopped at the entrance to the main palace building and planted his feet. With a controlled exhale, he scanned all angles, ready to launch another arrow, but found nothing to aim at. He looked to the stained-glass windows for some sign of life, but there didn't appear to be any light coming from inside. He frantically spun around with his bow nocked, fearing that a blade would sink into his back at any moment. After several turns, he lowered his bow. It was too quiet.

Acalan stepped gingerly up the shallow steps at the entrance and into the shadowy archway ahead, which led him into the main palace building. With an arrow readied and his fingers holding the bowstring tightly, Acalan was prepared to fire at any moment. The corridor he was walking down expanded into a long room with marble flooring, and the ceiling rose high above, causing the space to feel even emptier than it was. Simple seats arranged in uniform rows all faced away from him towards a barely lit throne. At the end of the room, a spectrum of colours dotted the backdrop. The high wall of colourless stone was accented in a Gothic style, with carved arches that protruded outwards.

The silence was interrupted when Acalan approached the throne. The clicking of heels against the marble floor echoed around the hall, filling the space. Acalan could feel his heart pumping in his chest. This was when he became aware that his breathing was no longer automatic.

'I didn't expect to see you again,' a familiar voice said calmly. 'You look terrible,' she insulted him as she emerged.

Virrel's long black cloak floated behind her, undisturbed by the still air. Several colours from the window reflected across the golden circle upon her flaming locks. Although there was nobody around for her to impress, she still looked flawless and seemed completely aware of this fact.

'Where is she?' Acalan demanded, pulling tight on his bowstring.

'I got it wrong with you, didn't I?' Virrel deflected, stepping up to sit comfortably on her throne.

'I'll kill you,' Acalan barked in a domineering tone and tears formed in his eyes as he endured the pain in his brutally beaten face.

'Well, wouldn't that just be typical?' Virrel laughed in a carefree manner, crossing her legs and making herself comfortable. 'I *knew* that was all you were good for,' she taunted.

Acalan took another step forward, disinterested in playing her game anymore.

'You're alone,' he pointed out. 'Nobody is going to save you.'

'So are you!' she teased, ignoring any tension that Acalan tried to impose. 'There's a really big difference between us, though, isn't there? I can handle being alone.' Her words bit at him before she pulled back, adjusting herself on the throne and starting afresh. 'You want her back, don't you?' she asked genuinely, her nasty tone replaced with a calm one.

Finding himself somehow disarmed by her words, Acalan's grip on his bow loosened.

'Tell me where she is,' he demanded abruptly.

'I can tell you. I'll even show you if you like.' She smirked at him smugly, the nasty tone returning once more.

'If you hurt…' Acalan started.

'She's fine!' Virrel interrupted him, recognising his concern. 'Listen. I think we should make a deal,' she continued.

Acalan remained silent, allowing her to make her case.

'You've caught me at an inconvenient time. You might have noticed that some of our citizens aren't behaving themselves.'

'They want freedom,' Acalan interrupted.

'They don't even know freedom. You have been to Jasebelle and seen how they conduct themselves,' she argued. 'Take these crates of bellum, for example. The outsiders think it brings them progress, but it is disorderly. It is dangerous,' Virrel monologued angrily.

Knowing that he had seen Jasebelle allowed her to speak freely; this information was otherwise unheard of on these shores. 'This city has kept them safe for generations, and this is the thanks I get.' Her features tightened, and her rant continued. 'They have decided to follow your example, which is very unfortunate.'

Virrel stood up once more and adjusted her dress. She exhaled in a jarring return to calmness and began to approach him with her palms open and facing him. 'I need to set a precedent.' She placed her hands onto his shoulders and made eye contact, her expression playfully feigning sorrow.

Although Acalan shrugged her off, she continued to pace around him, her eyes looking him up and down.

'Do you know what happens when bellum is misused?' she asked politely.

'I have a rough idea,' Acalan answered cautiously, reflecting on the explosion at the city gates.

'Great! Well, it's very dangerous, isn't it?' she fished for details, which he did not provide. 'That is why it needs to be locked away, but if the districts are so determined to see what happens, then I will show them firsthand,' she said ominously.

Acalan reflected on the cart that he had destroyed earlier. That pile of barrels was a drop in the ocean compared to the sheer volume being imported. 'I'm going to keep the Upper District; it was always my favourite anyway,' she joked with a sly grin.

Failing to understand the joke at first, Acalan then realised the consequences of his explosion being scaled up.

'Synnor has risen from nothing once, it can do it again.'

'Those people are innocent!' he argued.

'Well, I forgot that you've recently grown a conscience, but you've been doing this for years.' She indulged in the opportunity to mock him before forcing herself back to the topic. 'I was going to use the girl as an example and be done with it, but that will no longer suffice,' she stated simply. 'I can take you to her now, but let me be clear, you will be leaving immediately.'

Acalan stared at her, searching for signs of deception that were not present; her seemingly authentic stare met him in response. Acalan considered the temptation mindfully. When he had entered the palace, it would have been either him or Virrel who walked out alive, as he had not yet been aware of this option. If he could bring himself to accept, then he could save Iverissa and never look back. But the cost of his actions was finally in black and white: he would be damning an entire civilisation. Virrel's remarks crawled around in his head, making themselves at home. Acalan tried to convince himself that she was wrong about him, that he was more than a pawn, but couldn't.

'Fine,' he agreed reluctantly.

'Great!' she said giddily. Virrel walked around him, not remotely unsettled by the arrow pointed at her as she led the way towards the courtyard. 'I think you're cute together, by the way,' she jibed and wandered out into the sun, allowing the warmth to wash over her.

Acalan followed nervously, anticipating danger that was either not present or had yet to reveal itself. As they approached the main tower, Acalan took his eyes off Virrel and scanned the rooftops. As far as he could tell, they were completely alone. His shoulders jumped up involuntarily when a clunk caught him off guard. When he looked back at Virrel, it surprised him to see that she was already removing a key from the door and swinging it open.

The unwelcoming spiral staircase was murky. Mossy patches escaped from cracks between the stonework and crawled down the bricks. The stairs themselves were narrow and wound steeply upwards. Virrel was taking each step at a time. Acalan trailed behind and took longer, slower steps. He found it challenging to keep his balance; the steps were so tiny and there was no railing.

Initially, the purpose of this building wasn't clear to him. Every ten steps or so, they passed a closed doorway. Haunting moans could be heard from under the doors, but Virrel disregarded them as they progressed. Having climbed for some time,

Acalan wasn't sure how high up they were, but he was beginning to feel the burn in his calves.

'Almost there!' she said cheerfully upon noticing him tired. She didn't seem particularly bothered by the exercise, but she was significantly skinnier than Acalan. He was also still tolerating the pain in his muscles, having been beaten half to death. Eventually, the staircase ended at another doorway. Acalan tried to conceal his heavy breathing but leaned against the wall involuntarily.

Virrel placed her key in the lock and turned it slowly, causing no sound. From his position behind her, Acalan was unable to see the grin that spread across her face. Suddenly, she spun around rapidly and shoved him violently, causing him to tumble backwards and fall down several stairs. Fortunately, his shoulders bore the brunt of the fall rather than his head. He jumped up as quickly as he could but saw nothing through the door that was now hanging slightly ajar.

When he kicked the door open and stepped in with his bow drawn, he was immediately lunged at by a masked man wielding a razor blade. Acalan sank an arrow into the assailant and stepped back, allowing the body of his attacker to tumble to the floor. As it fell, it rolled to land upright, revealing bloodied scrubs. The scalpel that he had held clinked along the stone floor and hit the wall. Acalan swiped around his back to clutch the last arrow in his quiver and nocked it tightly.

The room was close and claustrophobic, with space only for a partially upright treatment chair. The chair appeared modified, with metal restraints at various points, all of which were propped open. Next to the chair was a small trolley containing a range of sharp and menacing tools that he didn't recognise, as well as a small metal dish of deep red liquid. From the opposite side of the room, light shone in through a large arched window, accompanied by a chilling breeze. Acalan heard confused and distressed wailing coming from the two figures who stood in the window.

'This is how it will always be!' Virrel's voice shouted over the crying. Acalan's eyes adjusted to see Virrel standing with her arm wrapped tightly around the chest and arms of her hostage.

Iverissa's bare legs were exposed by the treatment gown she wore. It fluttered in the wind that blew in from behind. Acalan could see that Iverissa's gown was bloodied at the front, similar to the scrubs of the man with the scalpel.

'What's happening?' Iverissa cried desperately. A piece of cloth was wrapped tightly around her eyes, pulling her white hair against her head. The white of the cloth matched her hair, although it was also harshly stained with crimson at the front. She struggled against the scalpel that Virrel pressed tightly into her neck, causing several drops of blood to run downwards.

'I control everything you care about, Acalan. I always have done, and I always will!' Virrel shouted frantically. 'Leave or I'll kill her!' she barked, stepping backwards towards the window ledge, teetering on its edge.

'You know I can't do that,' Acalan responded, stepping closer and escalating the situation. However, when he aimed the arrow, he hesitated. Even a perfect shot would likely take both of them over.

As he looked closely at Iverissa, he fought off the familiar feeling of learned helplessness and tried to maintain his focus. He could see that she shook like a leaf, visibly experiencing a mixture of cold and adrenaline. But when he looked closer, he noticed that one of her arms was shaking particularly violently under her captor's clutches. Several drops of blood were dripping from the arm and forming a small puddle on the floor; Iverissa was also gripping a scalpel tightly, albeit from the wrong end. She had cut her hand as she clutched the knife but refused to let go.

'I'll do it!' Virrel cackled menacingly.

'Stop!' Acalan shouted. 'I'm leaving, okay?' He attempted to de-escalate the encounter, taking a step backwards.

Virrel mirrored him, stepping one pace forwards, away from the ledge. As she pushed Iverissa forwards, her grip loosened for a moment.

This was just long enough for Iverissa to thrust her arm forward and swing the knife down, lodging it into Virrel's thigh. Both Iverissa and Virrel yelped as they struggled, but only Virrel cursed as she pushed Iverissa off of her and onto the floor.

When Virrel's eyes met Acalan's, it was the first time he saw dread in her expression. Acalan smirked back at her and launched his drawn arrow into her heart. Virrel stumbled backwards, and her frame locked up at the ledge of the open window. Her eyes widened as her vitality left her, and she tumbled backwards out of the room. The scene froze in silence before a sickening thud came from below. Fluttering could be heard from the seagulls outside, who fled the sound. Acalan took short, sharp breaths as he lowered his bow.

He then flung his bow to the floor, causing several thudding sounds that reverberated around the room. This sound caused further distress for Iverissa, who was sprawled over the floor. She wailed uncontrollably and continued crawling frantically away from the window.

'It's okay.' Acalan rushed over to comfort her.

She screamed and struggled against him, still unable to understand the situation. She kicked and pushed as she continued to drag herself along the cold stone.

'Iverissa. It's okay,' he repeated, causing her to slow and then lie still.

She flinched as he guided her arm onto him but did not push him away again.

'It's so dark,' she sniffled.

Acalan looked her in the face, but she didn't acknowledge it, her eyes still bandaged tightly.

'Why is it so dark?' she pleaded, shaking uncontrollably in his arms. Tears began to form in Acalan's eyes when he examined the stained bandages that covered hers.

'Everything is going to be okay,' he forced out the reassurance, trying to conceal the emotion in his voice.

'I love you,' he confessed quietly before falling silent. Then, he lost the battle for control of his emotions and cradled her in his arms.

XXVIII

Free

'The water is quite…still,' Acalan said, resting his weight on the railing and looking out over the sea. 'The sky is full of orange, and so is the water,' Acalan described the morning clumsily while the sun peeked over the horizon.

'I've seen the sunrise before, Ack,' Iverissa teased. 'What about the boats?' she asked calmly.

Acalan hung his head momentarily, smiling to himself before looking at her. Iverissa stood beside him with her back completely straight. Although her hands rested on the railing, she was not leaning forwards with him. The rounded golden rims of her black-tinted glasses were turned upwards as she held her head high, patiently awaiting a response.

'There are too many to count,' Acalan replied, looking back down at the shining waters that were occupied for the first time. 'It's a mix, though. About half and half,' he added.

'I don't know what you mean,' Iverissa stated.

'Well, some of them are the big Jasebelle ones, like the one that I was on,' he explained, scanning the enormous freighters that filled the backdrop. 'But there are lots of our new ones too, little wooden sailboats,' he said, realising there were more of these miniature vessels than he had initially thought. The larger ships were completely stable in the water, overshadowing the little ones bobbing around them.

'After all this, you're still describing things as us and them?' A familiar voice interrupted Acalan from over his shoulder.

When he turned towards the Grand Market gate, it delighted him to see Arthur approaching, hands in his pockets.

'Elena would be devastated if she heard,' Arthur teased as he joined the couple on the promenade. 'Hi Iverissa,' he added, leaning against the railing with them and looking outwards.

She nodded in response with a gentle smile.

'Okay, yes, they're all *our* boats,' Acalan corrected himself. 'Some of them are just much bigger than the rest,' he emphasised cynically, forcing eye contact with Arthur as he did so.

'We will get there eventually, Acalan,' Arthur said wearily. 'It's a lot of work to unite two nations, it takes time!' he added.

'Well, then it's a good thing we have you and Elena to rely on, isn't it?' Acalan teased, massaging Arthur's ego with his words.

'It's actually funny you mention that,' Arthur mused, beating around the bush while Acalan stared at him with raised eyebrows. 'I know it hasn't been long, but we are trying to get the right people in the right places while we have the chance.'

'What are you trying to ask us, Arthur?' Iverissa asked upfront, still facing forwards.

'Two things, actually. One each,' he responded in a more confident tone. 'For you Iverissa, to make a long story short, the library isn't fit for its purpose anymore.'

'How so?' she asked abruptly, turning her face in his direction.

'Well, there are a lot of books there, and many of them need to be organised and released to the public,' Arthur started. 'There are also a range of them filed incorrectly. Under non-fiction, that is,' he joked. 'Additionally, there will be many more arriving on one of those ships,' he continued, mirroring the smile that began to creep across Iverissa's face. 'It's going to be a big job; I think you may know the man who's overseeing it?'

'Right, and who's that?' she asked curiously, hanging onto Arthur's words.

'Talmu Olonelis,' Arthur responded, his eyes narrowing as he waited expectantly for her reaction.

Iverissa relieved him with a nod.

'I know him well; he will be perfect,' she stated in a genuine tone.

'Yes, we thought so too. He says he can't do it alone, though,' Arthur explained.

Acalan's head dropped once more. He smiled knowingly when he lifted his head back up, waiting to see the same realisation dawn on Iverissa's face.

'To be a bit clearer, he actually said that he *won't* do it alone. He keeps mentioning the same name,' Arthur specified, allowing his proposal to linger for several moments before she caught his drift.

Only then did her eyebrows rise suddenly, and her jaw dropped, leaving her mouth agape.

'Ah!' She laughed nervously, grinning as she processed the offer. 'I'd be honoured,' she agreed unreservedly.

'Excellent! I knew you would,' Arthur said, placing a hand on her shoulder. 'You don't have to start today. It's there when you're ready,' he added, appearing somewhat unsure of himself.

Acalan tolerated the awkwardness as he speculated on what Arthur had in store for him. He was already used to being a known face in the city, but Synnor's material change in circumstances had only increased his fame. A variety of gifts had arrived at his home, ranging from things like flowers to the coins that bulged in his pockets. Whether or not he deserved it, people seemed thankful, and he was financially stable for the near future.

'Acalan?' Arthur asked, snapping Acalan's attention back to the moment. 'Have you started working again? I'm sure children and parents alike would queue up around the block for one of your bows.' Arthur dug for information, using flattery as his method. 'For fun, of course, seeing that there will be no more trials,' he added.

'Not yet, but I may well do so.' The question caught Acalan off guard. He was still unsure of the implications of his newfound popularity at this point, so he had been keeping the workshop closed.

'Right, a shame,' Arthur said, looking expectantly at Acalan.

'No job offers for me, then?' Acalan deflected with humour, still unsure where this was going.

'Not an offer, no,' Arthur stated. 'Elena and I had an idea if you're open to ideas.'

'Moreso than ever,' Acalan replied. 'Go on then.'

'With Virrel out of the picture, her council has disbanded,' Arthur explained. 'Some of them fled, but I'm responsible for the prosecution of those who remain.'

'You deserve it,' Acalan interrupted, drawing raised eyebrows from Arthur. 'Finally, the career that you were seeking,' he clarified.

'Let me win first, then I'll agree,' Arthur remarked dryly, concealing his embarrassment at Acalan's flattery before returning to his point. 'We are in yet another unprecedented scenario, though, Acalan. Elena is –'

'Have you asked him yet?' Elena's familiar voice accompanied the sound of clinking glass from inside her satchel. This noise subsided when she halted at the railing and stood close to Arthur on his far side.

'To be honest with you, Acalan, we're just pushing around paperwork in the aftermath,' Arthur said, smiling subtly at Elena.

'Hang on!' she interrupted. 'We need to make sure nothing like this ever happens again!' she grandstanded at first before acknowledging his smirk and allowing her shoulders to relax once more. 'Sorry, force of habit,' she said with a shrug.

'The chancellor wants to share power with Synnor,' Arthur said, before giving way to Elena once more.

'That means that it will need its own people at the top,' she added. 'I'm in charge of organising some democracy over here,' she spoke with pride before kneeling down and unbuckling her satchel. 'There will be a new council, one chosen by its people and accountable for its actions.' Her explanation slowed as she produced wine glasses from the bag and tried to stand them upright on the bumps of the cobbles.

'We can't offer you a job, it wouldn't be in the spirit of the whole idea,' Arthur continued. 'Still, you're a hero to these people, Acalan, so we think that they would get behind you.'

'You want me to be a councillor?' Acalan asked. This suggestion bewildered him.

'I do, and so does he,' Elena said candidly, pointing towards Arthur. 'You're more familiar with those trials than anyone. If anyone could ensure that they won't ever happen again, it would be you.'

'I think that sounds good too,' Iverissa joined the motion with a smile.

'It isn't about what we think anymore, the city has the right to choose,' Elena specified. 'Anyway, it's an idea,' she said, not letting the moment linger.

'We aren't going to be prepared for any sort of election in the coming weeks; it will take some time.'

'Right…,' Acalan murmured, mulling over the idea as he looked out towards the bright orange sky. Much like the city and its people, it seemed that he had a choice to make. He could continue working out of his cupboard, crafting arrows and bows. The work would certainly be there for him if he wanted it, so why was his workshop still dark, filled with dust and behind a closed door? Maybe he was destined for more?

He smiled to himself and avoided eye contact with his successful and intelligent friends; everyone had found a place except for him. Continuing to stare out towards the horizon, Acalan realised that he was at peace with this. Somewhere along the lines, he had found a voice, and he didn't believe in destiny anymore.

'I'll think about it.' Acalan slid along the railing towards Iverissa, pressing his arm against hers and allowing her head to rest on his shoulder.

Both Acalan and Iverissa jumped as their tranquillity was interrupted by a sudden pop. A cork fired out into Acalan's line of view before plummeting into the sea below. He looked down towards the source of the noise and saw Elena clutching a bottle with a steady stream of frothy liquid escaping from its mouth. The sunlight reflected the shine of the label, and when Elena tilted the bottle to pour the wine, Acalan recognised it as Arthur's good bottle.

Elena filled the leftmost glass gingerly, holding its stem to keep it upright. Nodding with self-contentment, she passed the glass up to Arthur and began to pour another. He waited patiently while Elena filled two more glasses for Acalan and Iverissa. Acalan sipped on the wine and watched as the sun rose over a new world that awaited the man he would choose to be.

Acknowledgements

Hello again, reader. I hope you liked the book. It's a story that I've been trying to get to you for a *really* long time, and a few people have been particularly important to this journey over the years. I'd like to list them, thank them and mention what made them so helpful.

Mum, Dad and Sarah, thank you for asking how the book was going, even when it wasn't. Thanks for picking me back up when I have struggled and always encouraging me to bounce back.

Daniel Brooke, thank you for relentlessly chasing for a release over four years. It's out now, bro.

Euan Furness, thank you for lending me your enormous brain to find the mistakes. Your feedback has been invaluable towards making this happen.

Molly, Jack, Kayleigh and Darren, thank you for being such supportive and reliable friends over the years. Happy Birthday Molly!

Gerki's Group, and all their other aliases, thank you for helping me discover my passion for storytelling.

About the Author

When Scott Thompson is not working as an IT Professional, he is most likely running, cycling, bouldering or inflicting some other form of exercise upon his body. Failing that, you will find him playing Dungeons and Dragons or writing a story.

This project was undertaken by Scott in late 2019, shortly after graduating from university and before finding full-time employment in his field. A big part of his motivation for this project was the idea that this might be the remarkable thing he was supposed to do in his life. Over the years of this project, he found himself stuck in a loop of existentialism on several occasions. He struggled to scratch that itch for a while.

Eventually, Veil of Synnor, among other things, broke him out of this loop. A pretty neat story for interviews that he will undoubtedly lean on if anyone ever asks.

Four years was a little longer than he had planned, but the story was finally ready. Scott had experienced much more change than he would have liked along the way, but he was ready to start all over again.

Printed in Great Britain
by Amazon